L'S CURSE

A thrilling murder mystery with plenty of twists

M.J. TROW

A Schoolmaster Murder Mystery Book 6

JOFFE BOOKS

Revised edition 2024
Joffe Books, London
www.joffebooks.com

First published by Hodder and Stoughton
in Great Britain in 2000

This paperback edition was first published
in Great Britain in 2024

Cover art by Imogen Buchanan

ISBN: 978-1-83526-530-7

A NOTE TO THE READER

Please note these books were published in the 2000s, when social attitudes were different.

CHAPTER 1

The Old Millennium had just four minutes to live. Four minutes. Some people could run a mile in that time. In the good old days of impending nuclear destruction, it was all you had to hit that shelter or you could kiss your arse goodbye.

Peter Maxwell was a child of the Old Millennium. He could boil an egg in four minutes with just a little help from the National Grid. But this wasn't any Millennium. This was Peter Maxwell's Millennium and everybody knew that Peter Maxwell was mad. A year ago, the Dome had exploded with light on to a cynical and dubious Greenwich. A river of fire had allegedly roared down the Thames, the great and ancient artery burning and writhing, as though Hermann Goering's Luftwaffe had come back again or the City witnessed again the results of that one careless match in Pudding Lane. Curiously, only the organisers of the event had seen it happen, but hey, what's a little Millennium bug between friends?

That was then. Last year. Ninety-nine — the year of the flake in the ice cream. Only the historians held out against it — and a few mathematicians nervously followed. The cusp of two thousand to two thousand and one — that was the real Millennium, Maxwell had argued, to anybody who would listen in the staffroom at Leighford High, that fountain of all knowledge where the Great Man had been driven to drink. He had harangued his Sixth Form on the matter, but they were callow youths and it was ever a case of pearls before swine. It gave them an excuse, they reckoned, to party all over again and to celebrate twice, exactly as they whooped it up at eighteen and twenty-one.

He'd fought his way through the milling New Year crowds that thronged the aisles at Tesco's. There seemed to be offers on everything except the thing that mattered — the amber nectar that was Southern Comfort. 'Buy one, get one free?' he asked the cheerless woman on the till, the one who still had tinsel in her hair.

'No,' she answered with all the wit and repartee of her calling and Maxwell dropped the badinage while rummaging for his plastic.

So here he was, alone as he faced his version of the twenty-first century. H.G. Wells had assumed we'd all be dead by now, choked in the creeping red weed from Mars. But dear old H.G. hadn't lived long enough to discover that Mars was really made in Slough and it was actually brown. George Orwell had feared we'd all be cowed into impotence by Big Brother and his thought police. Maxwell chuckled and shook his head; then he caught sight of Tony Blair on the front page of his paper, smiling like a death's head at some New Year symposium and he suddenly wasn't so sure. Come to think of it, as Maxwell suddenly did, wasn't George Orwell's real name Blair? What with him and Tony and Lionel, it was quite a dynasty. Spooky, too.

The cat called Metternich lay in a tight curl on the pouffé, his tail up his nose, his nose behind his knees in that curious way that cats have. The Millennium, Old or New, meant nothing to him. He was just grateful that the cantankerous old bastard who was his master had grabbed that black plastic thing with the buttons and that, coincidentally, the telly had gone off. There was something about the nasal colonial whine of Clive James that got right up Metternich's arse. It played merry hell with his sound waves.

Maxwell looked at the black and white beast of Columbine through the amber distortion of his glass. 'Here's looking at you, Count.' It was a superlative Bogart and he sucked his teeth, becoming Maxwell again. 'Here's to the chase and the nightly hunt. Did you know there are more rats than people in this great country of ours today? I shall expect you, in the Millennium that's about to break, to do something about that.'

The sharp ring of that piece of white plastic shattered Metternich's moment. He didn't need the exhortations of the old bastard to encourage him where rats were concerned. He was a serial killer without conscience, the pied piper of Columbine and come early light he'd be out there, sniffing, scenting the wind, crouching with his belly prone — the Jeffrey Dahmer of Leighford.

'War Office,' Maxwell picked up the phone.

'Max. Happy New Year, darling.'

'Woman Policeman Carpenter,' Maxwell smiled. 'Excuse the formality, but you are on duty?'

She was indeed. At her end of the line, in the cheerless glass and brick of Leighford Nick, DC Jacquie Carpenter was back in the old routine. Peter Maxwell was the biggest thing in her life these days, although she'd die rather than let him know it, but she didn't believe his Millennium reckoning and found his addition a little shaky. So, for her, this was just another Hogmanay, another chance for drunken idiots to make her life that teensy bit more eventful. She was nearly thirty, attractive and bright and she'd refused to bow before the recent onslaught that decided ginger was the new blonde.

'You didn't go to the party, then?' she asked him, accepting gratefully the cup of tea from old Jock Haswell, the desk man.

'A party to me means Whig or Tory, replaced in time by Conservative, Labour and the other lot whose name now escapes me. It does not mean a good time. Anyway, you're . . .' He checked the clock across the lamplit room from him, 'two minutes early.'

'I'm out on the road in a minute,' she told him, 'at the witching hour. It's the Inspector's guess that the "fun" will be at Little Willy's about then. Then it might gravitate to the Grapes.'

'You be careful, Jacquie Carpenter,' he told her. 'What a detective constable is doing mixing it with midnight revellers is beyond me.'

'It's the bug, Max, I told you.'

'Millennium?'

'Flu. We're four blokes down on the usual rota. And don't get me on that, when the Millennium really is nonsense again.'

'Ah,' sighed Maxwell, 'I thought Y2K was a genital lubricant until I . . . oh, shit, there's someone at the door.'

'First footer?' Jacquie asked.

'As long as it isn't a left footer, we'll be all right. Abyssinia, Police Woman Carpenter. Cop you later.'

'Love you, Max,' she said, but he'd gone, the piece of plastic back in its cradle. She looked up at old Jock Haswell, smiling at her wryly and tapping his watch. 'Yeah, all right, Jock. Thanks for the tea,' and she went to find her car.

* * *

Peter Maxwell lived in one of those town houses so fashionable in the late seventies. 38 Columbine had four floors, from the Inner Sanctum that was Maxwell's attic to the little lobby where his kind postman left the bills. Maxwell wasn't expecting anyone. The closest he'd come to Scotland was to ass *Braveheart* to his video collection. So this couldn't be some kilted idiot carrying a lump of coal. Could it? And surely, not even the terminally nosy Mrs Troubridge, his next door neighbour, would be desperate for sugar as Big Ben struck. There again, Maxwell pondered as he reached the stairs, it *could* be a child. True, a child that would not see adulthood if he had his way, but it may be there was such among the alumni of Leighford High deranged enough to try to have a joke at the expense of the Head of Sixth Form. In his mind, Maxwell narrowed it down to two. Either it was Wayne Kerr, whose dad had a DIY shop in the High Street or it was Benny Jarvis, the school psychopath.

In the event, it was neither. At first sight, there was no one there at all, just a pile of rubbish lying on Maxwell's path. The Head of Sixth Form flicked on the outdoor light and looked right and left. It was midnight. From several doors away he heard a muted cheer go up and the tortured strains of *Old Lang Syne*. Otherwise, it was Columbine, its parked cars and orange lamps all part of the usual street furniture. Maxwell looked at the rubbish at his feet — a bundle of black plastic bags. He kicked it with his right foot. It felt solid, hard like granite against the velveteen of his slipper. He crouched on his haunches, with all the sang-froid a man the wrong side of fifty-four could manage. And he peeled back the wrapping. It was the hair he saw first, silver in the midnight light with its quartered moon, then the face, frosty, pallid, dead.

He stood up with the suddenness of Richard Dreyfus coming face to face with a Great White for the first time. He steadied himself against the doorframe, grateful for its solidity, its strength. He looked again from right to left, licking his lips that were bricky dry. The distant party was going on, with whoops and laughter. And in the middle of all this life, as Maxwell forced himself to look again, was death.

CHAPTER 2

'And I'd be telling you again . . . why, exactly?'

'Just in case, sir.' DS Martin Stone didn't want to be here. Not tonight. Not just as the new year dawned, looking suspiciously like the old. 'In case there's a little something, however small, you may have overlooked the first time.'

The detective sergeant was a kid, really, no more. He had large ears which Maxwell suspected hid gallons of wetness. Still, he seemed competent, not fazed by death at all.

The Head of Sixth Form was not a kid, though he taught several. His ears were largely hidden under a greying thatch of barbed-wire hair, but his dark brown eyes burned right through a man. Stone checked his watch. Today was the allotted day. A new year baby, a first footer. His and Alex's second. The head had engaged; the scans were good. It would be a girl — Samantha. Alex had already bought the Buzz Lightyear against the day when the infectious hunky toy came back again like a boomerang, a merchandiser's dream.

'It was virtually on the stroke of midnight,' Maxwell began again. 'The New Millennium.'

'Excuse me?'

Maxwell hated the Americanism, but he wasn't going to get into all that reasoning again, not with this lad and not now. There were more pressing problems. 'Two minutes to twelve,' he settled for.

'You were watching the clock, I suppose,' Stone prompted him, 'raising a glass. Er . . . you were alone?'

'Apart from my cat,' Maxwell smiled.

'Er . . . yes.' Stone could see no cat, on account of how Metternich had fled up the attic stairs at the first shrill screech of the doorbell that had announced the arrival of the boys in blue. He was crouched on an old chest, head low, ears flat, his bottle-brush tail relaxed now and swinging just slightly in the wind of his nonchalance. He considered huffing on his claws, but realising there was no one to witness the spectacle, thought better of it. What was the point, really? It was like silent trees falling in forests. You had to be there.

'And the doorbell rang?' Two floors below him, the young suit with the jug-handle ears was pursuing his inquiries.

'That's right.'

'You weren't expecting anyone? Family? Friends?'

'Haven't many of either,' Maxwell shrugged. It wasn't intended to elicit sympathy. And it didn't. It was just a statement of fact. Christmas. The New Year. They were the loneliest of times, like the dead of night, when a man can be truly, madly, deeply alone.

'You opened the door?'

'I did.'

'Was that sensible, sir?' the uniform spoke for the first time, as though trying to impress or just because it was his turn. He was taciturn in a nondescript sort of way, slowly turning his peaked cap in his hand.

'This isn't the Ratcliffe Highway, Constable,' Maxwell reminded him. 'There've been no murders on Columbine for, ooh, let me see . . .'

'An hour or so, sir,' Stone looked his man in the eyes.

'Yes,' Maxwell acknowledged. 'Sorry, bad taste.'

'You saw no one in the street; you're sure?'

'Not a soul. There was a party going on — number twenty-six, I think. There were lots of cars and the lights were blazing. I heard it rather than saw it.'

'And on the path?'

Maxwell raised his eyebrows and sighed. He'd seen corpses before. Before this questioning kid was born, he'd been to the hospital to identify the bodies of his wife and child; they who'd been on the wrong stretch of road at the wrong time. But this was different. This time, death had come to him.

'Looked like somebody's old rubbish,' he said. 'As if the bin men had suddenly raised two fingers to the world and piled up garbage on my doorstep annoyed at no Christmas tip. It was only when I looked closer . . .'

Stone shot a glance at the uniformed man. This was only his third murder inquiry, his first as detective sergeant. Murder took men in different ways. He didn't know Maxwell, couldn't guess which way he'd go.

'It was an old woman,' the Head of Sixth Form's voice came back stronger than ever. 'Seventy, seventy-five. Difficult to say. She was stiff, covered in hoar frost, which was odd, considering the ambient temperature.'

'Ten Celsius,' Stone confirmed. 'Very mild for January. What did you do?'

'Well,' Maxwell leaned back on his settee, clasping his knee and looking at his man. 'It was a classic choice between chucking up or floating away, but I went to a good school, so in the event I phoned you blokes. Record time, by the way. Well done.'

Stone nodded. He didn't want compliments at this stage. He wanted answers. And he sensed he'd get no more here. Time to move this on, take the matter upstairs. He stood up, along with the uniform and Peter Maxwell.

'Can you come to the station tomorrow, Mr Maxwell, to make a full statement?'

'You mean today?' Maxwell checked the large clock.

'Er . . . yes,' Stone nodded. 'I s'pose I do. John?' And the uniform nodded and made for the stairs, putting on his cap. 'Oh, by the by,' Stone turned to Maxwell, 'it's not every day someone leaves a stiff on a doorstep in the nice end of

Leighford, so expect a bit of pestering from the gentlemen of the press tomorrow, Mr Maxwell.'

'Should I mention your name, Mr Stone?'

'If I were you, sir,' the DS told him, 'I wouldn't even mention yours.'

* * *

'Bugger!' Jim Astley wasn't a believer in biorhythms, part of the folklore/feng shui bollocks a desperate people increasingly clung to in an age of secularism and disbelief. Not for him the mantras and healing crystals of the New Age. He was a scientist, well, a doctor anyway and anything you couldn't find in Gray's Anatomy was just so much mumbo-jumbo.

Today however he was off form. The problem was that old Roger McGuigan threw a bloody good party. Too good, as it turned out, because Jim Astley still had the mother of all hangovers by lunchtime the next day. Had any of the boys in blue with whom he occasionally worked asked him to blow into this, they would have been horrified at the result.

Some would say it didn't matter too much. Because Jim Astley only operated on the dead. In a sleepy seaside town like Leighford, he'd doubled for years as police surgeon and pathologist, but increasingly the younger men were tackling the live ones, coping with drunks in the cells and officiating at scenes of accidents. Increasingly they only called Jim Astley in when life was pronounced extinct. That didn't bother him much. In his heart of hearts, Jim Astley knew he was better than all of them. Except today. Today, he'd dropped his scalpel for the second time. He was still sharp enough not to turn however as the door clicked behind him. He didn't turn and he knew exactly who'd come in.

'Morning, Henry. Happy New Year to you.'

'And you, Jim.' Detective Chief Inspector Henry Hall had never liked mortuaries. They were cold and antiseptic, like a politically correct abattoir. But then, Henry Hall was a copper of the new school, a fast-track graduate who'd done his beat time with his eyes shut. He wasn't Astley's generation, the man who'd obtained his first 'subject' for dissection from Messrs Burke and Hare. Hall had almost grown up with computers rather than having them foisted on him.

But this was no way to go, to start a new year. He perched on the green plastic chair by the door. 'How was your Christmas, Jim?' he asked.

Astley grunted. That was years ago, wasn't it? It even seemed years since last night, when he'd taken Marjorie home before she embarrassed them both still further. Harping on about the Falklands when your hostess is Argentinean was perhaps a little insensitive. But then, that was Marjorie, through whose veins ran pure Gordon's.

'Time enough for pleasantries later,' the pathologist told the policeman. 'You are here, I presume, for answers?'

'That would be nice,' Hall said.

'Well, then,' Astley continued rummaging into someone else's soul. 'If you're sitting comfortably . . . Female Caucasian. Seventy-three, seventy-four, something of that order. Not very well nourished. What was the weight, Donald?'

'Fifty-four point one,' Donald answered. Anyone less like a mortuary attendant it would be difficult to imagine. Donald weighed fifteen stone if he weighed an ounce, martyr that he was to KFC and McDonald's. Colonel Sanders had been his godfather.

'She had mild osteoporosis and evidence of operation scars to both ears. I think it's a fair bet the old girl was pretty deaf. Loads of mastoid trouble. And — and this is a singular rarity in this day and age — she was a virgin. I wonder how in the twenty-first century you can get to be seventy-four and still be a virgin.'

'Lucky, I guess.' Donald was riffling through the paperwork.

'Be a dear, Donald,' Astley looked at his number two over the rims of his glasses, 'and make the chief inspector a cup of tea, could you?'

'Your wish is my command, master,' and Donald was gone through the heavy, plastic swinging doors, the Igor of Leighford General.

'Getting above himself, that man,' Astley croaked. 'He's been watching too much Quincy on the telly and might well find himself in one of his own body bags one of these days.'

'Cause of death?' Henry Hall had other fish to fry.

'My hands around his throat,' Astley grunted. 'Oh, I see. This one. Well, actually that's a bit of a puzzle. Come and have a look.'

Astley heard Hall's chair legs scrape back with a 'must I?' sort of sound. Hall looked over the pathologist's shoulder. The old woman lay on the slab, her legs splayed slightly, her tiny, shrivelled breasts separated by the y-shaped incision. Mercifully, Astley had not yet gone to work with his circular saw and her scalp was still in place — a thatch of silver hair above the peaceful, sleeping face.

'When I first saw the body, it was still in the process of thawing out. Do you want to tell me about that?'

'We assume it had been kept in a deep-freeze — for how long is your department.'

'Yes,' Astley lifted his glasses on to his green-capped cranium. 'I thought it would be. Raises all sorts of problems, that, about the time of death.'

'Knew it would,' Hall nodded.

'She was naked under the plastic bags,' Astley went walkabout in his white-walled mausoleum, 'so post mortem, she should have cooled about one to one and a half degrees per hour, extremities cooling faster than the trunk of course. But the freezing interfered with all that. It also cut across the usual rigor. Normally, she'd have been cold as a witch's tit after twelve hours, rigor kicking in after five. As it was, by the time I'd got to her, rigor was almost gone. Look,' he was back at the body again, 'the jaw moves freely, limbs quite mobile.'

Henry Hall looked away. Pulling the dead about was Astley's job, but there was a grotesquery about it, like some mad puppeteer pulling strings.

'Rigor is delayed by freezing; it doesn't start until after the thaw begins. So it buggers up the usual equation — normal body temperature minus rectal temperature divided by one point five . . . Not going too fast for you, am I?'

Hall had regained his seat and sat with his head against the wall. 'No,' he said.

'I won't bore you with the chemical analysis,' Astley went on, proud as always of his medical superiority, 'and some of that's still to do.' He turned to face Hall and put his glasses hack on the bridge of his nose, as though to add majesty to his next pronouncement. 'I'm estimating the approximate date — date, mark you, as opposed to time — at about December 20 to 22.'

'Before Christmas.'

Astley smiled and winked at the chief inspector. They weren't mucking about at Bramshill these days, were they? Hall's IQ was clearly off the scale.

'And the cause of death? The freezing wasn't accidental, presumably?' Hall wanted to know.

'Indeed not. When I peeled back the black bags, her arms were crossed over her chest in the traditional laying out position. She didn't die from exposure. And she didn't die from this, either.'

'Just tell me, Jim.' Hall didn't want any more glorious technicolour close-ups. He heard Astley chuckle as he bent over the corpse again.

'Oh, ye of little bottle,' the pathologist said. 'All right, then, the wussy way. She has a stab wound to the back of the neck. She must have been lying on her front when that was delivered or possibly in a sitting position. The knife you're looking for is double-edged, the blade at least four inches long.'

'Commando,' Hall was talking to himself. 'Special Services. Any survival store or mag sells them. Wait a minute — you said that wasn't the cause of death?'

'Indeed not. The stab wound was delivered post mortem. No blood. No bruising. Somebody impaled the old girl after she was dead. Now why, I wonder, would they do that?'

Hall was on his feet, peering at the corpse, despite himself. 'Frenzy? What kind of wound is it?'

'One sure, powerful thrust. No sign of anything frenzied. In my experience, such an attack would produce several wounds, rained down with speed, blurred by the old red mist. There's no indication, apart from the lack of clothes, of any sexual motive at all. No, the stab was an afterthought.'

'So what did kill her?'

'Ever heard me talk of Sir Ephraim Wallace?'

Hall hadn't.

'Splendid name, isn't it? Splendid chap, too. My old pathology teacher at Guy's.'

Hall thought Astley had graduated from Reading, but he let it pass.

'"The face," he would always say. "Look at the face. It holds a million secrets."'

'And what does the face tell you?' Hall asked.

'The eyes have it,' Astley told him. 'Petechiae. Tiny blood pricks in both eyeballs.'

'Suffocation?' Hall had met this before.

'Possibly. But I don't think so. Toxicology will confirm it later, but there's much fatty degeneration of the internal organs. Swelling of the liver, stomach, spleen.'

'Indicating . . . ?'

'Poison, dear boy. Possibly phallin. If I'm right, the poor old duck would have had chronic vomiting and diarrhoea. She'd have dribbled and her eyes would have watered uncontrollably. She'd have felt dizzy, had the grandmother of all headaches, before slipping into delirium and convulsions. If she was lucky, a coma would have put her out of her misery after eight hours. Could have been as much as thirty, though. Who was she?'

'I haven't the faintest idea. Jane Doe at the moment.'

'Hmm.' Astley turned back to the corpse. 'Just remember,' he murmured, 'a granny isn't just for Christmas.'

'Thanks, Jim.' Astley heard the door click open.

'Any forensic on the bags?' the pathologist asked.

'Clean as a whistle.' Hall held the door open for Donald returning with the tea, a beam and some biscuits. 'This one's a professional, Jim.'

'Ah, thanks, Donald.' Astley prised off one of his sterile gloves and took the proffered mug. 'This isn't happening, by the way, Henry.' He raised the tea, 'So unprofessional. I'd be struck off.'

Hall waved the sight aside.

'Tell me,' Astley joined him at the door. 'Is it right the old girl was found on Peter Maxwell's front doorstep?'

'That's right.'

'What is it about that bloke?'

'You tell me,' Hall said.

'This is not the first time — oh, Christ, Donald, no bloody sugar, for Christ's sake,' and he put the mug down before following Hall into the corridor. 'Not the first time friend Maxwell's been caught up in murder. There was that Jenny Hyde business a few years back; and that accountant chappie in the theme park . . .'

'On second thoughts,' Hall stopped him, 'don't tell me. He's like a bad penny, turning up when you least expect him.'

* * *

'Nobody expects the Spanish Inquisition,' Peter Maxwell murmured, looking out of his lounge window at the knot of paparazzi hanging around the open space where his front gate should have been, if only someone hadn't invented open planning.

Jacquie Carpenter had had the nous to leave her car streets away and had got in through Maxwell's back garden. 'How annoying have they been?' she asked.

He broke away, bored with the sight. 'On a scale of one to ten, eighty-three,' he said. 'I'm beginning to feel like Fred West at twenty-five Cromwell Street. Should I carry out a box wrapped in black plastic, do you think? Titillate them a bit?'

'Not funny, Max,' she scolded. That in itself was a landmark in their relationship. A year ago she daren't have said any such thing. Even now she wasn't sure how he'd take it.

'You're right,' he said and sat himself down below the display of cards and tinsel. 'God, when's Twelfth Night?'

'It scared you, didn't it, Max?' she sat opposite him, her stone-washed jeaned knees tucked under her chin, her auburn hair, usually worn up according to constabulary regulations, cascading over the shapeless Aran that covered her shoulders. 'Have you considered counselling?'

He looked across the room at her. 'They'll make a detective of you yet, Jacqueline,' he said softly. 'And, yes, it scared the shit out of me. But counselling? No, thanks; I've got my cat.' There was a silence. 'It's good of you to come. I know how difficult this must be.'

She shrugged. 'Just putting your mind at rest, sir,' she played the policewoman, 'as I would with any other member of the public.'

'Oh, thanks a bunch,' he scowled, teasing the skin from the top of his milky coffee. 'What've you got?'

'Max,' she growled in warning.

'Oh, come on, now, Jacquie. You can't do this to me.' He lapsed into his early Brando. 'I coulda been a contender.'

'I can't tell you . . .'

'This is the only counselling I need — involvement, immersion; the need to know. Who was she? That's all. Just that one question. No more. I promise.'

'Don't know . . .'

'Jacquie!'

'Honestly, Max,' she laughed. 'We haven't the faintest idea.'

'Handbag? Purse? Clothing labels? Laundry marks?'

Jacquie Carpenter had been on the force seven years now, woman and girl. She knew the routine, the basics of an inquiry. The irritating thing was, so did Maxwell.

'Nothing,' she smiled. 'She was naked . . . Oh shit!'

Maxwell smiled. The law, nil; Peter Maxwell, one. 'Sexual assault?' he asked.

'Max,' she was firm. 'I've already said too much.'

'Of course.' His criminal mind was kicking in. 'It's not likely at her age, but then, Albert de Salvo . . .'

'And she wasn't strangled . . . Oh, bloody hell!'

Maxwell chuckled. 'Tell me, Jacquie, what was your new year resolution? Tell Old Maxie everything he wants to know? That's very generous of you.'

'What have you told them?' She was suddenly on her feet, changing the subject, nodding towards the window, covering her back.

'Well,' Maxwell joined her at the window to wave at the increasingly bedraggled newsmen huddled in the rain, 'the bloke from the *Grauniad* and I had a discussion on the role of murder in New Labour's philosophy. I told the bloke from the *Telegraph* this would never have happened if William Hague was PM, which seemed to please him. I gave the *Mail* man a load of bollocks and the *Express* the total opposite — still bollocks, but different. Oh, and when the *News of the World* turned up I just got my chopper out — oh, saving your presence, Woman Policeman!'

She shook her head, smiling. 'Max, you're the end,' she said.

'Omega and Alpha, me,' sang Maxwell, still vaguely in the Christmas spirit. 'How long do you think they'll be out there?'

She checked her watch. Time to be elsewhere. 'The DCI's calling a press conference at six this evening,' she told him. 'That'll satisfy them for a while. Unfortunately, Max, they're a bit like that film. What is it? *Sometimes They Come Back* ?'

Maxwell nodded. He knew it.

She put down her coffee mug and held him by the shoulders, out of sight of the paparazzi's prying lenses. 'Are you all right?' she asked him.

'Awright.' He slid into his Barrymore with ease.

She screwed up her face, never sure of Peter Maxwell. He was Mad Max, not just nor-by-nor'west, but in all directions, to every point of the compass. He'd worn that mask for so long, even she couldn't see beyond it. She who loved him. She reached out and kissed him. It was enough. For now, it was enough.

* * *

Thanks to the miracle of reprographic technology, photographs of the dead woman were on the streets of Leighford by that afternoon. The house to house had begun. As many uniforms as Henry Hall could spare knocked on doors or rang bells or pushed paper through letterboxes. Everywhere the same story; the same shake of the head. 'Difficult to say, innit?' 'I mean, they all look alike.' 'Blimey, is she dead?' 'I wouldn't know my own grannie, mate, never mind somebody else's.'

A detective had visited Leighford General, next door to where the dead woman lay, checking records. But this was the National Health Service, the one run by Alan Milburn, not the one created by Nye Bevan and the inquiries drew blank. 'Ah, no, you see, all the ENT records were lost in the fire. You know, in '95. If she'd had the operation before that, we'd have no record of it. And I wouldn't bother asking Mr McGuigan if I were you. Patients to him are just numbers to feed his wife's Gucci habit — not that you heard that from here, of course.' Hospitals, especially junior registrars, were helpfulness itself.

So it was that they set up an Incident Room in the old Tottingleigh library, complete with VDUs and databases, those banks of information that could stem the tide of ignorance. And the Leighford force once again became eagle-eyed, adept under the diced headband at finding needles in the haystacks of unknowing.

So it was too that DCI Henry Hall held his press conference, giving the gentlemen of the press, the doyens of the fourth estate, just enough to keep them off his back for the couple of days he desperately needed. On his way in, towards the powerful lights to each side of the poking lenses and grey fur of the sound booms, he caught Jacquie Carpenter's arm.

'A word,' he said.

She slipped into the corridor. 'Sir?'

'Your friend,' Hall murmured.

'Sir?'

Hall shifted his feet. 'Don't get coy with me, Jacquie. Listen to those bastards in there. Baying for blood and they don't care whose it is. Maxwell. You've talked to him?'

'Yes, sir.'

The DCI looked into the steady grey eyes of the DC. He didn't like his people mixing it with Joe Public. But he knew that they were human too, with families and friends. There were bound to be relationships. But with Maxwell, it was different. The man had a knack of turning up in the middle of somebody else's pile of shit. And the annoying thing was he always came up smelling of roses. 'What has he told the press?'

'Nothing, sir,' she said. 'He doesn't know anything.'

'Jacquie.' He closed to her, anxious that the paparazzi should get no wind of this. 'I don't know how deep you're in with Maxwell. I don't want to know. But when you tell me he doesn't know anything, every alarm in my body starts to ring. Peter Maxwell always knows something. Usually, it's where the bodies are buried.' He turned to go, then turned back. 'And I don't necessarily mean that figuratively.'

Then he was gone, into the thick of it, facing the cameras and the music of the media.

'Good evening, ladies and gentlemen . . .'

* * *

Maxwell thought how much smaller Sean Holden looked in the flesh than on the screen. There he was on the local news that night, Meridian's man at the murder, standing outside

38 Columbine with a microphone in his hand, talking to camera.

'The body of an unidentified woman was found on this path behind me at midnight last night, as the old year turned.'

'Very poetic, Count, don't you think?' Maxwell stretched his feet in front of the coal-effect fire. The cat continued the habit of a lifetime and didn't answer. 'Still, I must put a lick of paint on that doorframe. Nothing like a murder for outlining one's need for DIY.'

'Police are regarding the case as one of murder. Detective Chief Inspector Henry Hall said at a press conference earlier this evening that the first task was to discover who the dead woman was.'

The face of a million secrets flashed on to the screen, causing Maxwell to blink for a second.

'Anyone with any information,' the reporter went on, should contact Leighford Police Station on 825311 or Crime Stoppers on 0800 555 111.'

'Why me?' Maxwell pressed the button on his remote and Sean Holden disappeared into the ether of the airwaves. And he found himself becoming Humphrey Bogart again. 'Of all the paths on all the estates in all the world, why did you have to be left on mine?' He caught the flick of Metternich's tail out of the corner of his eye. 'Of course, Count, you're right,' he said. 'That is a much more pertinent question, isn't it? — Who rang the doorbell?'

* * *

That was the year that Modular A levels were launched on to an unsuspecting world. Leighford High School had hung nervously back from the pilots at the end of the old century, largely at the behest of the educational dinosaur that was its Head of Sixth Form. The school's headteacher, James Diamond BSc, MEd, had been all for it, embracing the new examination structure rather as an idiot would embrace a boa constrictor. But Peter Maxwell had whispered the two dread words that were guaranteed to make any head teacher blanch and reconsider — 'league tables'. James Diamond had held off.

Now, however, there was no choice. The twenty-first century had caught up with Leighford High School and with it, Peter Maxwell. Modular A levels it was. And the first exams were now — January, wet and grey, with the temperature falling and the drizzle driving in from the west over the breeze-block and glass monolith that was Leighford High.

So it was that the laughingly called Spring Term began and a distinctly damp Head of Sixth Form wheeled in from the north-east, the spray flying off the spokes of White Surrey, his famous bike. Not for Surrey the rusty old bikesheds where the more robust kids chained their Meteors and Road Ragers. Peter Maxwell led the old white charger across the quad and hooked it lovingly against the wall of Food Technology.

'Saddle White Surrey for the field today,' he parodied Olivier's Richard III as he hobbled towards the side door. 'Look that my cycle clips be sound and not too tight. What, is my briefcase easier than it was and all my red pens laid into my desk? Ah, morning, Betty.' Maxwell was himself again. 'How are your boilers off for spots?'

'Doc' Martin's name wasn't really Betty. Neither did Maxwell know any guilty secret the man might have, perhaps in the silk underwear department. It was just that Maxwell called him Betty after the old English saying, itself a distortion of the Catholic prayer — 'All my eye of a yarn and Betty Martin'. No one else on the staff was old enough to remember it. As for Betty, the school caretaker, he was perfectly used to Maxwell talking to himself and quoting some crap or other. He was Mad Max. It was as simple as that.

'Fucked up, as usual,' he told him. 'Wouldn't be the start of term without that, would it?'

'Indeed not, Betty. Oh, Happy New Millennium.'

Mad, Martin mused. Mad as a March fucking hare.

Maxwell was down the corridor past T Eight, up the stairs and through the library, dripping rainwater from his army cape as he went. Miss Ratcliffe the librarian looked aghast. She'd been dreading the start of term as she always did, because the kids contrived to make her life a living Hell. To see the apparition she did however was the last straw.

'Morning, Matilda,' Maxwell boomed, sweeping off his saturated tweed cap. 'You can be sure,' he stood for a moment to take in the woman's narrow, sour face, as though she'd just sucked a lemon, 'that however ghastly we feel, the ducks are loving all this. I'll be in to talk libraries to you later, fear not. I just love it when you talk Dewey.'

Miss Ratcliffe had long ago stopped fearing anything from Peter Maxwell, least of all whether he might just, one day, get her name right.

He splattered along C corridor, where the neon strip was unaccountably flickering on and off. 'Thank you, Jason,' he thundered without turning round. 'I'm sure that when Mr Boston wants a lighting maestro for his next rattling good dramatic production, you'll be the first he'll call on. Until then, leave the bloody switch alone, there's a good pyromaniac.' Jason flattened himself against the wall until the wake of the Great Man had passed.

Maxwell crashed into his office and suddenly all eyes were on him. Lon Chaney Jnr stared at the caped crusader from behind his furry make-up as the *Wolf Man*; Alan Ladd smouldered at him through the smoke of his *Gun For Hire*; and a very badly drawn Orson Welles scowled at him from the poster of the Scottish Film. The cinema was Maxwell's second love. The decor of his office screamed Hollywood with just a hint of Ealing and Handmade.

'Thingee,' Maxwell had dropped his dripping cape and sprawled on his soft plastic chair, County Hall, teachers for the use of, with one of Mr Bell's telephonic apparati in his hand, 'Happy Millennium. When's the staff meeting?'

Thingee wasn't Pamela's real name either, but she did have the sure knowledge that Maxwell knew she was Morning Thingee as opposed to her afternoon oppo who was Thingee Too. And it wasn't really her place, as part time receptionist at Leighford High, to know such matters that were printed in the school calendar nearly a year before. But she also knew Mad Max.

'Two minutes ago, Mr Maxwell,' she said.

'Oops,' the Head of Sixth Form was on his feet. 'That's another New Year Resolution gone breasts up. Begging your pardon, of course, Thingee.'

'Mr Maxwell, I'm glad you rang, really. There's a policeman to see you.'

'Is there, now?' Maxwell sat down again. 'Tell me, Thingee, is he tallish, sandy hair, wears a three piece suit and rimless glasses? Could pass for our own dear Headmaster in a bad light — which, by the way, is the only way in which you can see our dear Headmaster?'

'Er. . . his name is Chief Inspector Hall,' Thingee answered. Maxwell nodded.

'Close enough,' he said. 'Show him up, would you?'

CHAPTER 3

'Happy Millennium,' Peter Maxwell shook the DCI's hand. 'Coffee?'

'No, thanks.' It had been a while since Henry Hall had stood in the office of the Head of Sixth Form. His youngest, Jeremy, was at Leighford now, in Year Nine, that luckless bunch of no-hopers picked on by all and sundry but mostly by the staff. He'd settled in surprisingly well, but he'd got to that age when he didn't want people to know his dad was a copper and he'd declined Hall's offer to drive him in that morning — 'No, I'll catch the bus, Dad; it's okay.'

'I understand you had something of a shock on New Year's Eve,' Hall took the proffered seat, easing the pile of exercise hooks to one side.

'You might say that,' Maxwell was brewing coffee on the low table near his desk.

'We've found out who she was.'

'Really?' Maxwell sat down opposite his man. He'd crossed Henry Hall before. He was a bland bastard. He was as inscrutable as Ming the Merciless, hiding as he did behind the blank lenses of his rimless specs. Men like Peter Maxwell wore their hearts on their sleeves. Men like Henry Hall probably didn't have a heart at all.

'Elizabeth Pride. Mean anything to you?'

Maxwell scowled, shaking his head. 'Not a thing,' he said. 'Should it?'

Hall raised his eyebrows. It was the gesture he used in lieu of a smile. 'I can't help wondering why anyone would dump a body on your doorstep, Mr Maxwell,' he said.

Maxwell smiled. 'The thought had occurred to me, Mr Hall,' he said. 'What do you know about this Elizabeth Pride?'

'I don't answer questions, Mr Maxwell,' Hall said. 'I just ask them.'

It was his best shot at avoiding cliché, but Maxwell wasn't having any. 'Humour me,' he said.

Hall hesitated. This was why he had come. He knew of old that Maxwell had his ways, his means of getting answers when the police could not. Against every rule in the book though it was, Maxwell had his uses. 'Well,' he said, 'the press will have it all by tomorrow anyway, so why not? Elizabeth Pride was seventy-four. She lived alone near the Chanctonbury Ring — Myrtle Cottage.'

'On the Downs?'

Hall nodded. 'She was a recluse. Lived with her cats and whatever memories she had. No known next of kin.'

'A spinster lady?'

'Widow, apparently. Husband died in the 'seventies. No children.'

'And nobody missed her, I suppose.'

'Exactly. She shopped in the local village, but had nothing delivered. Seems she was prone to wandering off from time to time anyway.'

'Flotsam,' Maxwell murmured.

'Sorry?'

'Flotsam. The floating debris of this great country of ours. Nobody noticed she'd gone. We're a long way from Jane Marple, Mr Hall.'

'Local postmistress identified her. Jesus, what's that?'

Maxwell laughed over the wailing siren. 'Well, it could be that ex-Comrade Putin has launched his nuclear strike, but I'd be prepared to bet it's the start of Lesson One. Ten C Eight. Oh, joy. Today, we're doing joined-up writing. You wouldn't care to swap jobs, I suppose?'

Hall was on his feet. 'Oh, no, Mr Maxwell. After all, you do mine anyway, don't you?'

The look on Maxwell's face said it all.

* * *

It was the moment that teachers the world o'er savour — the magic hour of four of the clock, when the tide of battle in school corridors recedes and the barbarian hordes drift away to lick their wounds and plan tomorrow's campaign. A few might do some homework.

'Knock, knock!' A curly head appeared around Maxwell's office door.

'Sylv!' the Head of Sixth Form was on his feet, and he took his visitor in his arms. Sylvia Matthews was Leighford's school nurse, the lady without the lamp. Six months ago, a hug and a kiss from Mad Max would have left her with weak knees and an iron lump in her throat caused by that age-old medical condition, the rising of her heart. Sylvia Matthews had loved Peter Maxwell for years. She still did. But she wasn't *in* love with him any more. She knew how hopeless it all was. And she knew about Jacquie Carpenter. And besides, Guy Morley filled her waking moments now. True, he was only, in Maxwell's sneering phrase, a supply teacher, but whatever Sylvia Matthews needed, Guy Morley could supply it.

'How was Christmas?' Maxwell asked, ushering her to a seat. 'The Millennium? The First Day?'

'Ah,' Sylvia's smile vanished. 'Trust you to wipe out a girl's dreams. I'm never ready for this one, Max, are you?'

'The psychological wrench of getting back to the Front?' he asked. 'No. "*I will go back tomorrow, from Imbros over the sea. Stand in the trench, Achilles, flame-capp'd and shout for me.*"'

'Absolutely,' Sylvia smiled, as usual blissfully unaware of what Maxwell was talking about. 'Just for the record,

Hannah Knightley isn't pregnant, Greg Smith's dad is inside again — GBH — and Mary McGee seems to have impetigo. I haven't seen a case in years. Sent her home.'

'Gentian violet,' Maxwell remembered. 'When I was at school, every other kid had purple splodges all over his face.'

'Ah, but then, they had red crosses on the doors when you were at school, didn't they?'

'Oh, ha,' he grimaced. 'Coffee, Sylv?'

'Scrummy. God — is that the state of your tea towel already? On the First Day?'

'Don't come the public healthier than thou, Sylv, please. As my old granddad used to say "You got to eat a peck of dirt". Mind you, he was dead at thirty-three.'

'Oh, come on, Max,' Sylvia suddenly blurted.

'What?' he queried in mock ignorance, looking for mugs.

'I saw the local news last night. I'd know thirty-eight Columbine anywhere. They found a body on your doorstep.'

'Did they?'

'Max!' She could bellow with the best of them, could Sylvia Matthews — a skill she'd acquired along with BCG testing.

'Oh, all right. Inspector Hall came a-calling this morning. After-sales care or something. Apparently, they've found out who she is. Elizabeth Pride — an old girl who lived up near Chanctonbury Ring.'

'Do they know who killed her?'

'Aha,' Maxwell chuckled. 'Slowly, slowly catchee monkey, I think is the order of the day.'

'Max,' Sylvia took his hand as he rummaged with the kettle, 'it must have been awful for you. I mean, finding her like that.'

'I'm all right, Sylv,' he smiled. 'But thanks for caring. Actually . . . what are you doing this evening?'

Sylvia raised an eyebrow. 'Are you asking me out for a date, Mr Maxwell?'

He tapped her wrist. 'You don't want to be so forward, young lady. No, it's just that I have a mind to watch the sunset over somewhere ancient and romantic — say, Chanctonbury Ring. And you have a car.'

'Max,' she tutted, smiling despite herself. 'You utter shit!'

'I hope I'm not interruptin'.' It was Mrs B., Leighford's Mrs Mopp, on her daily rounds. She could have been any age really — timeless, like Cleopatra. But she had the legs of Nora Batty. 'Ooh, them bleedin' kids don't get no better, do they? Don't Christmas seem a bloody age ago, eh? My Bert went on Boxing Day, y'know — still, it was a blessed release, really.'

Maxwell was well used to Mrs B.'s tirades. She 'did' for him at home as well as cleaning up behind the scattering classes at Leighford High. 'They don't, Mrs B.,' he answered her in question order. 'It certainly does. I'm so sorry about Bert. Was he a great age?'

'Well, only about three years for us, but to a budgie it's probably bloody Methuselah. Waddya think this is, Nurse?'

And Maxwell turned his head before something improper on Mrs B.'s person popped into view.

'Could be anything, Mrs B.,' he heard Sylvia say. 'Let's pop to my office, shall we? Max — half an hour?'

'Half an hour it is, Matron mine.'

'Got any ciggies, dear?' Mrs B. was asking. 'Only, some bloody kid's pinched mine. I won't be long, Mr Maxwell. Get your hooverin' done in a jiff. 'Ere, what about that poor old duck, eh? Dumped outside your house like that. It's a bleedin' shame, that's what it is. I blame that Tony Blair, y'know.' And she was gone with Sylvia in a cloud of Sanilav.

'Well, thanks for that, Mrs B.,' Maxwell poured a cup of coffee for himself. 'I'll get right on to Leighford CID and give that nice Mr Hall the benefit of your wisdom, shall I? They'll feel Mr Blair's collar in no time, don't you worry.'

* * *

They took the coast road to Sompting, then north on the A24, past golf courses without number to the high ground of the South Downs Way. As Sylvia's Clio snarled on the gravel of the English Heritage car park, they could see the Victorian splendour of Worthing along the coast and the pier at Brighton a grey spur jutting out into a greyer sea.

'So much for the sunset,' Sylvia switched off the engine. 'Is that it?'

She was looking across the headland, away from the sea at the tree encrusted slopes, on a horizon of blackness to her left.

'Don't knock it,' Maxwell unclipped his seat belt, ''til you've tried it.' And he got out. She locked the car with the flourish her remote gave her and did her level best to keep up with his stride. Mad Max wore a tweed jacket and his old college scarf looped around his neck. The cycle cape he'd discarded in the bowels of the Clio and he'd lowered the shapeless tweed cap firmly against the biting wind.

'Bit brass monkeys up here, Sylv,' he commented, ever a faithful barometer. 'Right, here we are,' he stood with his feet planted either side of a grassy ridge, the blades blown flat with the wind of the centuries. Above him the tree-topped ramparts were dark and ageless in the gathering night. 'It's cold in there even on a sunny day, believe me,' he told her.

'What is it, Max?' Sylvia couldn't make out the shape.

'The prosaic, historical answer is that it's an Iron Age hill fort. Perhaps it housed a hundred or so people. People like you and me, without our veneer of sophistication. Perhaps they watched Caesar's legions rolling from the east like an unstoppable tide. Listen.'

Sylvia did.

'Hear that?'

'Only the wind,' she frowned.

'Exactly. They say the birds don't sing here.'

'Birds don't sing at dusk anyway,' she comforted herself out loud. 'Not at this time of the year at least.'

'How are you at running backwards?' Maxwell asked her.

'What is this?' she snapped, getting frightened now as the night drew on.

He leaned towards her. 'They do say,' he growled, 'that if you run seven times backwards around these trees, the devil will appear for your soul.'

'Bollocks,' she snorted, clinging on to her sense of the here, the now. She was a child of the twentieth century and a woman of the twenty-first. She knew from long, deep talks with Mad Max it was only education that was running backwards.

'Quite right,' he chuckled. 'That can only happen at midnight on Midsummer Eve. Mind you,' his voice grew cold again, 'they say if you hear the beat of a horse's feet and the swish of a skirt in the dew . . .'

'Max! For God's sake, shut up, will you?'

'Nothing like a spot of Kipling between friends. Come on, Sylv. Got your torch? Myrtle Cottage must be down this way.' And he was gone, striding down the leeward slope away from the winds of the sea, away from the ghosts of Chanctonbury.

'How do you know?' she was running now, anxious to stay by his elbow.

'Know what? About Chanctonbury? Years of experience, my dear. Oh, and a brain the size of the Great Plains.'

'I mean,' she clutched her shoulder bag to help her balance on the uneven tufts of the slope, 'the whereabouts of Myrtle Cottage.'

'Well, while you were doing what women will, filling the car with petrol, changing your tyres or reboring the engine or whatever, I popped into the shop and asked directions.'

'Why didn't I think of that?' she asked him.

'You will, Oscar,' he patronised. 'You will. Aha, Eureka.'

Myrtle Cottage was particularly unprepossessing in the half light. There was clearly an unmade road to it from the east, but God alone knew where that came out and in any case, Maxwell had his bearings from the direction of the Ring.

'Victorian,' he said, looking at the dull red brick and the little windows. 'Possibly a little earlier.'

Sylvia fumbled in her bag for the torch and trained it on the front door. 'What's that?' she asked.

Maxwell couldn't tell her at first. A bunch of herbs swung under the little porch, at the mercy of the breeze that was lifting from the west.

'It's garlic.' Sylvia answered her own question as soon as her nose got close enough. 'Who hangs garlic over their front door?'

'Elizabeth Pride, evidently,' Maxwell said. 'Shine that thing on the lock, will you, Sylv?'

'Max,' she did as she was told. 'You're not going in there?'

'I haven't dragged you all this way to marvel at the architecture of the place,' he said.

'Why have you dragged me all this way?' It was perhaps a question she should have asked before.

'It was a little gem dropped in my lap by the chief inspector.' He was rattling the iron knocker, testing the door. 'Myrtle Cottage, Elizabeth Pride's address.'

'Wasn't that a little careless of him?' she asked, looking around at the house's dark windows.

'No,' he leaned his shoulder against the wood, 'Nothing that Henry Hall does is careless. He wants me in on this . . .'

'Why?'

'"Ours not to reason why", Miss Nightingale. Ready for a spot of b and e?'

B and Q Sylvia had heard of. 'What?' she asked.

His answer was a sudden charge of the right shoulder and the front door crashed back. 'Shit! That hurt!'

'Max!' she sounded half strangled in the dark. 'You've broken in.'

'That's what I like about you, Sylv.' He took the torch from her and let its beam wander the room. 'Your grasp of essentials. Mr Hall's generosity did not extend to him letting the door key fall out of his pocket on to my office furniture, so if we're to make headway . . . Needs must, when the devil drives.'

'We're to make headway?' she repeated.

'Sylv,' he found a switch, but it didn't work. He turned to face her, holding the torch so that he could see her, those shining eyes, that trusting face. 'Sylv,' softer now. 'Nobody dumps a body on my doorstep and says "That's Africa". I want answers.'

'Leave it to the police, Max.'

'The police,' he took her hand, 'seem happy enough to leave it — or at least part of it — to me.'

'What about Jacquie?'

'Who?'

Sylvia knew when to leave it alone. Max wasn't in the talking vein tonight.

There was a hiss and a scream and a cupboard door flew open above Sylvia's head.

'Jesus Christ!' She felt her heart thump and was glad of Maxwell's arm around her. His torch beam picked up the cause of the commotion immediately as a grey cat, old and frightened, crouched on a table, hissing at them, teeth bared, ears flat.

'Mrs Pride had cats,' Maxwell said.

'Do tell,' Sylvia was slowly returning to some sort of cardiac norm. 'Max, this place. It's like a time warp.'

It was. If it had ever had electricity, it wasn't working now. The cupboards with their glass doors were pure 'fifties. There was a single table with a plastic cloth, and two chairs. Rusted taps leaned over a stone sink of the type Kensington Sloanes paid a fortune for. There were still dishes in it, grubby with old food, partially licked clean by the rasping tongues of the cats.

'Pantry,' Maxwell wandered into it, a tiny lean-to off the living room. He was conscious of padding on ancient lino, worn smooth to the contours of the flagstones beneath. He flashed the torch around the room again, lingering in corners, letting the light creep along the cobwebbed ceiling. 'No one's lived here for a while,' he said. 'What do you think, Sylv?'

She tried the taps. Nothing. Not the merest of drips. 'Gives me the creeps.' The smell itself was enough — dank, derelict, dead.

Maxwell was rummaging in the cupboards. There were plates, cups, tins of cat food. A box of fairly ancient Weetabix he didn't want to investigate. The whole place reeked of tom

'Have the police been here?' Sylvia asked him.

'Presumably,' he nodded. 'If so, they'll have taken anything relevant away. Do you fancy upstairs?'

'No, Max.' He could rarely remember her voice so firm.

'Just a thought,' he cleared his throat, 'Hello, what's this?' The torch beam fell on a calendar, dusty and stained, pinned to the wall with a rusty drawing pin. The page was opened at December and someone had written for the 21st the words 'Thomas grey' twice. And on the 20th, in an unsteady hand, 'Good St Thomas, do me right and let my true-love come tonight. That I may see him in the face and in my arms may him embrace.'

'What is it. Max? Is that writing?' Sylvia couldn't make it out in the wobbling circles of the torch beam.

'Elizabeth Pride's last will and testament,' he said.

'Max,' he felt her arms snuggle into his and her head on his shoulder. 'Can we go now? I don't like this place much.'

* * *

Peter Maxwell looked up the name Grey. There was Edward, Viscount of Falloden who rolled up the maps in 1914 and never saw a lamp for the rest of his life. There was Jane, briefly England's queen until Bloody Mary took exception to her; and there was Zane, who wrote cowboy stories. With the alternative spelling of 'Gray' Chambers edition in Leighford High's library the next day gave him the poet who wrote Odes at a distance from Eton and was positively elegiac (for reasons best known to himself) about the churchyard of Stoke Poges.

Why, the Head of Sixth Form mused as he stirred his umpteenth coffee that day, should an old recluse make a big deal about a dead poet whose name she couldn't even spell?

'Jessica,' he growled to the tarty girl deep in conversation at the back of his classroom, 'I'm not sure Mr Diamond half a mile away in his office quite caught that last bit, covering last night's fumblings down the Front. Where were Lee's hands, exactly? Would you like to show us?'

Jessica looked outraged. You couldn't even have a private chat these days without some old perv wanting to know more. She looked at Maxwell. Still, poor old bugger. He probably wasn't getting any. You had to feel sorry.

'Mr Maxwell?' It was Helen Maitland, his loyal Number Two, at his elbow, the vast and good woman the sixth form called The Fridge on account of her bulk and her tendency to wear white.

'Mrs Maitland,' public schoolboy that he was, he was already on his feet, bowing low. Jessica continued her blow by blow-job account of last night.

'Sorry to bother you, Max, especially with Ten C Three, but can I introduce Crispin Foulkes? Peter Maxwell, Head of Sixth Form.'

'Mr Maxwell,' Crispin Foulkes was probably thirty-three, with a mane of golden hair and a serious set to his mouth, 'delighted to meet you,' and the men shook hands.

'Crispin's the new social worker in the area,' Helen explained. 'I'm introducing him to all the Year Heads.'

'Bad time?' Foulkes nodded in the direction of the class.

'No, not at all,' Maxwell chuckled. 'Two thirds of this lot will be on your couch by sunset anyway. Are you based at the Barlichway?'

'For my sins, yes. It seems to have its fair share of problems.'

That was an understatement. The Barlichway Estate was a disaster area. For a while in the mid-'eighties, when Toxteth burned and Broadwater bled, the Barlichway was a no go area. Its bleak windy terraces and 'sixties concrete were daubed with the anarchic art of the spray gun — and bad spray gun at that — and murky men sold powdered death in its empty shadows.

'Where were you before?'

'Erdington.'

'God,' Maxwell scowled.

'Quite,' Foulkes laughed. 'At least here you get sea glimpses.'

'Oh, we do that.' There was an electronic shattering of the moment. 'Ah, the bells, the bells.' Maxwell launched into his Charles Laughton's Quasimodo. 10 C 3 had seen it before. They ignored him.

'Homework!' he thundered at them. Now they listened, moaning as is the wont of fifteen-year-olds. 'Have a look at the question on page fifty-eight. I want at least three sides of exercise book and when do I want it?'

'Yesterday!' came the shouted answer and the stampede for the door began.

'See you, sir,' called the last kid.

'They like you,' nodded Foulkes.

'They hate my guts,' Maxwell smiled. 'But it gives them something to kick against and I'll get them through GCSE History or die in the attempt — the old motto of the Foreign Legion. Join us for a coffee?' He held up the mug he'd pinched from Special Needs last term.

'Eight A Four, Max,' Helen was making her excuses, already blocking the corridor on her way to D Block. 'See you again, Crispin.'

'Sure.' He waved.

'Salt of the earth, that woman,' Maxwell said. 'In here,' and he led the man next door into his office.

'Jesus!'

'Ah, one of my little hobbies.' Maxwell waved to the film posters.

'One of them?'

'The other one's teaching History,' the Head of Sixth Form winked. 'Sugar?'

'No, thanks.' Foulkes took the soft, low seat. 'I'm sweet enough.'

Maxwell was used to clichés. 'So what made you become a social worker?' he asked.

'That's very good,' Foulkes beamed.

'What is?' Maxwell was boiling his kettle.

'The way you said "social worker" without the merest hint of contempt.'

Maxwell looked at his man for a moment, then exploded with laughter. 'Just because you're paranoid,' he said, 'doesn't mean everybody doesn't hate you.' It was his turn for cliché.

'I'm used to it,' Foulkes said. 'Let me answer you by throwing the question back — why did you become a teacher?'

Maxwell thought for a moment while pouring Foulkes's coffee, then he became all of the Magnificent Seven rolled into one. 'After a while,' it was pure Steve McQueen, 'you can call EWOs and Ed. Psychs by their first name — maybe two hundred of 'em. Daytrips you've been on — five hundred. School dinners you've had — a thousand. Home, none. Wife . . .' his pause was longer than in the film, 'none. Kids — millions of 'em. Prospects, zero.'

'I . . .'

But Maxwell hadn't finished. It was Yul Brynner talking now, 'Places you're tied down to: one. Kids you step aside for: none.' Now it was Robert Vaughan. 'Insults swallowed: none. Enemies: none,' and he caught Foulkes's astonished gaze and smiled, 'alive.'

'You're having me on, Mr Maxwell,' said Foulkes.

'I am,' Maxwell laughed, handing Foulkes his coffee. 'And that's Max, by the way. But being a teacher is a little like being a gunfighter in a way. It's you and your six slugs of knowledge against a whole mean town of ignorance and indifference. Sorry,' he raised his mug. 'It's Thursday. I get a little poetic on Thursdays. Talking of poetry, what does a social worker know about Thomas Gray?'

'Thomas Gray?' Foulkes repeated. 'Nothing, I'm afraid. Why do you ask?'

Maxwell crossed to his desk. 'Thomas grey, Thomas grey.' He twisted the dog-eared calendar on his desk around so that it faced Foulkes.

'I didn't know you were a student of folklore, Max,' the social worker perched on the edge of his chair to get a closer look.

'Neither did I,' Maxwell said. 'What do you mean?'

'Well, here. The rhyme's not quite right. It should be Saint Thomas Grey, Saint Thomas Grey, the longest night and the shortest day. Saint Thomas was the patron of stone cutters and carpenters.'

'Doubting Thomas?'

'The same.'

'So you are a student of folklore, if not a professor, Mr Foulkes?'

Foulkes laughed. 'Oh, not even a student, I'm afraid. And that's Crispin, by the way. Look, you've got it here, on the 20th — "Good St Thomas, do me right. . ." St Thomas's Eve, a night to foretell the future, but to be wary of ghosts.'

'Ghosts?'

'What is this, Max? Somebody's heirloom?'

'The calendar? I wish I knew. Let's just say it came into my possession and I'm trying to make some sense out of it.'

'Can I have a look?'

'Of course.'

Foulkes flicked through the tattered pages with their strange, fusty smell. 'Max, where did you get this?' he asked slowly.

'It's not important,' Maxwell said, then he caught the look on the man's face, 'Is it?'

'Er . . . no,' Foulkes said. 'No, not at all.'

There was a knock on Maxwell's door and a pale bespectacled youth stood there.

'Right, Nigel,' the Head of Sixth Form said, 'give me a minute, would you?'

'No,' Foulkes was on his feet. 'I've got to be going. Thanks for the coffee, Max. I've got an appointment with your deputy head . . . Mr Ryan, is it?'

'Oh, bad luck,' Maxwell sympathized. 'One of the worst things Spielberg ever did, saving Mr Ryan. Turn left, then right, then follow the snail trail. Can't miss it.'

And Foulkes shook his hand. 'See you again.'

'Depend on it,' said Maxwell and turned to the geek bearing no gifts. 'All right, Nigel, now before I ring the Admissions Tutor at Peterhouse and reduce the man to a quivering wreck, tell me again why they've rejected you.'

CHAPTER 4

Henry Hall sat behind his desk in his office at Leighford nick. Opposite him sat Martin Stone, his new sergeant, whose eyes strayed when they could to his watch and whose mind, intermittently, was with the woman he loved, waddling round the semi in Chalgrove Park waiting for the contractions to start for real. Opposite him too sat Jacquie Carpenter, altogether more focused, altogether more together.

'Astley, then, Martin,' Hall opened the file in front of him.

'You didn't tell me he was a miserable old sod, guv,' Stone began.

'Some things detective sergeants have to learn for themselves.' It was the nearest the DCI was ever likely to get in the direction of humour.

Stone checked his notes. This was his first case with Hall. He didn't want to put a foot wrong at this delicate stage. 'The toxicology report confirmed Dr Astley's suspicions,' he said. 'He was most particular about that — that he'd been right.'

Jacquie smiled. That was the comforting thing about Jim Astley — there was absolutely no possibility of his being wrong.

'Organic poisoning had been administered to the dead woman a minimum of eight hours before she died. *Agaricus phalloides* is the scientific name apparently — phallin to the likes of you and me. Mushrooms.'

'Does he know how it was administered?' Hall asked.

'Sir?'

'Poisonous fungi are usually bitter to the taste and you can smell them three rooms away. Most of them are highly coloured too.'

'There was nothing like that at Myrtle Cottage,' Jacquie remembered. 'No food at all, in fact.'

'Except?' Hall looked at her over the rim of his glasses, like a professor gently prompting his student.

'Except . . . oh, my God.'

Stone looked from one to the other. 'You can't be serious. You mean Elizabeth Pride ate cat food?'

'Why not?' Hall shrugged. 'It's full of nutrition if you believe the manufacturers' hype.'

'And it's got flavours — mackerel, chicken, turkey.' Jacquie was suddenly aware that both men were staring at her.

'Cat lover, are you, Jacquie?' Stone asked. It was an innocent question.

'No,' she said, and omitted the cliché 'but I know a man who is.'

'Did Jim Astley stick his neck out and say what type of mushroom?'

Stone shifted in his seat. 'That's why I was late getting here,' he said. 'I had the whole lecture, the full monty. Apparently — and I quote — there are nearly two thousand larger fungi in the UK, of which two hundred are edible and ten are poisonous. Astley's problem is that he doesn't know — nobody does — the time lag between the old girl taking the stuff and the first symptoms. If they were late onset, say upwards of eighteen hours, he'd go for *Amanita palloides* — Death-Cap.'

'Looks and peels like a common mushroom,' Jacquie said.

'Thanks for the woman's touch,' Hall murmured. 'Relevance?'

'The old girl could have eaten them by accident, sir.'

'That's as maybe,' Hall was leaning back, his hands behind his head, 'but she didn't then stab herself in the back of the neck, climb into a package of bin-liners and deposit herself on Peter Maxwell's doorstep, having carefully rung his doorbell first.'

There was no real answer to that and Jacquie didn't give one.

'No one thought to take any food samples, I suppose, from Myrtle Cottage?' Hall checked. 'The cat food? Whatever was on those plates in the sink?'

'Er . . . I was just going to get on it, guv,' Stone grinned.

'The first time, Martin,' Hall said softly. 'When you know me better, you'll learn I like things like that done the first time.'

'Yes, sir. Sorry. But there's no real harm done, is there? I mean, nobody will have been snooping? We didn't give the old girl's address.'

It was Hall's turn to shift in his chair. 'No,' he said, 'indeed we didn't. Jacquie, how's the Incident Room getting on with next of kin?'

'It's early days, sir,' she told him.

'That's right,' an unflappable bastard was Henry Hall, 'but we both know, Jacquie, about cold trails. It's been four days.'

'There was a husband — er . . . She checked her notes. 'Edward. Died in '79.'

'Did he live at Myrtle Cottage?'

'We don't have any other address at the moment,' she said. 'Uniform have talked to the locals at Wetherton where the old girl occasionally did her shopping.'

'And?'

'Nobody really liked her. One or two felt a bit sorry, but she wasn't easy. Help her across the road and she'd bite your head off — you know the sort of thing.'

Hall did.

'Had something of a reputation, though.'

'Reputation?' Stone asked. 'As what?'

'Oh, you know,' Jacquie chuckled. 'As a witch.'

* * *

The truly great thing about Friday is that it marks the end of the working week. Peter Maxwell wrapped his scarf around his neck, snapped his cycle clips into position and pedalled hell-for-leather over the darkening fields heading for the flyover and home.

'Those things'll kill you!' he roared as he rattled around Smokers' Corner at the far end of the Sports Hall. Three consumptives sprang apart, dawdling as they had been on their way home in order to light up. 'That's in the long term. In the short term all three of you are in detention next Thursday. Have a nice day!' and he'd gone, whistling down the wind.

* * *

Now, Peter Maxwell had a vice. Well, actually, he had several. But that evening, he sat in the lamplit attic at 38 Columbine and indulged in his favourite. Before him on his desk lay a white plastic man beside a white plastic horse, 54mm high and correct in every detail. This was the three hundred and eighty-ninth figure to join the great diorama he was creating in the centre of the room. Beneath the roof's apex, three hundred and eighty-two such plastic men sat painted and ready to ride into the Valley of Death. It was an expensive and time-consuming hobby, but it filled the dead hours of Maxwell's life. And one day, all six hundred and seventy-eight of Lord Cardigan's Light Brigade would be saddled and waiting. By then, Maxwell computed, he would be retired and too broke to buy any more. At the moment however, though he'd rather Mr Blunkett never found out, he had the paint, he had the glue, he had the money too.

'Couldn't borrow your lesson plans for Year Thirteen, could I, Max?' his green Head of Department, Paul Moss, had once had the temerity to ask.

'Lesson plans, Paul?' Maxwell's basilisk stare had frozen more sensitive men. 'What they?'

No, Peter Maxwell had far more interesting things to fill his time with than something as trivial as education.

'Yes, of course he rides a grey, Count,' Maxwell was talking to his cat again. 'Have I taught you nothing about the Light Cavalry in all these years?'

Evidently not. Metternich twitched an ear and yawned ostentatiously. 'Trumpeter Hugh Crawford, Number 1296 4th Light Dragoons. All trumpeters of the cavalry rode grey horses for ease of identification, except in the Scots Greys, of course, where it would cause a little confusion. There the trumpeter rode a black or a bay.'

As if to show his passionate fascination, Metternich rolled a little way and placed his right leg behind his right ear, before pedantically licking his bum. 'Kama Sutra, page 194,' Maxwell murmured, unimpressed by the beast's agility. He had after all seen it all before. It was only the fact that he'd been to a good school that prevented him from doing the same.

'Crawford was Canadian actually, born at Fort George. He was taken prisoner in the Charge, but Sam Parkes of his regiment saved his life. Left his wife behind at the depot at Brighton,' he carefully rested the plastic trumpet across the soldier's shoulder, concentrating hard with the glue stick in his other hand, 'which, as you know, is just up the . . . Shit!'

The phone's harsh ring shattered the moment and Metternich was gone like a cat out of hell, down the attic stairs.

'War Office,' Maxwell reached the receiver seconds later.

'Hello?' a rather startled voice said from the other end.

'Who's that?'

'Mr Maxwell?'

'Yes.'

'Oh, you don't know me. I'm Ken.'

'Ken,' Maxwell lolled back in his swivel chair, 'how's Barbie?'

'Er,' there was an attempt at a giggle. But Ken Templeton had heard that one before. 'I was wondering if I might . . .'

'Double glazing? Got it. Treble, in fact. Car? Don't drive. Medical insurance? I'll take my chances with AIDS, TB, swamp fever . . .'

'No, no. I'm ringing on behalf of Beauregard's.'

'Beauregard's?'

'Does the name mean anything to you?'

'It does indeed. Pierre Gustave Toutant Beauregard was one of the gentlemen of the South from West Point. Rather an ace general, as it happens. Took part in that little spat the Americans had among themselves a few years back.'

There was a pause. 'Oh, really? Well, no, this has nothing to do with him. We're a new fitness club recently opened in Leighford.'

'Ken,' Maxwell interrupted. 'It must be a very depressing business trawling through the phone book . . .'

'No, no, Mr Maxwell. You were recommended. This isn't a cold sell, I can assure you.'

'St Benedict himself couldn't have had one colder, Ken, I can assure you.' And he put the phone down, desperately scrabbling on hands and knees for the tiny trumpet that had fallen God knew where.

'Recommended?' He suddenly knelt up and fetched himself a smart one on the corner of his desk. 'Who the hell would recommend me for a fitness club? I, who put the potato into couch. Dear God in heaven, is this what the twenty-first century is going to be like?'

* * *

Peter Maxwell wasn't exactly a party animal. It was commonly believed in the staffroom at Leighford High that the last one he'd been to was the night they relieved Lady Smith. In fact the old duck had more right to be relieved than anybody at Leighford knew — Maxwell had been busy that night.

But it was Saturday. And Jacquie had asked him. And she did know a few vital Ju-jitsu holds that were guaranteed to make a man's eyes water, should he refuse. Besides, he wanted to talk to her.

'Tell me about Myrtle Cottage,' he said in the green glow from Jacquie's dashboard lights.

He didn't see her knuckles whiten on the steering wheel, nor the muscles in her jaw flex. 'Where?' she asked, and felt his eyes burning into her as he lolled sideways, his head on her shoulder. Peter Maxwell had invented body language — the fawning adulation of a lap-dog and the inquisitional skills of the Gestapo all rolled into one. 'Oh, all right, but first . . .'

'I know.' He straightened up again and raised both hands. 'Not a word to Bessie and I've never seen you before in my life, have I, darling?'

'That's not what I was going to say — although, yes, it'll do for starters.' She swung the wheel and purred onto the flyover, the tail lights of cars magic in their road-spray radiance. 'What I was going to say was — how did you know about Myrtle Cottage?'

'Ah, well,' Maxwell wriggled lower in his seat to ease the numbness in his left buttock. What had possessed Jacquie to buy a Ka? 'Therein lies the essential schizophrenia of today's police force, my dear. On the one hand, there's you, the dutiful detective constable who clams up. On the other, there's your boss, the DCI, with as clear a case of verbal diarrhoea as I ever saw.'

'Hall talked to you?' There was a distinct wobble in Jacquie's road positioning and from nowhere a horn blasted the night.

'Indeed,' Maxwell still had his two fingers in the air. It was the knee-jerk reaction of the lifelong cyclist.

'When? Where?'

'Last Tuesday. At school. You know, you're getting more like Mrs B. every day.'

'Thanks. What did he say?'

'Told me the dead woman's name and where she lived.'

'Christ.' Jacquie looked at him for as long as staying alive on the flyover would allow. 'Why?'

'Am I your DCI's keeper?' Maxwell asked her. 'Maybe he felt lonely, needed a chat; perhaps he's a one-man pilot scheme for Jack Straw's Freedom of Information Act; I don't know.'

'This is weird, Max.' She was shaking her head and frowning.

'No more weird than someone leaving a frozen body on my doorstep. But now the cat's out of the bag, so to speak, Myrtle Cottage?'

'The old girl lived there,' Jacquie shrugged. 'SOCO have been all over it. Nothing that would indicate how she died or who killed her.'

'How did she die?'

'Oh, no,' Jacquie laughed, joining the queue to the A27. 'We may have something going here, Max, you and I — I hope we have . . .' and she looked across at him waiting for confirmation, while he stared stoically ahead. 'Bastard,' and she thwacked him — lovingly — around the ear. 'Even so, I can't go into any of that — you know I can't. What if I came snooping around Leighford High?'

'You'd find an open book,' he said. 'Several hundred of them, in fact. We have no secrets. Legs Diamond, the Headmaster, is an ineffectual nerd; his deputies Bernard Ryan and Roger Rabbitt are slightly worse. David Boston, Head of Drama . . .'

'I think you're deliberately missing the point, Max,' she interrupted him.

'You're right,' he beamed, 'but that's what points are for.'

'Here we are,' she tucked the Ka in behind a Range Rover so that it looked like the dot of an exclamation mark. 'Willoughby's.'

'His name isn't really Willoughby, is it?' he asked as he disentangled himself from his seat belt.

'You are not to be rude,' she warned him, eyes flashing with laughter. And he was still doing his terribly hurt impression as they reached the front door.

By half past ten, Maxwell had lost the will to live. Whoever Willoughby was, he had either never heard of Southern Comfort or the crafty bugger had locked the good stuff safely away. Maxwell had chatted over the row of the '90s music and found himself belting out the one blast from the past he recognised — 'The Mighty Quinn' — with the rest of them.

'Tell me,' a thirtysomething brunette had suddenly appeared on the arm of his settee, thighs on a level with his nose, 'why Willoughby hasn't already introduced us?'

Maxwell took in the slightly bleary make-up, the lack of bra and the fuck-me shoes and drew his own conclusions. 'I've just been lucky, I guess. Not that I've met Willoughby yet.'

The woman's eyes widened and her lips formed a silent o. Then she tapped his modelling arm playfully. 'And you're such a bitch. I like that in a man,' and she squeezed herself between Maxwell and the settee arm, a feat that surprised them both.

'I'm Prissy,' she held out a limp hand that was festooned with gold.

'Surely not?' he frowned and took it. 'Maxwell.'

'I know. Isn't it awful? Ciggie?'

He shook his head.

'Mummy had this thing for Cilla Black — well, they were different days, that's the only excuse I can think of — so when I came along, Priscilla it was. Everyone called me Cilla of course until I was fourteen. Then I rebelled. Lost my virginity at the same time.'

'Congratulations.'

'Oh, no,' Prissy slurred. 'It's one of the easiest things I've ever done. Are you with anybody?'

'With in the Biblical sense?'

Prissy looked a little confused. 'You naughty man,' she trilled, lighting up. 'Not one of your vices, then?' She waved the fag in his face.

'No.' He coughed for effect. 'Actually, I came with Jacquie Carpenter.'

'Oh, Jacquie.' Prissy blew smoke down her horsy nostrils. 'Lovely girl. Shame she's filth. Oh, you aren't, are you?'

'No, no. Good Lord, no. Scum.'

'I'm sorry?'

'I'm scum. A teacher.'

'Oh.' That piece of information usually produced results like that. 'Look, your glass is empty. Can I top you up?'

Before Maxwell could reply he'd have to be getting along, she'd found a bottle from somewhere and refilled his glass. 'What is it you teach?' Prissy asked.

'Oh, the usual,' he smiled. 'Children.'

There was a pause before she giggled. 'You silly man. What age group?'

'The terrible teens,' he told her.

'Oh, frightful.' She gulped at her glass. 'Still, I bet there's quite a bit of teenaged totty has the hots for you, though, eh? We did in my day. Course, that was a boarding school.'

'Don't tell me you had a groundsman hung like Bow Bells?' Maxwell sighed. St Trinians he could do without.

Prissy closed her eyes. 'Well, if it's stories you like, Maxwell . . .'

'Maxwell?' The owner of that name had never been so glad to hear a male voice in his life. 'Mr Maxwell?'

'Er . . . yes.' A crop haired young man had plonked himself down on the other side from Prissy. 'Well, this is extraordinary. I'm Ken.'

'Ken?' Maxwell looked blank.

'Ken Templeton — from Beauregard's. I was talking to you last night. The phone call.'

'Really?' Maxwell shifted as much as he could. 'It seems longer ago.'

'This is an amazing coincidence.'

'Yes, isn't it?' Prissy leaned across, her smile a mask of tightness. 'Look, Ken, why don't you go and find that silly little wife of yours and give us all a break?'

Ken leaned across Maxwell. 'I don't think this is the time or place, Prissy, dear . . . Mr Maxwell, have you reconsidered Beauregard's?'

'Well, I . . .' Maxwell felt Prissy fingers sliding up his thigh. 'As a matter of fact, I have. Shall we?' And he hauled Ken upright and bowed curtly to Prissy as they left.

The two of them climbed over assorted bodies in the hall. 'Do you think Willoughby would mind if I used his phone?' Maxwell asked Ken.

'I'm sure he wouldn't. Now, about Beauregard's . . .'

'Ken, look,' Maxwell slowed his man down. 'I can see that under that shirt beats a heart of gold and pecs of steel. But look at me, my trackless waists.'

'Nonsense, Mr Maxwell, just a bit of toning, that's all. I hear you're a keen cyclist.'

'I get from A to B,' Maxwell shouted over the cacophony from the lounge, 'but I must get a taxi tonight.'

'Nonsense,' a voice he recognised was at his left ear, car keys jingling in the dim light. 'I couldn't let you.' Prissy rested her arm against the doorframe, the contours of her body moulded into her party dress.

'I hope you don't think you're driving anywhere.' Someone snatched the keys from her hand. Prissy spun round to face him.

'Give me those keys, you bastard, or you know what's going to happen, don't you?'

The plump-looking man with the crimson face faltered for a moment. Then, aware that everyone was looking at him, he managed a grin. 'Well,' he winked at her, 'just 'cos it's you, Priss.' She arched an eyebrow and snatched the keys back before twisting her stiletto into his foot as she turned. He winced and leaned back against the wall.

'Max, good Lord, hello.'

'Kr . . . Crispin,' Maxwell turned at the slap on his back. 'Tonight's just full of surprises.'

'Well, it is. I didn't know you knew Willoughby.'

'I don't.'

'Well, for God's sake, you've just been talking to him. Willoughby Crown, this is Peter Maxwell.'

'Mr Maxwell,' Crown shook his guest's hand.

'I'm sorry but I have to be going,' Maxwell said. 'I'm afraid my lift had to leave early.'

'Jacquie C.,' Prissy said. 'It was all very exciting. Her bleeper thing went off. Some sort of emergency.'

'I was trying to get Mr Maxwell to join the club, Crispin.' Ken was one hell of a persistent salesman.

'Yes,' Foulkes smiled, 'Yes, that is a good idea.'

'You're a member?' Maxwell asked him.

'Oh, just a bit of weights. Nothing heavy. Prissy fences, don't you, darling?'

The woman suddenly threw her right leg forward and her straight arm pinned Peter Maxwell to the wall.

'Oh, for fuck's sake.' Willoughby wandered away.

'What a riposte!' Foulkes winked at Maxwell. 'No, you really should get along to Beauregard's. It's a bit of fun. Besides,' he became as sotto as the thumping CD would allow, 'I wanted to talk to you about something.'

'Oh,' Maxwell extricated himself from Prissy. 'What's that?'

'Calendars,' said Foulkes and he swirled away to join the dancers in the other room.

'Shall we?' Prissy was still dangling the keys.

Maxwell looked around for agony and loss, but all his allies had deserted him. Ken had been whisked away to the kitchen to have his drink refilled, Willoughby had retired hurt. He turned back to Priscilla, queen of the desert.

* * *

It may have been the longest ride of Maxwell's life, like the one the bit players always took in the back of the Mob's cars in B movies. But Maxwell wasn't in the back, he was in the front of Prissy's Shogun and it wasn't his imagination that her party frock rode up higher with every gear change. If he'd lived any further away than the other side of Leighford, it would have become a rather attractive hat.

'What did you make of Crispin?' she asked him as they roared along the flyover.

'Nice bloke,' Maxwell said when the G-force of her driving let him.

'For a social worker, you mean? God, yes. Namby-pamby bloody job.'

'What do you do, Prissy? For a living, I mean?'

'As little as possible. Daddy was a merchant banker with a decidedly dicky ticker. I was an only child. A perfect combination, really. I'm one of those people the Lefties can't stand — a woman of independent means. Tell me, Maxwell, can I ask you a personal question?'

'You can ask,' Maxwell smiled.

'You and Jacquie. Are you an item?'

'Now,' Maxwell leaned across to her, an easier task in the Shogun than it had been in the Ka. 'Why would you want to know that?'

She hit the accelerator hard and the Shogun lurched to the right, hurtling past a BMW on the one side and the crash barrier on the other. 'I like you,' she said, staring straight ahead. 'I like men in general, but you're . . . I don't know, different.'

'Must be the cut of my G-string,' he winked at her.

'That remains to be seen,' she purred.

'First left beyond the lights,' he told her.

'Will you join Beauregard's?' she asked him.

Maxwell shrugged. 'I might,' he said.

'Well, that would be good.'

They reached 38 Columbine a little after twelve. It was Sunday morning and the lamps still glowed their eerie orange. A large, rangy black and white cat prowling the privet, took one look at the woman in the Shogun's driving seat and beat a hasty retreat. That wasn't the one Maxwell had gone with. The car, the smell, it was all different. This one, even through the closed window, reminded him of himself — a hunter, a creature of the night. What was the old bastard doing, playing with fire like that? He'd tackle him about it later.

'You're stone cold sober, aren't you?' Maxwell had slipped off his seat belt.

She turned to him, the engine still idling. 'Of course. What did you expect? A lush?'

He shrugged. 'I don't really know.'

'Maxwell,' she was looking hard at him. 'I've been watching you tonight.'

'Oh?' He felt like a prize bull in a show ring. He was old enough to remember when farmers had such things.

'You're a listener, aren't you?' she asked.

'Goes with the territory,' he said. 'But I should warn you I'm no good with anybody over eighteen.'

'I don't suppose you've formed a very good impression of me,' she said and sounded like a little girl again. The fatale seemed to have vanished from her femme. He took in the cleavage, pale in the dashboard's glow, the powerful thighs below the stretched dress.

'I don't form impressions,' he said.

'Maxwell. You know I've heard of you. Before tonight, I mean.'

'From Jacquie?' he asked.

'No. Not from Jacquie. You're a knight errant too, aren't you?'

'Depends on the damsel,' he said, feeling for the door handle.

Her hand snaked out to his chest, her fingers sliding over his shirt. 'This damsel is in distress, Maxwell,' she said, her face taut, her front gone.

'What kind of distress?'

She looked away suddenly, biting her lip in the half light. 'You solve murders,' she said.

Maxwell blinked. 'Do I?' he asked.

'Oh, for fuck's sake,' she snapped at him. 'You're like a bloody psychiatrist.' Then softer, 'There's . . . there's something . . . sinister happening at the club,' she said. 'At Beauregard's.'

He waited. There wasn't going to be any more. Not there. Not then.

'Would you like to come in?' he asked, half-dreading the answer. She hit the ignition and crashed the Shogun into gear. 'No, thanks,' she said. 'I'd better get back.'

'To the party?'

'Yes,' she tried to smile, 'to the party. I live there, Maxwell.'

'You . . . I see. So Willoughby . . .'

'. . . is my husband, yes,' she said quietly, 'but that's just a cross I have to bear. No one's afraid of Willoughby, Maxwell.' She flashed her indicator, revving the engine. 'Except Willoughby, of course.'

And he waved as he dropped down from the Shogun and watched her drive into the night.

CHAPTER 5

Metternich raised his lion's head and scented the wind. Bacon sarnies. Heaven. That meant it must be Sunday morning already. What was the betting He Who Must Be Ignored would ruin the appeal of any scraps he might leave by plastering them all with that noxious brown stuff.

'Running low on the old HP, Count,' Maxwell called through from the kitchen, as though it were somehow the cat's fault. He had to get back to Myrtle Cottage, that less-than-chocolate-box place in the folds of the Weald, his only link with the woman who had ended up on his doorstep. He needed the daylight and he needed time. He looked at the pile of A-level essays on his coffee table, taunting him, haunting him.

'Later, everybody,' he muttered, finishing his coffee. 'Today belongs to the late Elizabeth Pride.'

When he'd gone, the black bomber, the great white hope, slunk off the pouffé and checked out Maxwell's plate. Yup! Just as he thought — that brown stuff was all over the sliver of bacon the old bastard had abandoned. Metternich sneezed in disgust and wandered away.

Maxwell left White Surrey in the shed. He couldn't call on Jacquie; she was too sensitive about the whole business.

Neither could he bother Sylvia again — it hardly seemed fair. So he swallowed his pride and caught a bus. That way he saw a lot of the West Sussex countryside at an incredibly leisurely pace and overheard conversations that normally only Alan Bennett is privileged to hear.

'I had an accident this morning, Beryl.'

'Oh, dear.'

'I used my spray deodorant, you know . . . down there. Only it was polish.'

'Oh dear.'

Maxwell didn't dare look around in case the old girl in question slid the length of the aisle.

* * *

Chanctonbury stood silent in the hoar frost. Shortly before dawn the cold had come and the brass monkeys scampered and chattered over the uplands, still silver in the mid-morning. He felt his feet crunch on the grass as he left the road and he saw the rooks wheeling and bickering as they skirted the tall trees on the Ring. He paused on the ridge, as the iron men of the Iron Age had before him and looked at the broad sunlit sweep of the valley below. He saw the winter-hard furrows of the ploughlands and the knots of sheep huddling along the hedgerows for shelter. A single tractor rattled its way across the hill, a solitary black and white dog padding in its wake.

Myrtle Cottage looked larger in the sunlight, nestling against a bank of dead brambles that coated the hillside like the barbed-wire tangles in the trenches of Christmas 1914, silver and deadly. Maxwell strode down, glad of his scarf and gloves, his breath snaking out and wreathing behind him as the wind took it.

It was only when he reached the cottage's rusting gate that he realised he was not alone.

'Hello,' a voice called. Standing in the lee of the cottage was a man, perhaps thirty, perhaps not, with a sleeveless sheepskin jacket and a scruffy flat cap. His dark face was hidden in the shadows and he was smoking a roll-up between pinched lips.

'Morning,' Maxwell switched to cheery mode.

'What do you want?'

'Peter Maxwell,' the Head of Sixth Form was through the gate and on the broken bricks of the path. '*Littlehampton Mercury*. Is this Elizabeth Pride's house?'

'Was,' the man said. He was still leaning on the cold brickwork, like Shane when the Ryker boys came threatening Van Heflin.

'Yes, terrible, isn't it? Mr . . . er . . . ?'

Now the man straightened. 'Whaddya want to know my name for? Your bloody paper?'

'Just doing a piece on the murder,' Maxwell told him. 'Did you know the old girl?'

'I might of.'

Maxwell knew kids like this. Chips on their shoulders Harry Ramsden's would be proud of. He flipped out his wallet, watching the man's reaction and reminded himself of Sir Robert Walpole's wisdom — 'every man has his price.'

A crisp tenner stood stark in his fist. 'How well?'

'Well enough,' and the man had snatched it.

'Shall we go inside?'

'No.' The answer was sharp, sudden, emphatic.

'All right,' Maxwell smiled and rested himself on the low wall that circled the garden, 'but I'll need a bit more than "well enough" for a tenner.'

'Like?'

'Like your name for a start.'

'You'll only use it.'

'No, no,' Maxwell assured him. 'It's the paper's policy not to print anything which is unattributable. It's also the paper's policy not to print names if we're asked not to.'

'Cruikshank,' growled the man after some hesitation. 'I live yonder.'

'Yonder?' Maxwell wondered if he'd stumbled into a time warp, if the old continuum had come round and smacked him in the face.

'Who's this, Joe?' another voice made both men turn.

'Some reporter bloke,' Joe said, dragging on the stub.

'What's he want?' The newcomer was a broader version of the first, a shapeless willy cap pulled down over his ears.

'Information about Elizabeth Pride,' Maxwell told him.

'Bitch, she were,' the newcomer snarled, squatting on the dead woman's wall along from Maxwell, shading his eyes from the watery sun.

'Indeed, Mr . . . er . . .'

'Cruikshank.' He grinned a gappy smile. 'Same as him.'

'I thought I detected a likeness,' Maxwell said.

'I'm not surprised she's dead.'

'Really?' Maxwell raised an eyebrow. 'Why's that?'

'Had it coming, didn't she?' Joe said, throwing his fag into the weeds.

'Killed our dog,' muttered the other one.

'Killed? Really?'

'You're like a fuckin' stuck record, mate.'

'Easy on, Ben,' Joe said. 'Bloke's only doing his job.'

'Have the police talked to you yet?' Maxwell asked.

'The police don't talk to us, mate. And we don't talk to them.'

'See, we're travelling people,' Joe volunteered. 'Romanies. Rubbish, we are. Vermin. We steal and vandalise and rape, don't we, Ben?'

Ben sniggered. 'Every chance we can get,' he said. 'Look, we don't steal horses and sell pegs and lucky lavender any more and we ain't got one of them fancy sod-off gyppo vans neither, so why don't you stick your poncy nose into somebody else's business?'

'If you're hanging around Elizabeth Pride's house,' Maxwell said, 'I think you are my business.'

'Do you?' Ben had shambled to his feet.

'My brother told you.' Joe was closing along the path. 'The old cow killed our dog.'

'Why?' Maxwell asked.

Both brothers grunted. 'Why not?' Joe asked.

'Because she fuckin' could,' Ben growled.

'What we don't know is how,' Joe went on. 'One morning it was right as rain. Next day she looked at it. Just bloody looked, mind. Nothing else. Dropped dead right in front of us.'

'So you killed her?' Maxwell was chancing his arm.

'That's right, mate,' Ben said softly. 'With this.' Suddenly there was a knife in his hand, glinting in the sunlight. Maxwell hadn't moved. 'Now, why don't you fuck off?'

'While you still can,' Joe underscored the situation for his brother.

For a moment Maxwell hesitated. Either of the brothers could just about pass for his sons. They were leaner, tougher, nastier, more armed. Time enough for valour on some other field.

'Well, that's settled then,' he smiled. 'I'll just have a look round.'

'No you won't, mate.' It was Joe who blocked his path.

'You don't wanna go in there, son,' Ben assured him.

'Really? Why not?'

'Look,' he pointed to the door. 'Know what that is?'

'Garlic.' Maxwell basked in Sylvia Matthews' reflected glory. He didn't know one plant from another, though the smell would have given it away in time.

'Precisely,' Ben snarled. 'Now, you take heed of that, mate. And off you fuck.'

Maxwell smiled. 'It's been . . . an education,' he said, tipped his hat and retraced his steps up the rise to the Ring.

* * *

The dead man lay cold in the North Transept, his hands clasped on his chest, his sword at his side. Somebody, be it Cromwellian soldier or souvenir hunter had taken his legs away. No wonder he was frowning under the rim of the bascinet.

'Sir John Viney,' a voice called from behind him. 'Commanded the left wing at Crecy.'

'Three leaves azure on a field argent,' Maxwell said, his voice ringing slightly in the vaults of the church, 'Viney. The old canting ploy. A pun on the owner's name.'

'Ah, a student of heraldry,' the voice said. 'I'm impressed.'

So was Maxwell. It had been a long time since he'd translated cross-hatching from a sepulchral brass. The owner of the voice padded into view, a tall, white-haired spectre of a man who wore his tell-tale collar back to front. 'Would you care to hazard a date?'

Maxwell took in the jupon with its folds and the extent of plate armour. The knight's likeness glinted dully in the afternoon light and the stained glass threw blues and golds onto the stone canopy on which he lay. 'Thirteen seventy, thirteen eighty,' he guessed.

'Thirteen seventy-two,' the vicar beamed. 'Now I really am impressed. Andrew Darblay,' he extended a sinewy hand.

'Vicar?' Maxwell asked.

'Rector,' the old man smiled. 'But who's counting?'

'Peter Maxwell.' Maxwell shook the man's hand.

'Just visiting our lovely old church?' Darblay asked. 'Or are you early for Evensong?'

'Either or,' Maxwell said. 'You've a fine collection of tombs.'

'The Vineys built this place,' the rector told him. 'Sir John's father endowed it. His great grandson built the Lady Chapel and his great-great-great-grandnephew put in what laughingly passes for central heating. Are you an historian, Mr Maxwell?'

'Of sorts,' Maxwell confessed, 'but I'm actually here on less pleasant matters.'

'Oh?'

'The murder of Elizabeth Pride.'

'Ah.'

'I understand she shopped here in the village.'

'May I ask your interest?' Darblay tried to get the measure of his man. College scarf. Too much hair for his strict Anglican tastes, vaguely resembled a greying hippy.

'*Littlehampton Mercury*,' Maxwell explained on the grounds that if you're going to lie, be consistent about it. 'I'm writing a piece.'

'Oh,' Darblay smiled wryly. 'So you're a paparazzi, are you?'

'No,' Maxwell shook his head, smiling too. 'I am a reporter.'

The old man took him by the arm and led him down the transept, turning briefly to bob before the altar. They turned into the nave. 'In my less charitable moments I sometimes think that when the Good Book tells of "tax gatherers and others" it refers to journalists. Then my sense of Old Testament history takes over and I know better.'

'Good to hear it,' Maxwell smiled.

'Would you care for a small sherry?' Darblay asked him.

'A small sherry would be delightful.'

The Rectory at Wetherton was one of those unpretentious fourteen bedroomed jobbies that really miffed people and had turned the Victorian deferential tenant into the Marxist yobbo of the twentieth century consumed by the politics of envy. Darblay pointed out his magnificent rhododendron bushes, the superiority of his wisteria and showed Maxwell the lake where the herons dipped of a summer's evening.

38 Columbine would have fitted quite snugly into Darblay's hall and his study could easily have swamped Leighford High's gym. Still, Maxwell said nothing, preferring to wallow in his own hyperbole. The old cleric's sherry was particularly old peculiar to a palette corroded and destroyed by the delicious bite of Southern Comfort, but it hit the spot well enough on a freezing Sunday afternoon.

'I'm not sure I can be that helpful,' Darblay stretched before the open fire. 'Old Mrs Pride wasn't one of my parishioners in the fullest sense.'

'She was married in the church?'

'You'd have to consult the registers. We're not allowed to keep them any more, alas. They've all been consigned to Winchester and, what is worse, placed on microfiche.'

Maxwell tutted. That annoyed him too.

'I wouldn't mind,' Darblay went on, rubbing a cadaverous finger around the rim of his glass, 'but it's only done for the convenience of the Americans. You'd be amazed how many of them we get in the summer, trying to find their roots.'

'Hairdressers' nightmare,' Maxwell nodded solemnly. 'You didn't visit her, I suppose?'

'Mrs Pride? No, I'm afraid not. Oh, I did make one house call, so to speak. A long time ago, when I first got the parish. Sticks in my mind, though.'

'Oh?'

'Don't you people tape record interviews?' Darblay asked, 'Or at least take notes?'

'No need,' Maxwell tapped his temple. 'Photographic memory.'

'How fascinating!' Darblay put his glass down and leaned forward. 'I have a theory . . .'

'Er . . . Mrs Pride?' Maxwell wanted the man back on track.

'Oh, yes. Yes. Well, I went up to her house, the one near the Ring. No one answered for what seemed ages. I was just about to go when she appeared. It was odd, really. A sizzling hot day — August 1, I remember — and I didn't hear a thing. Not a rustle of clothes, not the padding of feet. She was just . . . there. At my elbow. I confess, Mr Maxwell, I was startled. I was even more startled when we got talking.'

'Oh, why?'

'Well, I introduced myself and said I hoped we'd see her at church. Do you know what she did? She spat.'

'Really?'

'As God is my witness. Spat, then and there, quite volubly, on the garden path. Then she asked me if I knew what day it was — that's how I remember it so well. I said "Yes. It's August 1st." "Lammas," she said. "It's Lammastide."'

'Lammas,' Maxwell repeated.

'Loaf Mass,' Darblay explained. 'Symbolic of the beginning of the harvest. I said to Mrs Pride "Are you a farming family, then?" She just laughed.'

'And that was it?'

'Yes, Mr Maxwell, it was. I never went back. Not to Myrtle Cottage. I'm not ashamed to admit old Mrs Pride frightened me. There was something . . . unreal about her. It's impossible to describe. Oh, I've met people who are anti-clerical before and since. Humanists, atheists, don't-give-a-damners — they go with the territory; and my back, like my church, is broad. But there was something different about Elizabeth Pride — and I'm not being melodramatic when I say . . . she was pure evil.'

* * *

'"Pure Evil", Count,' Maxwell sipped his Southern Comfort, his bum on his sofa, his feet on the coffee table. 'You had to be there, really, corny as it sounds.'

The cat was unimpressed. It was the concept of church mice that interested him most in Maxwell's story.

'There we were, tucked up in his study, only a little smaller than the Bodleian, toasting our toes — in his case lissom, clerical, printless; and we were talking about a poor old soul as if she was Beelzebub. But the thing of it is, Count, this calendar.' He shook it at the animal, for all the good that did, 'Elizabeth Pride . . . listen to me when I'm talking to you — I'll be asking questions later . . . Elizabeth Pride made a big thing about Lammas tide, August 1st. And here, it's one of the few dates she's circled on her calendar, the one I lifted from the cottage.' He read from the tattered paper, 'Fly over moor and fly over mead, Fly over living and fly over dead, Fly ye east or fly ye west, fly to her that loves me best. Not exactly Manic Street Preachers, is it?'

Metternich yawned. What was the old duffer on about? He was always the same when he sloshed that amber stuff down his throat. Why didn't he stick to pond water and the odd slurp of gold top?

'You'd have liked the Reverend Darblay,' Maxwell assured his companion of an inch. 'Like something out of Trollope, he was — and I mean that in the nicest possible way . . .' Then the A-level essays caught his eye, sitting, like the sword of Damocles, dangling over the edge of his coffee table. 'Oh, all right!' he shouted at them.

Metternich saw his moment and slunk away. Once the old bastard picked up papers that was it — an hour or two of effing and blinding, all in the cause of scholarship, all for the sake of an A-level grade. And he heard him humming as he reached the cat flap, 'One man went to mow, went to mow a module . . .' The rest was silence and the nightly slaughter on Columbine Avenue.

* * *

Beauregard's was a little out of town, on the curve of East Hill beyond the station. Maxwell recognised it at once as the Leighford Institute, a solid block of Victoriana with a mock marble facade — built in the days of self-help as a library for the working man. That nice old picker-up of prostitutes, Mr Gladstone, was at Number Ten and beer was tuppence ha'penny a pint.

It had changed somewhat now and a rather spotty youth peered at Maxwell from the Perspex anonymity of an entrance booth just inside the front door.

'You a member?' the youth asked with all the charm of a pit bull.

'No,' Maxwell told him. 'I'm just sampling the place.'

'That'll be six pound fifty.'

'No, no,' Maxwell smiled at the lad. 'Sampling the club, not buying the premises.'

Either the spotty lad had heard them all before or he was a stranger to levity. 'Six pound fifty, please,' he said.

Ah, the magic word. Maxwell was a sucker for Old World niceties and he coughed up. 'What do I do?' he asked.

'Turn left through there,' the lad pointed to the end of the corridor. 'You'll see what's available on the wall. You're not going swimming, are you?'

'Er . . . I don't think so. Why?'

'No, it's just that I gotta ask about verrucas and that; whether you got any.'

'Well, I did have one an old aunt left me. Took it to the Antiques Roadshow a while back. But I put the damn thing down a while ago and can I find it?' he winked at the lad. 'You have a nice evening, now.'

Maxwell perused the hearty things on offer on the huge noticeboard at the bottom of the stairs. From beyond the double doors he heard the tell-tale squeal of trainers on polished floors and the erratic high-pitched thud of squash balls on walls. The odd 'Fuck!' reminded him of the appalling agony as that malevolent bit of rubber hit his own flesh for the first time years before, when the Cantab sports clubs beckoned. He turned left, past lockers without number where flab fighters hung their day clothes before doing battle with their chocolate addiction.

'Well, well,' he heard the voice before he saw the silhouette ahead of him, a towel round its neck. 'Tripped over any good bodies lately?'

'Dr Astley. It's been a while.'

'It has.' The police surgeon sauntered into the light, considerably more crimson than when Maxwell had seen him last. 'I didn't know you were a member.'

'I'm not,' Maxwell told him. 'Just heard about the place and was idly curious. You?'

'Oh, a spot of squash. My club's having a bit of a face lift at the moment, so I thought I'd give this place a whirl. Rather inferior, I think you'll find.' His deferential whisper rang down the corridor.

'Is there a bar here?' Maxwell asked.

'I should bloody well hope so,' Astley chuckled.

'Well, lifting a tincture is about all my right arm can take this evening. Time for a drink?'

'Mr Maxwell,' Astley's eyes narrowed behind his specs, 'the last time we met, you thoroughly spoiled a little private evening I was having with a few friends.'

'Did I?' Maxwell was all innocence. 'I'm most dreadfully sorry. Let me make amends by getting the first round.'

'You were quizzing me then about a murder, I seem to remember.'

'Was I?' Maxwell frowned. 'How extraordinary.'

'What is?'

'How history repeats itself. This way?'

Peter Maxwell knew Jim Astley of old. The pair had never liked each other, but that was the way of it. Armed with Disraeli's famous dictum about royalty and flattery and a trowel, Maxwell went to work with all the gung-ho of Alan Titchmarsh.

'But what I can't understand,' he leaned forward, frowning, twisting his lips, the lost student at the knee of the master, 'is why the old girl was frozen.'

'She'd been kept in a deep-freeze, old boy,' Astley was lolling back in Beauregard's Bar, the brandy swilling around the base of his glass. This was his second. Sleuthing was costing Peter Maxwell a fortune.

'Froze to death, eh?' Maxwell nodded, eyes widening.

'I didn't say that,' Astley hedged. Should Maxwell buy the man a third or was his vanity enough to tip him over the edge?

'No,' Maxwell chuckled. 'No, you've lost me now.'

Astley sighed. The man before him was after all only a teacher. What was it Bernard Shaw had said? Those who can become doctors, those who can't, teach? Something like that. 'She was poisoned, Mr Maxwell,' he said. 'Death-Cap, if I'm any judge.'

Men like Jim Astley were judge and jury. Thank God British justice didn't depend entirely on them. 'Mushrooms?' Maxwell blinked.

'The knife was a red herring.' Astley was leaning forward now, warming to his theme.

'Knife?'

'Yes . . . look, Maxwell, I mean,' he was suddenly glancing around him, watching walls, 'you do realise how utterly confidential all this is? I mean, you can't use this information, you know.'

'Of course not,' Maxwell shrugged and folded his arms. 'No, it's just for my peace of mind, that's all. After all, it's not every night you find a body on your garden path. Tell me about the knife.'

'Nothing much to tell,' Astley shrugged. 'It was double-edged, driven between her vertebrae. A downward thrust.'

'Poison and a knife? What are we looking for, a schizophrenic?'

'We aren't looking for anything,' Astley told him. He downed his brandy and snatched up the hold-all. 'Unless of course you're using the royal "we", Mr Maxwell. Thanks for the drink.'

'No problem,' Maxwell stood up. 'Perhaps we could have the odd game of squash, some time.'

'I don't think so,' Astley said. 'I'm not sure we're in the same class.'

'Oh, I am,' Maxwell winked.

He finished his Southern Comfort as the good doctor swept away in a cloud of undiluted superiority. In the corner two tallboys were having a conversation about weight training, each of them in a lurid track suit with white silhouetted figures down the seams. The barman was drying glasses and puffing on a distinctly non-PC fag. Otherwise the place was deserted. Maxwell picked up his coat and made for the door. The corridor was dimly lit and echoed to his footfalls. He turned a corner and strode for the stairs.

Perhaps he wasn't looking where he was going. Perhaps he was too lost in thought over the forensic facts that Astley had thrown at him. Perhaps he really believed his head was harder than Beauregard's brickwork.

Perhaps Nostradamus had been right and the blackness that swept over him was indeed the Millennium night — the end of the world.

CHAPTER 6

'How are you feeling?'

The voice was muffled at first, like somebody mumbling down a tube of rolled up carpet. The face too was a blur, a badly focused camera, a shadow of a shadow. It had long hair, he was sure of that, and smelt of a warm tent in the summers of his childhood.

'Ow!' Ever the master of wit and repartee was Peter Maxwell.

'Steady,' the voice was clearer now. 'You've had a nasty bump on the head. Don't get up too quickly.'

He found himself sitting upright, his temples feeling as if they'd been squeezed through a mangle. There was a screen in front of him and a table with bloody cotton wool. A rather luscious girl was bending over him with a roll of bandage in her hand.

'I'm not sure we'll need this,' she was saying.

Maxwell felt the back of his cranium and immediately wished he hadn't. Whatever the opposite of frontal lobotomy was, he'd just had one.

'Would it be too corny to ask where I am?' He tried to focus on her.

'You're in sick bay at Beauregard's,' she told him. 'A floor down from where we found you. I'm Sophie, by the way. Sophie Clark.'

'Peter Maxwell. Are you a nurse?'

'Please,' the girl snorted. She was the Nordic type, with cascading blonde hair she'd recently unleashed from a braid, a grey top that stretched across a formidable chest and black Lycra cycling shorts that would have had most of Maxwell's boys drooling. Come to think of it, they had Maxwell drooling. 'I'm an Aerobics instructor. But I happen to have a First Aid certificate and Prissy and I were the first to find you.'

'Prissy?'

'Prissy Crown. She says she knows you.'

'Not Biblically, I assure you.'

Sophie laughed, rolling up her bandage and tidying things away on a tray. 'You mustn't mind Prissy,' she said. 'She means well. Just has a thing about men, that's all.'

Maxwell was quite relieved. At least that was men plural and not any man in particular.

'What on earth happened to you?' she asked him.

'I was hoping you'd tell me.' Maxwell experimented with turning his neck. 'The last thing I remember is a blinding pain and I must have passed out. Did I walk into a wall? I did that once in Basingstoke. I remember being so appalled by the architecture of the place, I attempted suicide by running slap into a pillar — not of the community, you understand, a brick one.'

'Any teeth loose?' Sophie was pulling his lips about.

'Not that weren't loose before.' He gently prised her fingers away.

'Sorry,' she smiled. 'Follow my finger.' She held it up and his dark eyes swivelled with it. 'That's fine. No, I really don't know how this happened, Mr Maxwell. You've got one helluva lump on the back of your head and the skin's broken. Not worth a stitch, I don't think. The bleeding seems to have stopped. I'd have it checked though, if I were you.'

'Casualty? No thanks, I haven't got that long to live.'

She stood up, tall and powerful in her workout rig. 'You weren't walking backwards, were you?'

'To Christmas?' Maxwell's Neddy Seagoon was inspired, but it was lost on Sophie Clark.

'Max, for Christ's sake, I've just heard.' An hysterical-looking Ken Templeton crashed in, towel round his neck and looking positively flushed in a nasty turquoise track suit. 'Are you all right? Sophie, is he all right?'

'He's fine, Ken,' the girl said softly, calming him down.

How on earth did it happen?' Ken asked, looking from one to the other.

'Just me,' Maxwell made light of it, 'being a silly bugger. Sorry to be such a nuisance on my first visit.'

'Max,' Ken knelt in front of him like a medieval knight offering allegiance to his king. 'We'll waive tonight's entrance fee. I'm sorry you were charged in the first place. It's on the house, okay? First six months, free. What do you say?'

'I'd say you were a man nervous of litigation, Ken,' Maxwell smiled. 'And don't worry, I'm not the suing type.'

'Oh, no,' Ken blustered. 'I wasn't thinking of that, at all,' but he did seem to Maxwell to be amazingly grateful. 'Let me at least run you home.'

'My bike . . .' Maxwell began.

'You can't possibly ride that,' Ken insisted. 'We'll shove it in the back of my Space Wagon.'

'Ken . . .'

'Not now, Sophie,' her boss broke in. 'Can't you see Mr Maxwell's all in?'

'Thank you, Sophie,' Maxwell eased himself off the couch, wobbling a little at first as his head reconnected with his feet. 'You've been very kind.'

'That's all right,' she smiled. 'I'll give your love to Prissy, shall I?' But she wasn't looking at Maxwell when she said it. She was looking at Ken.

* * *

The lights never burn blue in an Incident Room. When he was a kid, Henry Hall had read novels about Scotland Yard, when the detectives of yesteryear turned down the oil lamps, lit their pipes and pondered the problem, still wearing their trench coats and trilbies, looking for 'chummy' before they subdued him with a left hook. The men in front of him didn't smoke pipes; neither did the women, but it was rumoured that old Jane Cruikshank did.

'So what have we got, then?' he asked by way of summation at the end of another long day. Through the haze of ciggie smoke, DS Stone was on his feet. This was the eighth night of the investigation, the new year just eight days old. And still the Stones waited, as the back pains worsened and the twinges continued and the clock ticked.

'House to house have come up with a gypsy encampment, guv. At least, it's a mobile squat more than anything. Family named Cruikshank plus assorted dogs and a goat.'

'Where is this?' Hall asked.

'Below the Chanctonbury Ring, mile or two from Wetherton.'

'They were neighbours?'

'After a fashion. Seems they'd known — and hated — each other for years. Something of a feud between the Prides and the Cruikshanks going way back. Nobody can remember how it started, but it was centred on the two old women.'

'Anybody talked to this . . . Jane, is it?'

'Jane,' nodded Stone, 'granny. Rules her grandsons with a rod of iron by all accounts. And no, sir, nobody has yet. She wasn't at home when the lads paid a visit. We didn't get much out of the grandsons, either. I've run them both through the computer. Benjamin, the older one's got form. Theft, spot of GBH. Joseph's cleaner, but it's only a matter of time.'

'Where did the feud story come from?' Hall wanted to know.

'Mostly goss from the locals. The Rector especially — a Reverend Darblay. By the way, there's a bogus reporter out there.'

'I'm not sure we've got time . . .'

'I just thought, guv,' Stone was a copper on the climb, too bright for his own good, 'anybody who's posing as a reporter's got an agenda we ought to know about.'

'All right,' Hall nodded after a pause. 'What do we know?'

'Kev, you've got this one.' Stone sat down.

Kev had. Kevin Brand was a large florid man with prematurely silver hair combed forward in a way that Caesar would have understood. He swayed to his feet, 'Reverend Darblay phoned to say a bloke whose name he couldn't remember called at his church yesterday looking for info on the Elizabeth Pride killing. Nice bloke, apparently. The old boy used the word' — and he checked his notepad, so unused was he to the concept — '"charming".'

'How did he know he was bogus?' Hall asked.

'Said he was from the *Littlehampton Mercury*,' Kev told him.

'And?'

'Littlehampton hasn't got a Mercury.'

There were chuckles and rhubarb all round. 'Does he want a job on the Force, this Vicar?' somebody asked.

'We could do with God on our side,' somebody else chipped in.

DCI Hall raised his hands to calm things down. He knew the signs. Seven days in and the strain beginning to tell. Tonight it was banter, still good-natured, still generous. By tomorrow it would turn bitchy and the cliques would develop. Blokes would get their own coffee and nobody else's or expect the girls to get it, which would raise feminist hackles and the rot would set in. He'd seen it before. It destroyed a team's concentration, ground it down and broke it apart so that before long nobody was looking each other in the face.

'We need to talk to Jane Cruikshank,' Hall said. 'Jacquie?'

'Sir?' She felt the eyes burning into her, the only female detective in the room.

'Tomorrow morning. First light. I want you and a team of uniform at this gypsy camp. How many people are there, Martin?'

'Er . . . just the two grandsons and the old girl, guv.'

'Right, Jacquie. See Mr Williams, will you? I want a team of six big blokes behind you and I want Jane Cruikshank in Interview Room One at the nick by nine o'clock. Do you foresee any problems with that?'

'No, sir,' she said.

'Good.' Hall was on his feet. 'Ladies and gentlemen, it's been a long day. Let's close it down.'

Jacquie Carpenter didn't like the mob-handed approach. She appreciated Hall's need for a woman, but the boot through the door bit was not Jacquie's style. She saw Inspector Williams that night, on her way home and arranged for the heavies at dawn.

'Shooters, Jacquie?' Williams had asked her. He'd tangled with gyppos before. 'We're not talking tactical team here, are we?'

'No, thanks, sir,' she smiled. 'Best not upset more people than we have to.'

Tom Williams was a wise old copper. He nodded and let it go.

* * *

She swung the Ka into her driveway and sat for a moment looking at the circles of her headlights illuminating the garage door. Then she sighed, switched off the ignition and made for the house. The first thing she saw was a shiver of the ivy, the one her dad had trained to climb the trellis by her front door. Then she saw him, a man in the shadows, moving towards her.

'Jacquie?'

'Oh, Jesus, Crispin. What the fuck are you doing, hiding like that?'

'Sorry,' his breath snaked out on the raw night. 'I was waiting for you and it's sort of parky out here.'

She undid the lock. 'There are such things as phones, you know.' Then she saw his face. 'You'd better come in.'

She led him through the hall and into the lounge, throwing her scarf and coat onto the settee. 'Can I get you a drink?'

'I'd kill for a cocoa,' he said, trying to get the circulation back into his hands.

'How did you get here?' she asked him. 'I didn't see a car.'

'No. I jogged.'

'Jogged?' she rummaged in the kitchen, finding a saucepan and ferreting for the milk. 'Oh, of course. Beauregard's.'

'Shame you had to leave the party the other night,' he leaned on her breakfast bar, 'just as things were hotting up.'

'Really?' she cocked an eyebrow. 'Don't tell me — Prissy.'

'And your friend Maxwell, yes. She took him home.'

'Oh?' Jacquie wasn't very good at indifference.

'Just thought you ought to know.'

Despite herself, she turned to face him. 'Did you run all the way from Beauregard's and risk frostbite just to tell me that the local nympho gave a friend of mine a lift?'

'I haven't come from Beauregard's,' he said. 'And I think Mr Maxwell's got bigger problems than Prissy.'

She put the milk bottle down with a louder thud than she intended. 'What do you mean?' she asked.

Foulkes straightened, then he crossed to the door as if to check they were alone. He crossed back to her. 'Jacquie, what do you know about Lammas?'

'About what?' She was fiddling with the gas.

'What about Beltane? Samhain?'

She stopped fiddling and looked at him. 'Crispin, are you all right? I haven't the faintest idea what you're talking about.'

'Jacquie.' He took her hand, turning off the gas with the other. 'Look, never mind that. Come and sit down.' He led her into the lounge and sat her down on the settee, perching beside her, half turned so that he could look her in the face. 'Tell me what you know about Peter Maxwell.'

'Max?' she blinked, 'Why? What's all this about, Crispin?'

'Just humour me,' he said, but there was no humour in the grey eyes, the serious mouth.

'All right,' she sighed. 'Peter Maxwell is Head of Sixth Form at Leighford High. He's a widower, but he doesn't let on about that . . .'

'How do you know about it?' he cut in.

'Oh, he let it slip one day.'

'Go on.'

'Well, let's see. He went to Cambridge, Jesus College, I think. He's an historian — an MA. He's got a cat called Metternich.'

'And he solves murders in his spare time,' Crispin said.

Jacquie looked at him. 'He has helped us in the past, yes,' she nodded.

'Isn't that a little . . . unusual?'

Jacquie laughed. 'Max is an unusual man,' she said. 'You know the kids call him "Mad Max"?'

'How unusual?' he wanted to know.

'How? . . . Look, Crispin, this is daft. Why do you want to know so much about Maxwell?'

'When I went to Leighford High . . .'

'You've been there?'

'Yes, it's part of my patch,' he explained. 'About a quarter of their kids come from the Barlichway. I expect I'll be in and out of there like a yoyo. When I was introduced to Maxwell, he had a calendar on his desk.'

'So?' Jacquie couldn't fathom where this was going.

'It was a shabby calendar, looked old. But it was for last year.'

'I still don't . . .'

'There were certain dates on it, with rhymes written alongside them.'

'And?'

'One was Saint Thomas's day, December 21, the old Winter Solstice — "*Thomas Grey, Thomas Grey, the longest night and the shortest day*".'

'He does have something of a poetic streak in him,' Jacquie nodded.

'Another date — and I'm working backwards through the year — is Samhain, Shadowfest, Calangaef, the Festival of the Dead.'

'You're talking about Halloween,' Jacquie realised.

'When the witches ride,' Foulkes nodded. 'Then there's Beltane. The Germans call it Walpurgisnacht, the night of the May queen and her marriage to the horned god.'

'Crispin . . .' Jacquie's voice was quiet.

'Lammas was another date marked, when the ancient sun god Lugh was worshipped. They made kirn babies for him — corn dollies. Though once of course they were real children.'

Jacquie Carpenter was a woman of the here, the now. 'I don't see the relevance . . .'

'Neither do I,' said Foulkes. 'Yet. Jacquie, when did we last meet?'

She moved away, wrapping her arms tightly around her waist. If she hadn't exactly been dreading this moment, she hadn't exactly been looking forward to it either. 'Crispin,' she said firmly, 'that was then.'

He stood up too. 'After we finished,' he said, 'I moved to Nottingham. Did you know that?'

She shook her head.

'I worked on the Broxtowe case, or at least, its aftermath. Do you know about that one?'

'Satanic abuse, wasn't it?' she asked. 'Black magic?'

'That's right. I was in the thick of it. It's there I picked up all this folklore nonsense. Except, it isn't nonsense. Not to some people. To some people it's real and it happens.'

She spun round to face him. 'What, old crones on broomsticks?' she jeered. 'Black cats . . .' and the words froze on her lips.

He walked to her, putting his hands on her shoulders, looking steadily into her shining eyes. 'What colour did you say Maxwell's cat was?'

* * *

She couldn't remember a lovelier sky. It was the colour the French call *aurore*, the dawn, like bars of distant fire glowing between the fading purple of the night. She looked ahead to where the couple of coppers were taking up position on the grassy banks, white with the magic frost of another winter's morning. The walkie talkie crackled to life in her hand.

'We're in position, Jacquie. Over.'

'Copy that, John,' she answered him. 'Any sign of life? Over.'

'I can see a goat. Couple of large dogs. Still wish we'd brought ours. Over.'

'All right. Simon, are you there?' she turned to scan the patrol cars parked at crazy angles on the field behind her.

'Ready, Jacquie. Over.'

'Right. You know the signal. I'm going in.'

She clicked the radio down and left the car. From each side two oppos with shoulders like wardrobes crunched on the frozen ground.

'All seems a bit OTT for one old duck,' one of them muttered.

'One old duck, and two assorted males, one with a record of smacking,' she reminded him. 'The DCI wants no cock-ups.'

'Yeah,' the other one muttered. 'And I want a Lamborghini.'

Jacquie smiled and shook her head. She was scared too.

There was a sudden explosion of barking and the snapping of chains against timbers as the dogs scented strangers and sprang to life.

'That's far enough!' it was a growl rather than a shout and all three coppers stopped in their tracks. The dogs fell silent.

'Shotgun!' one of the uniforms shouted and they scattered, flinging themselves for cover. Jacquie rolled behind an abandoned mattress, soaking in the frosty grass and smelling to high Heaven. She expected the rip and roar of a twelve bore. She got nothing except a hollow chuckle.

'Well, well, our brave boys in blue.'

It was a woman's voice, she realised. 'Police,' she said, straining to make out any movement ahead. The gypsy camp was a ramshackle collection of huts clustered around a mobile home that clearly wasn't mobile any more. The two black and white dogs, mangy, vicious, were standing, ears flat, teeth bared, straining at the chains that held them and snarling at the intruders. The woman's voice snapped at them and they were silent, both of them dropping to their haunches and looking sideways at the caravan.

'What do you want?' the woman's voice again.

'We want to talk to Jane Cruikshank,' Jacquie called back. 'Just a friendly chat.'

'Friendly be buggered,' came the reply. 'There ain't no such thing with you buggers.'

Jacquie rolled onto her back, keeping her heels on the ground and her head below the curl of the mattress. She whispered into the walkie talkie, 'Simon. Keep back. You and Bill split up and join the others on each hill. John, Bucko, do you copy that? Over.'

There was muffled acknowledgement over the airwaves. 'John, can you see anything? Over.'

'Shotgun barrel. Left window of caravan. Can't see who's holding it. Over.'

'Are you Jane Cruikshank?' Jacquie had rolled onto her front again, glancing to each side as the dark blue shapes of Simon and Bucko crept alongside her, out beyond the hedges, skirting the rise to each side. She prayed that whoever was on the other end of that gun couldn't make them out in the still half light.

'My boys ain't done nothing,' the voice called. 'They ain't even here.'

'It's not your boys, Mrs Cruikshank,' Jacquie called. 'It's you we came to see.' She rolled over again, hissing into the plastic. 'Bucko, John. Can you move in? Over.'

'I'm there,' she heard Bucko respond. Then his line went dead.

'John?' Jacquie didn't like the silence. 'What's happening? Over.'

There was a pause. 'Bucko's coming down. I can see him. Over.'

Jacquie rolled back. She could see him too. A dark shape that circled the camp. She didn't move, her nose pinched and blue with cold, the water soaking through her clothes from the mattress. Steady, she found herself almost whispering. Bucko had a night stick, one of those American imports that gave the law an edge. But Bucko was packing too much linguini and no copper ever made was a match for the speed of a trigger. She'd only ever seen one shotgun blast — both barrels at close range. She didn't want to see it again.

'Jesus!' all the intercoms crackled into life at once. What the fuck was Jacquie doing? Bucko crashed sideways, ripping his trousers on the gorse. On the far side from him, John dropped to his knees, tumbling over the stiff white tussocks, rolling into a bush to steady himself. The two coppers who had dropped with Jacquie were still there, watching in mute astonishment as the slim girl in the black bomber jacket got up and started walking towards the camp. Towards the woman. Towards the gun.

* * *

'Old bags!' DS Martin Stone had had enough. 'Couldn't you just kill 'em?' Perhaps DCI Henry Hall was the wrong man to put that question to. The pair's eyes met across a crowded Leighford police station a little after breakfast that day.

'Personally, no,' was Hall's straight-faced reply, 'but it's our task to find a man who might.'

'Sorry, guv,' Stone looked like a man who'd been up all night.

'No news yet, then?' Hall leaned against the doorframe.

'Another false alarm last night. Just before one. Raced round to the Maternity Unit getting funny looks from the speed trap unit on Wildman's Hill. All hands to the pumps and nothing. It's getting us down.'

'How's Alex coping?'

Stone shrugged. 'Like you do.'

Hall winked and slapped the man's arm. That was as avuncular as the tight-lipped bastard got. He who had gone through all this three times. He went into the small dark rectangle that was Interview Room One. There was no window here; just the cold whiteness of artificial light bearing down on the sparse grey hair of old Jane Cruikshank. He nodded at the WPC sitting bolt upright by the door. He took in the small, almost frail old woman sitting in the pool of light in the centre of the room, a table and machinery in front of her.

He pulled back the chair opposite and sat down, switching on the tape recorder to his right. 'DCI Hall commencing interview number two at nine thirteen. Has anybody given you a cup of tea, Mrs Cruikshank?'

The hard grey eyes narrowed and she pursed her lips. 'Nobody's given me the time of day, sonny,' she told him. 'Just asked me questions. That kid, that sergeant of yours, he's a tosser, ain't he?'

'He's got a lot on his mind,' Hall said softly, leaning back in his chair. 'Marianne, get Mrs Cruikshank a cup of tea, would you? Mrs Cruikshank, you don't mind that the WPC is leaving us alone, do you?'

Jane Cruikshank cracked a broad gappy grin. 'Don't worry, sonny,' she said, 'you'll be safe with me. Three sugars, ducks. And lots of milk. I like my tea milky.'

Hall nodded at Marianne. 'WPC Fisher leaving the room at nine sixteen.' He waited for the door to close.

'I don't know nothin' 'bout them tyres,' she told him.

'Mrs Cruikshank, neither do I,' he said. 'Have you been told you can have a lawyer present?'

She spat savagely to her left. 'Yeah, that young tosser told me. What do I want with a lawyer? My boys will sort this out, you'll see. I don't want no lawyer.'

'Your boys,' Hall was leafing through the interview notes Stone had left on the table, 'your grandsons, er . . . Ben and Joe.'

'That's them.' The old girl nodded, as though chewing on an invisible pipe stem. 'They're not bad boys, mister. We're not like other people. Not settled. They ain't got much schooling one way and another. Me, I was born in a Vardo wagon. I remember doing the horse fairs before the war. Course, they was different days . . . Why did you bring me here?'

'Why did you threaten my officers with a shotgun?'

'I got a right,' Jane Cruikshank sat bolt upright on her dignity. 'Wakin' folks up — Godfearing folks, mind you — at some Godforsaken hour. 'T'ain't natural. I got a right.'

'Do you have a licence for the gun?'

''T'ain't mine,' the old woman told him. 'I told you, we're not like other people.'

'No, you can break the law whenever you like, can't you?' Hall looked at her. Like Stone, he felt the red mist rising. He'd met them before, society's misfits who knew all their rights and none of their responsibilities. He, who had once been so tolerant, so reasonable. He was starting to feel like Attila the Hun. The door's click saved him from throwing the book, and possibly the table, at old Jane Cruikshank.

'WPC Fisher returning at nine twenty,' he checked his watch.

'What?' the old girl took the cup that cheered, for all it was in a nasty pale institution green. 'No chocolate biscuits? I was hoping for a Penguin.'

'What's this?' Hall suddenly produced from his jacket pocket a tattered rag doll, perhaps six inches tall, with string tied crudely to form a bulging head and limbs.

Jane Cruikshank's lips froze inches from her cup. 'Where did you get that?' Her voice was like winter, her face a fungus grey.

'Have you seen it before?' he asked her, ignoring her question.

'No,' she said, shaking her head slowly, not taking her eyes off the doll. 'Not that one . . .'

'Not that one,' Hall took up the theme. 'Another, then? One like it?'

'No,' she shook her head faster. 'No, nothing like that.'

Hall leaned back, keeping the doll in his grip, in her eye-line. 'You're not telling me the truth, Mrs Cruikshank,' he said. 'My officers found this in your caravan this morning.'

'What?'

'It was stuffed down behind your chair — the old rocker in the corner.'

'That's a lie,' the old girl growled. 'I've never seen it before. I don't know nothing about poppets . . . Why am I here? What are you talking about, you tosser?'

'You know perfectly well why you're here, Mrs Cruikshank. DS Stone explained it to you. You're here in connection with the murder of Elizabeth Pride.'

Jane Cruikshank stared into Hall's eyes, then she threw the tea all over him and smashed the cup and saucer on the floor. WPC Fisher was on her feet in an instant, but Hall's hand checked her. He calmly wiped the liquid dripping from his glasses and looked at the old woman, quivering feet from him.

'Get me a fucking lawyer,' she snarled.

* * *

Jacquie had finished her report nearly an hour ago. She'd proofread it on the computer screen, printed it out, proofread it again. She didn't want to face the DCI. Not today. What she'd done had been stupid. She'd faced a madwoman with a shotgun, endangering not only her own life but those of her colleagues as well. The DCI didn't go for heroes. She knew that. There were procedures to be followed, a book of rules. What was the point in writing them if they weren't followed?

'Jacquie?' the DCI's head popped around the door in the Tottingleigh Incident Room. 'A word?' And she followed him into his office.

At first she stood there, paper in her hand.

'The report?' he asked her.

'Oh, yes, sir. Sorry.'

He sat down behind the desk, scanning the pages, putting a finger across his lips. Only then did he look up.

'She called it a poppet,' he said.

'Sir?'

'The rag doll you found in Jane Cruikshank's caravan. She called it a poppet. Any idea what that means?'

Jacquie shrugged. 'Sweetheart, darling?' she guessed.

He let it go at that. 'She's never seen it before,' he said.

'What? Oh, come on, guv.'

'I've been in this business a long time, Jacquie. I know the signs. Believe me, she hasn't seen it. But she was afraid of it.'

'Afraid?' Jacquie blinked. 'Why?'

'That's what I'd like to know.' He picked up the Biro on his desk and tapped with the end of it. 'Get me Peter Maxwell,' he said.

'Sir?'

Hall stood up. 'This morning, Jacquie, you behaved with extraordinary recklessness facing what might have been a loaded shotgun. I don't like heroes. Heroines I like still less. If you can't handle being part of a team — this team perhaps you picked the wrong job. And since when do you help yourself to private property like this doll without a search warrant?'

Jacquie had been expecting it, but the speed of attack took her by surprise, caught her off balance. 'I . . .'

'The old girl's demanding a lawyer. When he gets here, you can kiss this . . . evidence . . . goodbye. Now don't add coyness to stupidity. Call Peter Maxwell.'

'Sir,' and she left before the tears started.

CHAPTER 7

She lay sprawled in his arms as the chimes of his grandfather clock announced eleven.

'Whatever happened to Sandy Gall?' he asked her.

'What?' Jacquie cocked her head to look up at him, slumped on the settee as he was.

'Train of thought, really. News at Eleven used to be News at Ten and Sandy Gall was an old newsreader. Do they go to a sort of journalists' graveyard, do you think? Or does the devil grab their souls and force them down to the Other Place to read everlasting autocues?'

'It's funny you should mention the devil,' she murmured, nestling her head in the warm space between his neck and his chest.

'Is it? Why?'

'Oh, nothing. Just a conversation I had last night. Look,' she sat up again, 'are you sure you're all right?' She was frowning into his face.

'Just because I suddenly remembered Sandy Gall doesn't mean I've got galloping concussion.' He crossed his eyes over the bridge of his nose, 'And both of you should be aware of that.'

She laughed. With him. Because nobody ever laughed at Peter Maxwell. Not more than once, anyway. 'Even so,' she scolded, 'you're being very coy about what happened.'

'Coyness be my friend,' he said, reaching across for his Southern Comfort.

'I want to know,' she insisted.

'Shall I switch on the tape recorder, Woman Policeman?'

'Max, please. This is important.'

'All right,' he chuckled, humouring her. He looked into the steady grey eyes, the soft mouth. 'If you want to know, I think somebody hit me over the head.'

'What?' she was frowning again, not grasping the significance of what he was saying.

'I'd been talking to Dr Astley . . .'

'Oh?'

'One piece of interrogation at a time, please,' he batted aside the question he knew was hovering behind the parted lips. 'I'd got up to leave the bar. I was walking along a landing.' He closed his eyes to remember it. 'The stairs were to my left. A corridor stretched ahead, leading to the squash court spectator galleries, I think. There was a thud — that must have been my head saying hello to something hard. You will note, detective, that I do not have my wounds before.'

She had noted that. She'd already kissed and stroked the swollen ridge at the back of his skull and recognised it as the impact of a wall or door.

'Baseball bat,' Maxwell offered as another solution.

She reached round and ran her fingers through his iron-grey curls again until he winced. 'Sorry,' she bit her lip the way that women do. 'I think a baseball bat would do a bit more damage, Max,' she said.

'In the hands of Robert de Niro, yes.'

'De Niro?'

'Al Capone in *The Untouchables*. You remember the scene — somebody had looked at him funny so he spread their brains out over the breakfast table. Just another everyday story of psycho folk.'

'But why should anybody want to knock you out?' she asked.

'Children are definitely getting more stupid,' he answered her in riddles. 'When they're ten, they ask "Why is grass green?" But when they're five they ask "Why is grass?" Now, that's an altogether more imponderable one, isn't it? The Big One. But an even bigger one is that you've just posed, love of my loaf. Who would want to knock me out? Well,' he twisted his lip in thought, 'I've been at Leighford High now the best part of twenty years. Pissed off a lot of kids in that time.'

'Not enough for ABH, Max, surely?'

'You've never seen one of my lessons,' he winked at her.

'No,' she smiled, 'I haven't. And I'd like to. I dropped History early on at school. Too many dates.'

'Cobblers!' he cuffed her playfully around the ear. 'All right, when you ever get time off again for good behaviour I'll work with you on A level. How about that?'

'I'd never get beyond Walpole,' she laughed.

'My dear girl,' he said, eyes wide with impressedness, 'Knowing the man's name gets you a D grade these days. Maybe I can still pull a few strings at Jesus — call in some favours, you know.'

And they laughed together in the lamplight.

'You've been here for hours,' he said.

'You're right.' She stretched and sat up again. 'And I should be going.'

'That's not what I meant and you know it.' It was his turn to scold her. 'What about this morning's phone call?'

'Oh, that,' she dismissed it. 'The DCI had his arse in his hand. It was my fault really.'

'What was?'

'It's nothing, Max. I fouled up. Went in alone when I should have waited for back-up. It wasn't important.'

'Jacquie,' he was looking hard into her face, her clear eyes. He held her cheeks in both hands. 'There's something you're not telling me.'

‘Hall wants to pick your historical brains. I rang Leighford but they told me you were teaching.’

‘I’ve heard that rumour too,’ he nodded, ‘and I’ve been waiting all evening for you to tell me what the bloody hell he wants.’

She hauled herself away from him, gently, holding his hands as she got up. ‘Sorry, Max,’ she shook her head. ‘I’m not exactly the DCI’s blue-eyed girl at the moment. You’ll have to wait until tomorrow.’

‘I shan’t sleep, you know.’ He was on his feet too, his arms around her neck. She draped her arms over his.

‘Neither shall I,’ she said. And he kissed her, ‘But . . .’

He got her scarf and coat and saw her to the door. ‘I’ll walk you to the car,’ he said.

‘No,’ she turned to him under the light over the door, ‘I’ll call you tomorrow. Let me know what Hall says.’

‘Depend on it,’ and Maxwell kissed her again.

Neither of them heard the dark Peugeot purr away into the Leighford night, its engine muffled, its headlights off. He watched her crunch away over the freezing driveway, the one where Elizabeth Pride had lain nine nights ago.

‘I suppose you’d better come in,’ he muttered to the menacing black and white beast sidling between his feet. Thank God, sighed Metternich on an outward purr. He thought she’d never go.

* * *

Teachers, at secondary schools at least, have free periods. They’re not free at all, of course. Even an NQT can tell you there’s no such thing as a free period. They’re a single hour in the day when you can at last get to grips with that pile of marking that’s been building since 1975. Or, if you’re very lucky, you can cover for Miss Whatserface who hates the job and is continually and inexplicably missing on the days she’s got 10C6, so you’ve got them.

Today was a treat for Peter Maxwell. He hadn't been nabbed for cover and his marking was more or less up to date. Wednesday was pure luxury, a two hour stretch, including lunch when, if he was careful, he wouldn't see a kid at all. But today, a tall man in a dark car picked him up in the car park and took him away.

'Did you see that?' Bernard Ryan, Leighford's Second Deputy, was watching from his eyrie in C block. He was that most dangerous of teachers — one with too much time on his hands.

'Hm?' Deirdre Lessing, the Senior Mistress, flapped her leathery wings as she hung upside down in the cupboard next to him.

'Maxwell going off with some bloke.'

Deirdre straightened and stared after the vehicle just vanishing through the front gates. 'Doesn't surprise me,' she sneered. 'He's a funny age.'

The tall man took the flyover beyond the Shingle and skirted the rolling open ground of the Dam before cutting through the back doubles north of Tottingleigh. The Green Man's doors were welcoming as ever and sparkled silver in the icy sun of a January midday.

'What's your poison, Chief Inspector?' Maxwell asked at the bar of the Snug. Hall didn't appreciate Maxwell's humour and he'd never heard of William Palmer, the Rugeley poisoner who'd supposedly made the phrase famous.

'Orange juice, please.'

Maxwell's face said it all. 'Thank you, my dear,' he beamed to the girl behind the bar. 'Muriel, isn't it?'

'No.' She made no attempt to lodge her chewing gum anywhere.

'Well,' he said, 'worth a try. And a Southern Comfort, please.' He shot a glance at Henry Hall. 'Large.'

Henry Hall found a seat near the fire. The place was all but deserted.

'If you're having lunch,' the girl-who-wasn't-Muriel said, 'the stroganoff's off.' That little news item didn't surprise Maxwell one bit. He paid up and carried the drinks to the corner.

'Here's to a bloody war and a sickly season,' he gave the old cavalry toast.

'Cheers,' said Hall more prosaically.

'May I say you've been unusually tight-lipped on our way here,' Maxwell reproached him, 'and whereas I'm flattered by the attention . . .'

'Don't be,' Hall urged him. 'What do you make of this?'

Maxwell took the little bundle of rags that Hall had placed on the table next to the Trumans' ashtray. 'It's a doll of some kind,' he said. 'Why?'

'You're an historian, Mr Maxwell.' Hall leaned back. 'I thought perhaps you'd know something about its significance.'

Maxwell looked closer. Someone had marked eyes at different levels and a crooked smile on the face in black marker pen. There was a similar patch of red felt tip at the back of the neck and a white-headed pin had been stuffed into it.

'Dressmaker's pin,' Hall answered the unspoken question. 'You can buy them anywhere. The rags appear to be bed linen, old, unremarkable. The string tying the limbs and neck is your common-or-garden hardware store.'

'Where did you get this?' Maxwell asked.

'I can't tell you that,' Hall told him.

Maxwell leaned back, feeling the coarse cloth in the palm of his hand. Henry Hall was a cryptic bastard, the boss of the girl who had come to fill the yawning gap in his life. Clearly the DCI still had his arse in his hand. 'Then I can't help.'

'Mr Maxwell, we routinely call in experts of various kinds to help us with our inquiries.'

'Our inquiries?' Maxwell checked him.

'Police inquiries,' Hall clarified.

'And what kind of expert am I?' the Head of Sixth Form wanted to know.

'That depends on what this is,' Hall's face was expressionless behind the rimless specs.

'All right,' Maxwell sighed, 'but I'm chancing my arm here, you understand?'

Hall nodded. Ten days into a murder enquiry and he was ready to take a few chances.

'It's not my period, of course,' Maxwell was covering his back. He saw Hall's knuckles white around the orange juice and almost let a smile escape. 'I've never seen a real one, only photographs, drawings . . .'

'Mr Maxwell.' The voice was firm. Curt.

'I think it's a poppet.'

'A what?' Hall was in mid-swig as he said it and his face turned pale.

'A doll,' Maxwell shrugged, 'used in sympathetic magic.'

'You'll have to pass all that by me again, Mr Maxwell,' Hall put the glass down, leaning forward now, all ears.

'Like I said, it's not my period, the witch fever. Reformation and beyond. Sixteenth, seventeenth century. Black and grey witches used to make these dolls in the likeness of a victim . . .'

'A victim?'

'Yes,' Maxwell put the doll down and took up the menu. 'I fancy a ploughman's, I think.'

'What sort of victim?

'Anybody they didn't like. It was vital the victim knew he was a target or the doll wouldn't work.' He leaned forward until he was filling Hall's face. 'I couldn't help noticing the pin in the neck and the red ink. Anybody you know been stabbed in the neck recently, Mr Hall?'

For once the dull eyes blinked, the steady gaze fell away. Hall picked up his menu. 'Ploughman's?' he said, nodding. 'Sounds good.'

* * *

Henry Hall unleashed Peter Maxwell back on the unsuspecting waifs of Leighford High that afternoon, watching as the cantankerous old bastard made his way across the quad, confiscating walkmen and chewing gum, those twin evils of the twentieth century lingering on into the twenty-first. For a moment, Maxwell fancied he heard the warble of a mobile phone, then thought better of it. No one would dare — not in his hearing.

Hall drove like a madman back to the nick as the sun died and a raw biting wind rose from the north-east.

'Martin,' he all but collided with a still waiting DS Stone in the foyer. 'What news on Mrs Cruikshank?'

'Abusive and tight-lipped in almost equal measure,' Stone told him. 'Shame euthanasia isn't on the menu.'

'Who's with her now?'

'Jacquie Carpenter.'

'Right.' And he checked himself before opening the door.

'DCI Hall entering the room,' Jacquie spoke for the benefit of the tape recorder, 'at two twenty-eight.' The DC looked tired and pale, like police officers do when faced with a suspect who's clammed up, who knows her rights, whose lips are sealed.

Hall scraped back the chair next to his DC. 'For the record,' he spoke clearly, 'I am showing Mrs Cruikshank the rag doll I showed her yesterday. You said it was a poppet, Mrs Cruikshank.'

The old woman sat as if frozen, her narrow shoulders hunched, her hands flat on the table in front of her. She looked at the doll, then at the man. 'Where's that fucking lawyer? He's supposed to be here by now.'

'What is a poppet, Mrs Cruikshank?' Hall was pursuing his inquiries.

Jane Cruikshank leaned back, folding her arms with a finality that was frightening. 'I ain't saying nothin' to you people. Not no more.'

For a moment Hall stayed sat there, his elbow still on the desk, the doll in his fist. Then he stood up. 'Very well. Thank you, Mrs Cruikshank. Interview ended at two thirty-two. You're free to go.'

'Eh?' the old girl blinked, looking up at him through watery eyes.

'That's it. We're finished. There's still the little matter of the shotgun, of course. We'll sort that out later.'

'I . . .'

Jacquie was on her feet too, the tape recorder switched off.

They waited until Jane Cruikshank had reached the door. 'Oh,' Hall's voice stopped her with impeccable timing. 'Your poppet,' he said.

He wouldn't have believed a woman of her age could move so fast. 'I told you,' she growled. ''T'ain't mine.' And she was already striding down the corridor, calling back, 'I never seen it before.'

When the door had closed, Jacquie made to follow. 'Let her go,' Hall said. 'What happened to her brief?'

'Legal aid,' shrugged Jacquie. 'Could be anywhere.'

Hall nodded. 'Some kid still wet behind the ears.'

'What was all that about the doll, sir?' she asked.

'Hm? Oh, the poppet.' Hall was making for the door. 'You'd better ask Peter Maxwell.'

* * *

'Still nothing, then?' It was almost a knee-jerk reaction. You saw Martin Stone; you asked the question. The DS was thinking of pinning badges to his lapels — 'No news yet'.

He shook his head, peering through the gloom of a January afternoon. 'We'll just have to wait for God's own time,' he said.

Jacquie Carpenter looked at him for a second. She didn't know Stone well, but she hadn't got him down for the religious type — God's policeman.

'I appreciate this, by the way,' the DS was saying, joining the traffic on the flyover, 'on your own time and all.'

'I just wish I thought it would lead to anything,' Jacquie was unscrewing the flask. 'Cuppa?'

'Great. No, I know it's a long shot, but it's the little things in murder, isn't it? The devil's always in the detail.

I couldn't get out of my head Kev's info about that bogus newsman. Who is he? What does he want?'

'Just some creep,' Jacquie poured with the expertise born of hours on the road; visits, surveillances, a thousand follow-ups to a thousand leads. 'A ghoul. The world's full of them, Martin.'

He took the flask top, grinning at her. 'So young, so cynical,' he said.

'Maybe. But even if this vicar can give us a good description . . .'

'It doesn't get us any nearer the murderer of Elizabeth Pride, no, perhaps not. And that's Rector, by the way; the Reverend Andrew Darblay.'

* * *

The Reverend Andrew Darblay wasn't home. He was lying in the nave of his own church, laid out like the great knight whose tomb was spattered with his blood. His feet faced the altar and his arms were crossed over his chest, his right hand clutching a crucifix which was upside down. His head was thrown back, a dark crimson pool radiating out like a liquid cushion beneath it, making the ancient stones slippery and the heavy-duty carpet stiff. His sightless, sunken eyes were fixed on the floral bosses that studded the roof, his face pale against the blood and his mouth twisted as though with boredom at the view he had looked at now for too long.

Stone had made the phone calls to Leighford, stabbing out the basics his colleagues needed to know. An ambulance, photographers, the SOCO team and the guv'nor, who'd probably be SIO when the time came — they'd all be on their way now, snarling up the A25, hurtling through the quiet country lanes. There'd be no wailing sirens, no flashing blue lights — all that was for *The Bill* and *Liverpool One*. Stone estimated fifteen minutes before their arrival, perhaps more. That gave him some time to steal a march, even a few Brownie points.

'The attack began there,' he told Jacquie, pointing to the first blood spot by the West door. She followed the trail. She was all right with this one, as all right as you can be when you find a man with his skull smashed and his brains all over his place of work. Her initial reaction was to vomit, then to run, but she'd resisted both. She wasn't going to play the girlie in front of Martin Stone. All her working life she'd been aware of that one, ready for the snigger, the smirk, the chauvinistic inference that she couldn't cope. 'I'd say he ran, maybe stumbled would be more accurate, across that way.'

They stood together at the font, with its tell-tale brown drips of blood marbling the stone. 'He was still alive here; see, he slipped sideways, round behind these pews.' Jacquie solemnly followed Stone and the blood trail to the Gothic tomb. 'And here, he rested for a while. What were they doing? Having a breather? A chitchat? There's a lot of blood.'

'Had he hit him again?' Jacquie squatted to check the direction of the spurts.

'I'd say so,' Stone was checking the angles of the church. 'Back there, a second blow at the font. Here, a third. It was the fourth that brought him down. Slap bang in the aisle.' The DS crouched over the body, lifting the left elbow just a little. 'Rigor,' he said. 'He's been dead some time. I dare say Astley will have some words of wisdom on that. Jesus.' Stone had been looking behind him, towards the altar with its canopy and its stained glass. He was on his feet now, Jacquie beside him. A great deal of blood had saturated the white altar cloth, dripping down from something dark and slimy on the altar itself. On either side, two tall black candles stood unlit in their brass candlesticks and someone had painted something on the polished Victorian tiles at their base.

It was a circle with a star of five points.

* * *

'Max, how the hell are you?'

He didn't recognise the voice. Not at first. Earlier in the evening he'd wrestled with the complexities of his Year 10 coursework marking. Was that piece of plagiarised misspelt drivel a level 4 or level 5? The worst aspect of all this was that people often mistook him for the sort of teacher who gives a fuck. But, then, that was because they were right.

Now, he'd put away his red pen, hied himself to his attic, put the gold-laced Crimean forage cap on his head and settled down to the important things — breathing life into 54mm pieces of plastic.

'It's Prissy,' the voice crackled on the other end of the phone, 'Prissy Crown. I've been meaning to call you since the other night. How's the head?'

'Oh, it's twice its usual size,' Maxwell said, 'but that's because I've been named Leighford High's Teacher of the Year for the thirty-eighth year running. It's quite embarrassing. I really must turn down the Bolly and the fortnight in Klosters this year — give somebody else a chance.'

'I was worried, Max,' she ignored him.

'No need,' he breezed, searching frantically for Trumpeter Crawford's bridoon rein among the bits of plastic on his desk. 'It was my own fault.'

'Well, that's just it,' she said after a pause. 'I'm not sure it was.'

He stopped ferreting. 'I'm sorry?' She had his attention now.

'Max, look. I can't talk over the phone. There's something going on, at Beauregard's I mean. Do you fence?'

'Fence?' He nearly fell off his chair. 'Well, I used to, but, Christ, Prissy, that was years ago. I've been on the piste of a different kind since then.'

'I'd meet you elsewhere, but I'm competing tomorrow night at the club. Can you make it, say, half past six? I can get you togged out. Are you an epée man?'

'Sabre,' he said. 'But Prissy . . .'

But she'd gone. He hung up and looked at the cat. 'I'll have you know,' he said, 'that in my day at Cambridge, I was a beau sabreur of beaux sabreurs — and a pretty good fencer, too. Ah,' he leaned back, hands behind his head, reliving the Granta days, 'the sins of the flèche.'

* * *

Jim Astley was at it again, green-gowned the next morning, bent double over the dead. In his more fanciful moments he saw himself as one of those embalmers of ancient Egypt, pouring chemicals into Pharaohs, tipping them upside down and hooking their brains out through their noses. They had worshipped baboons and jackals and ibis. He worshipped science. Who was to say who was right?

'Lizzie Borden with an axe,' he murmured as he carefully tweezered pieces of shattered skull out of Andrew Darblay's brain, 'gave her father forty whacks. When she saw what she had done, she gave her mother forty-one. Or is it the other way round?'

'Are we talking axe then, doc?' Donald was brewing the coffee in the corner in the less-than-clinical procedure the two adopted when they were alone.

'Just being folksy, Donald.' Astley had not looked up. 'Put it down over there, will you? Don't want Douwe Egbert's messing up the scene here. Mr Hall won't be pleased.'

He adjusted the angle of the microphone as he moved to the left posterior occiput. 'How many pieces of cranium over there, Donald?' he asked.

'Er . . . sixteen.'

'Right.' He twisted hard to the left, 'Make that seventeen,' and the piece of bone clattered into the kidney dish. 'For the record, the deceased died as a result of four, possibly five blows to the skull. The weapon is your archetypal blunt instrument, consistent with a metal rod.' He looked up. 'Couldn't be as corny as the Reverend Darblay in the chancel with the candlestick, could it? Definitely metal — I'll confirm that microscopically later — and definitely with well-defined corners, not your smooth tube idea. Note the tell-tale crescent-shaped depressions. The killer is right-handed, both from the wounds to the occiput and the blood spatter pattern I observed on the deceased's clothing and at the scene. SOCO will confirm this — or if they're wise they will. Our man — and with all due deference to Ms Borden, I'm pretty sure it is a man — is pretty strong. One blow in the right hands would have been sufficient, but this guy seemed to enjoy it. The instrument was swung like a club, probably with both hands and the final blow delivered as Darblay was falling. He tried to . . . oh, thanks, Donald,' and he deftly slurped the coffee as he put his hand round the mike, 'tried to defend himself — Darblay, that is. Note the contusions and severe bruising to the back of both forearms. Pinky of the left hand is broken; again, I'd say, defensive wound.

'All wounds to the head were delivered when Darblay was on the move — witness the relatively defined extent of fracture fissures. A great deal of pulping and laceration to the brain . . .' he smiled benignly at Donald, and lapsed uncharacteristically into Hercule Poirot, 'ze little grey cells, n'est-ce pas?'

It was a bit before Donald's time and he'd always refused to watch David Suchet on principle.

'. . . severe haemorrhage and rupture of blood vessels are the cause of death.' Astley straightened, feeling his back go again and made a mental note to get that buxom piece Sophie Clark working on it that night at Beauregard's.

'What's this heart thing all about, then?' Donald was busy with his tape measure in the corner.

'Now,' Astley slipped his mask off his neck from where he'd draped it to drink his coffee. 'That is curious. The blood it's swimming in — or was before it dried up — is human. And I'd be prepared to bet it's Darblay's. But the heart itself is that of an *ovis aries*, the common sheep and before you ask I haven't the first bloody idea what breed it was. The most interesting question of all of course is what it was doing on the high altar of your typical English perpendicular church. Luckily, Donald,' and he prised off his rubber gloves, 'you and I need not concern ourselves with such imponderables. That sort of conundrum we can safely leave to Mr Plod.'

CHAPTER 8

'You know, you're actually pretty good,' Prissy Crown purred, patting the hard wooden bench beside her. Hard it may have been, wooden it certainly was, but to Peter Maxwell it was bliss itself. He had pulled muscles where he didn't know he had muscles and his hair was plastered over his forehead under the mesh of the mask.

'Was, dear lady,' he wheezed. 'And you're being kind. I was only ever B-team material.'

'Sophie, tell him.' Prissy needed a second opinion.

'Your riposte needs work,' the taller girl said. They both looked resplendent in their whites. Maxwell had borrowed an old pair of track-suit bottoms and trainers from Lost Property at school and his fencing jacket didn't fit him anywhere. 'I gather you're not used to the electric?'

'My dear girl,' he sought refuge in his towel to wipe the sweat from his eyes, barely remembering to tilt the mask back first. 'When I was fencing, there was a young bloke called Cyrano de Bergerac who was the club's teaboy.'

He noted with dismay the vacant look on both their faces, 'De Bergerac, seventeenth-century swordsman, big nose? . . . Jose Ferrer, Gerard Depardieu? . . . Oh, forget it. Suffice it to say I'm rusty.'

Prissy was sitting with her face close to his. 'You certainly impressed me with a sabre. How are you with a foil?' And she was on her feet, hauling him upright. 'Sophie, do the honours, will you?'

The blonde girl trotted off to check the machinery, then re-hooked the contestants to their wires. Maxwell checked the weapon Prissy had given him. It was light after the sabre and nestled neatly into the palm of his hand.

'There's something very phallic,' Prissy said, 'about a man with a sword in his hand.' She stroked his arm and wandered to her place on the piste.

Minutes ago, they'd paired Maxwell up with Ron, who had the face and body of an old-age pensioner and the speed and reflexes of Superman. What Maxwell hadn't known was that Ron was Beauregard's secret weapon. They always trotted him out to face newcomers, especially any who had the rashness to claim experience. They just switched Ron on and let him loose. Maxwell's button hadn't touched him once whereas Maxwell's jacket was metaphorically cut to shreds.

'En garde!' Sophie Clark called them to order. Maxwell crouched, his left arm behind his back, his knees bent, the point of his blade in a line with Prissy's mask. He felt and heard their blades slide together. 'Fence!'

She drove him back with a series of attacks, fast, hard, the steel ringing in the otherwise deserted gym. The competition wasn't for an hour yet and the opposing team hadn't shown up. A couple of spectators lounged on the rail of the gallery overhead. Prissy was grunting with the effort as she lunged at the end of the piste. Maxwell saw it coming and flicked the blade aside, catching the girl under the ribs. Her squeal and the buzz coincided and Sophie yelled out the score.

'A palpable hit,' murmured Maxwell.

'Lucky!' was Prissy's verdict and she may have been right. Maxwell sensed he wouldn't have it so easy next time. Again he faced her, her blade probing his defences. His legs were tired, his lungs tortured and the mask didn't help. It blurred his vision and suffocated him so that he found himself using less than orthodox methods to beat her back. Prissy was grunting again, her teeth bared under the mask, her nostrils flaring.

'Fuck!' and her lunge went wild. This time his point prodded her midriff and the buzzer sounded again.

'All right,' she snarled, en garde again. 'This time attack me, you bastard.'

Maxwell stood there. 'A lady always makes the first move,' he said and parried her thrusts. He wasn't ready for the flèche however and she hurled herself at him, aiming low and thudding the point into his crotch.

'Foul!' Sophie shouted. But Prissy wasn't listening. Recovering her balance, she went for the attack again, crouching like a puma on the scent, her hair flinging out behind the grips of the mask, the blade a blur in her gloved hand. They were off the piste now, Maxwell retreating every tortured step, desperately keeping her point away from his throat. The pain in his groin was mind-numbing and his eyes watered behind the gauze.

'Prissy!' Sophie was yelling, but the woman's blood was up and there was no stopping her now. Her cord had unhooked itself and she was free of its electric encumbrance. She lunged again, the blade higher this time and Maxwell scythed to the left. He felt his back against the gym wall and had nowhere else to go. His own cord was trailing on the ground, detached from his jacket. The steel slashed and scraped and Maxwell used all his force to hold the girl's sword arm down. She ripped off the mask, panting with the exertion and he did the same, assuming the bout was over. In an instant their lips were together and her tongue probing as her foil had done. Maxwell dropped his foil and firmly disentangled himself from the woman. Their bodies straightened. Maxwell felt Prissy's groin grinding against his own and he gently but firmly held her at arm's length.

'Let's call that a draw, shall we?' he asked, looking steadily down at her.

'Good idea,' Sophie was alongside the pair, relieving Prissy of her foil. 'Time for a cold shower.'

'Sounds good to me,' Maxwell winced. He was still coming to terms with three feet of tempered steel colliding with his gonads. Whatever Prissy had had in mind a minute ago, she was likely to be disappointed in all sorts of ways.

Prissy smiled and licked her lips. 'Thanks, Maxwell,' she said. 'See you after the competition,' and she winked as she flounced away, rolling her hips with more sway than was strictly necessary.

'Sorry,' Sophie said. 'She can get a bit carried away at times.'

'Doesn't wear a sword to bed, does she?' Maxwell asked, watching her go.

Sophie paused. 'Do you want to find out?' she asked.

Maxwell's eyebrows rose. 'Don't tell me between Aerobics and Fencing, you also run a dating agency?'

Sophie pulled an odd face, an expression Maxwell hadn't seen before. 'You'd be amazed at what goes on here,' she said.

* * *

Maxwell had showered and checked his multiple bruises. He'd stashed his gear into his hold-all and was just creeping along the landing, close to where he'd had his odd encounter of three nights ago. He'd hoped to reach the side door and winch himself gingerly onto the saddle of White Surrey, before Prissy Crown noticed he'd gone. He nearly made it too.

'Max!'

He turned. Prissy had changed out of her fencing whites and was standing in the foyer below, a skimpy black top stretched over her breasts, the nipples like organ stops. Her hair hung wetly around her shoulders. He waved.

'I think I owe you a drink,' she said.

'Actually, Prissy, I must be getting back . . .' And he loitered down the stairs.

'Just one for the road,' she added softly and linked her arm with his.

'What happened to the competition?' he asked.

She shrugged. 'Suddenly didn't give a damn,' she said.

Beauregard's Bar was dark, with coloured lights rotating in myriad patterns across the ceiling. This wasn't the one he'd talked to Jim Astley in on his last visit. This one was lit with lava lamps and thudded to rock music. It was for members only and energetic young things were gyrating in the swirling light show in the centre, myriad shafts bouncing off the ceiling.

He bought them both drinks and tried to sit as far from Prissy as possible. That wasn't easy. With the instincts of a man-killer, she insinuated herself alongside him and sat with her breasts on display on the table, her cleavage like a poor man's Grand Canyon.

'I'm sorry if I hurt you,' she said and proceeded to massage Maxwell's groin.

'That's okay,' he gently moved her hand away.

She leaned back, lolling now on the plush length of the seat, her legs splayed, her jeans undone at the top. She sipped her daiquiri, 'I'm glad you came, Maxwell,' she purred. 'I'm frightened, you see.'

Maxwell had seen fright before. In many people, at many times. Some cried, some whimpered, some screamed. Others sat there, rocking, silent, their limbs numb with fear, paralysed by the booming thud of their own pulses. What he had never seen was a woman so frightened that she was flaunting her not inconsiderable body and giving him the come on.

'Of what?' he felt it his duty to ask.

'Ken,' she said. 'Willoughby. Sophie. They're involved in something.'

'Involved?'

She sat up, leaning forward again. 'Are you fucking Jacquie Carpenter?' She was looking into his dark eyes.

'No.' He could still just about manage polite-mode. 'I'm drinking a Southern Comfort and talking bollocks to a mad woman.'

She slammed down her drink, her face white with fury. Then she softened, smiled. 'Yes,' she said. 'I suppose you would think that. Oh, Maxwell, I'm sorry. It's none of my business, but I get . . . so intense.' She rummaged in her bag, pulling out a small foil packet. 'Do you?'

He shook his head. He didn't need that. Fifty valium a day was enough for Peter Maxwell. She sighed and stashed it away again. Just her luck to be stuck with Mr Squeaky.

'For some time now, Willoughby . . . Willoughby's been going out, at odd hours. He told me it was bridge. But that's bollocks. He's been seeing Sophie.'

'I'm sorry,' Maxwell said.

Her eyes caught his. 'No, you don't understand. I don't give a flying fuck about that. Willoughby and I went our different ways as far as bed went years ago. If he was just slipping Sophie one now and again, nolo problema. But Ken's involved.'

'Ménage a trois?' Maxwell suggested.

'You're missing the point.' Prissy was twisting her fingers together, trying to make sense of it all in what passed for her mind, 'I'm not talking about sex, Maxwell, it's something altogether . . . well, sinister isn't too wide of the mark.'

'Hello, people.' They both jumped at the voice barking at them over the thumping music.

'Hello, Cris.' Prissy sounded less than pleased to see Crispin Foulkes. To Maxwell, the social worker was like the Seventh Cavalry, all bugles and buckskin jackets and salvation. He might as well have been whistling the 'Garryowen'.

'Mind if I join you?' Foulkes asked.

'Suit yourself,' Prissy said, snatching up her bags. 'I've got to be going. See you round, Maxwell,' and she smiled at him.

'Something I said?' Foulkes asked as they watched her go, hips swinging into the night.

'Don't ask me,' Maxwell said. 'I only fend the woman off.'

'Sexually?' Foulkes sat down in Prissy's place.

'That too,' Maxwell nodded, 'but I was thinking of a fencing bout. Ever faced her?'

'No fear,' Foulkes laughed. 'I'm not man enough. Anyway, I'm no fencer. Tried it once at school. Hopeless. No, I'll stick to the weights. Bit of judo, that sort of thing. I'm glad I bumped into you.'

'Not as glad as I am,' Maxwell beamed. 'Let me get you a drink.'

'Actually, Max, I won't. Not here. I wanted to have a chat, but I can't hear a blasted thing above this row. Look, my flat's not far away. Fancy a Chinese?'

'Do you know, I do,' Maxwell said. 'Must be all this wrestling I've been doing.'

* * *

Maxwell fished around for the last bit of crispy duck and pushed the carton away. 'Excellent,' he said. 'Mind you, I shall want another in a minute.'

Both men laughed. Foulkes' flat was in a wing of a Victorian house, still redolent of spring sunshine with new emulsion and furniture wrapped in polythene bags. Only the essentials were out and working — cooker, freezer, telly, computer. The social worker had apologised for the mess. He'd only been here since December and his caseload was already so huge, his social life was on hold.

'So you thought I was some sort of warlock,' Maxwell said, sipping the cold beer Foulkes had poured him.

The social worker raised both his hands, laughing. 'I'm sorry, Max,' he said. 'Idiotic of me, I know, but after the things I saw in Broxtowe . . . Well, you wouldn't believe it.'

'I thought that was all tosh,' Maxwell said. 'Satanic abuse and so on.'

Foulkes shook his head. 'I have to keep an open mind. It's like child pornography on the Net. Perverts say it's harmless — just computer images. But they're not, Max, they're real children. And they're being abused somewhere in the world every day of the week. Then there was all that business in North Wales last year.'

'But I don't see how my calendar . . .'

'Midwinter Solstice, Beltane, Lammas, Samhain, four of the eight major Sabbats of Wicca, the Old Religion. I suppose I'm paranoid now, looking for the links wherever I go.'

'But it's not my calendar.'

'Not?' Foulkes looked up from his remaining noodles.

'Look, Crispin,' the Head of Sixth Form sat upright, facing his man. 'If I tell you something, can you assure me it'll go no further? It could get someone I know into a lot of trouble — not to mention me.'

'Confidentiality goes with my territory, Max,' Foulkes said. 'Like the confessional and the Official Secrets Act all rolled into one.'

Maxwell nodded. 'I half-inched the calendar from the house of the old woman I found on my doorstep on New Year's Eve.'

'Yes, I read about that. Elizabeth . . . what's her name . . . Prior?'

'Pride.'

'What were you doing there? At her house, I mean?'

'That's a long story,' Maxwell said, 'and I can't go into it now. Does that make any difference? I mean the fact that the calendar was hers not mine?'

'It might,' Foulkes said, deep in thought. 'You seem very well informed about this business, Max. Would I be chancing my arm to suggest that the friend you want to protect is Jacquie Carpenter?'

Maxwell raised a hand. 'Now, come on, Crispin,' he said. 'That's not quite cricket. And I didn't say the person I know is a friend, did I?'

'Touché!' Foulkes laughed, acceding to the cryptic old bastard's point.

'Don't,' Maxwell shuddered. 'Too many painful memories.'

* * *

They'd told Martin and Alex Stone that if nothing had transpired by Monday, they'd have to induce. With little Janey it had been easy — like shelling peas as the midwife had put it. But this one was different, a big bugger with a bone idle streak. Martin Stone was picturing the moving scan in his mind when he heard his name echoing down the long corridor of relevance.

'Martin?'

'Guv?'

The DCI was looking at him, inscrutable as ever. Damn! That was a few demerits in anybody's book. Stone was on his feet, telling himself to concentrate. He hadn't taken in Simon Reilly's photographs of the laid-out corpse of the Reverend Darblay, nor the nastier ones that closed in with chilling full frontal morbidity on the shattered head. Perhaps it was just as well. He'd had the nightmares before and he didn't want all that in Alex's lap. She had enough to contend with.

He reached the front of the Incident Room as someone snapped off the carousel's smoky beam and the neon strips restored mock daylight.

'Andrew Darblay?' Hall reminded the man of his mission.

'Yes, guv, thank you. The Reverend Darblay was sixty-three. He'd been rector of Wetherton for nearly twenty years.'

'Family?' somebody asked.

'A wife, Dorothy, died of leukaemia a while back. No kids. He was well-liked by the churchgoers, a dwindling band of course these days. One or two we've spoken to found him a bit of a fuddy duddy . . .'

'Goes with the territory, doesn't it?' somebody asked.

'Part of the Oxford Tripos whatsit, isn't it?' There were sniggers all round.

Henry Hall sensed the change of mood. Before they'd found Darblay, the air crackled with suppressed tension. No leads on old lady Pride, brick walls, tight lips. Now, with the dead rector, there was expectation in the wind. A different body, in a different place at a different time. He let the ribaldry subside. Men and women with laughter on their lips were at ease with themselves. They got on with their work, even, in a curious sort of way, enjoyed it.

'We spoke to his housekeeper,' Stone went on, 'a Mrs Spooner. She doted on the man and is very upset by it all. Said he hadn't an enemy in the world.'

'She would, wouldn't she?' somebody asked.

'Nothing in the parish council?' Hall prodded. 'Often a centre of intrigue in my book.'

Stone wondered what book it was that his guv'nor was using. 'We haven't seen everybody yet, sir,' he said. 'It may be something will crawl out of the woodwork.'

'What do we know about his last movements?' Hall wanted to know.

'Jacquie?' Stone took a chair and watched the girl take centre stage.

'Mrs Spooner usually arrives at seven thirty to cook breakfast,' she told the team. 'Mr Darblay was always up by the time she got there and the house was unlocked. He was usually in his study working on his sermons and they'd have a cup of coffee together.'

'And on the morning in question?' Even fast-track graduates like Hall lapsed into policespeak every so often.

'She couldn't find him,' Jacquie said. 'That didn't bother Mrs Spooner. The deal was if he wasn't in the house, she'd brew the coffee and leave it in the filter machine. He was either in the church or out walking. That happened on average a couple of times a month.'

'That morning he was in the church?' Hall asked.

Jacquie nodded. 'Dr Astley gives the time of death as between six and eight. The local bobby says the church was never locked . . .'

'Isn't that a bit unusual?' Hall queried.

'Darblay insisted on it,' Stone piped up. 'Said — and I quote Mrs Spooner "*God's house should always be open*". We're assuming at the moment that he went to the church, perhaps to get something from the vestry, and disturbed somebody already there.'

'Which brings us to the desecration,' Hall nodded. 'Who's got anything on that?'

'I've been doing a bit of digging, guv.' Kevin Brand was on his feet. 'Mind you, the Net's a bit dodgy on all this.'

'Go on.'

'Black candles on the altar is not your standard C of E, but you can buy 'em, mind, almost anywhere these days. It's very Goth, apparently, whatever that means.'

'Mrs Spooner had never heard of Darblay owning any black candles,' Jacquie filled in.

'The heart on the altar was that of a sheep . . .'

There was a ripple of suppressed laughter, while Brand kept going. 'Wetherton's a rural area, farming community. Any one of a thousand people had access to a sheep carcass.'

'What's the fingerprint score?' Hall asked.

'Hundreds, guv,' Brand shrugged. 'The lab are doing their best, but there's choirboys, servers, cleaners, the women that do the flowers. The candles are clean, though. Our boy was careful with that. I'm working on the graffiti as we speak.'

'How far have you got?' the DCI leaned forward.

Brand sighed, waiting for the sniggers. 'It's what they call a Pentagram. It's usually drawn in the air with an athame . . .'

'Whatname?' somebody called.

Laughter.

'It's a sword,' Brand kept going.

'The thing on the altar was done with a sword?'

'No, a finger. The Pentagram's called a Witches' Star and sometimes a Goblin's Cross. Its point faces downwards — that means black magic, devil worship.'

Hall quietened down the whistles and cat calls.

'You've been watching too many Blair Witch Projects, Kev, me old mucker!' It was the last bit of nonsense Hall was going to tolerate. 'Jacquie, Martin, any history of this sort of thing at Wetherton?'

'None reported, guv,' Stone said. 'It's bloody weird, though.'

'Yes,' Hall mused. 'I'm beginning to think it is.'

* * *

'I'm glad we stayed in,' Jacquie raised her glass to Maxwell. 'I'm not sure I'm ready for *Sleepy Hollow* again — too many heads.'

'Darblay,' Maxwell nodded. 'I wondered if you wanted to talk.'

'Yes,' she said, then quicker, 'no.'

He caught her gaze.

'Damn you, Max. Is this what it's always going to be? One compromising situation after another?'

'Always?' he arched an eyebrow. 'Now, that's a long time, Woman Policeman. The Twelfth of Never. Is either of us talking always?'

She looked at him, across the polished pine of her dining-room table, his lasagne gone, his wine half drunk, his eyes bright and kindly in the candlelight. 'I don't know,' she murmured. 'Are we?'

He smiled. 'Darblay,' he said again.

She leaned back in her chair, 'I've got cheese and biscuits or bananas and custard.'

'Temptress!' he shouted. 'I'll make a start on the cheese and bickies, please. The rector seemed a decent enough bloke.'

'What?'

He was being domestic, collecting up the dishes, humming 'One man went to mow, went to mow a modem . . .' Not that he had the first idea what a modem was.

'Max!' She was at his elbow, racing him into the kitchen. 'Are you telling me you knew Andrew Darblay?'

'I met him, yes.'

'What? Some time ago?'

'Ah,' he was illuminated by the fridge-light, 'Stilton.' It was an excellent Homer Simpson. 'Last Sunday.'

'You shite!' She spun him round. 'Never mind the Stilton. Talk to me.'

'Aha,' Maxwell chuckled. '"*But it's saviour of 'is country when the guns begin to shoot*".' Kipling was a little lost on Jacquie Carpenter and she continued to face her man down. 'All right,' he said. 'You put the coffee on. I'll crumble the cheese. And we'll talk about the dear, dead days.'

'Don't tell me,' Jacquie relaxed her grip from his shoulders. 'You were talking to Darblay about his beautiful church.'

'Yes, I was actually.'

She fussed with the filter. 'It didn't look so beautiful smeared with his blood.'

Maxwell stopped in mid-crumble. 'God, Jacquie, I'm so sorry.' He put the crackers down and took her face in his hands, kissing her softly. 'Here I am being a cryptic bastard and you're up to your elbows in somebody else's blood. Was it terrible?'

She shrugged. She always felt like a little girl in Maxwell's arms. She held his hands, warm and strong and safe. She felt like crying. It had been a tough three days. 'You've seen your corpse too,' she said.

He sighed. 'It's the season,' he said. 'Winter. Isn't this the deadly month — January?'

'We're not talking about the weather, Max,' she shook her head.

He looked at his girl, quiet, sensible, solid Jacquie, the face of an angel and the heart of a man. 'Swap you, then,' he challenged her. 'Over coffee. Over cheese and bickies. Here and now,' he swung his hips coyly, lapsing into his deep South. 'Ah'll show you mine if'n you show me yours.'

She laughed despite herself. Despite the dead face of Andrew Darblay that grinned at her from every fold in her curtains, every knot in her pine. 'All right,' she said, clipping him on the chin. 'But you first.'

'Done,' he said and instantly became Jim Carrey as *Ace Ventura*. 'I was the second gunman on the Grassy Knoll.' Then he was Maxwell. 'Mr Hall, for reasons best known to himself, dropped me Elizabeth Pride's address. It was only a short step from there to Wetherton and the local man of the cloth.'

She clicked her fingers. '*Littlehampton Mercury*,' she said. 'I might have known.'

'It's not an alias I often use,' he told her. 'Bit suspect?'

'No such paper. DS Stone took me all the way to Wetherton to check on you. Darblay reported a bogus newspaperman to the blokes at the Incident Room. Rang in specially.'

Maxwell chuckled. 'Pretty astute clergyman there. How did he die?'

'Not just yet.' The coffee gurgled in the corner. 'What did Darblay tell you?'

'Ooh, let me see.' Maxwell scraped back a chair and buttered a cracker. 'That Elizabeth Pride was pure evil.'

'Evil?' Jacquie frowned. 'That's rather an old-fashioned word.'

'Andrew Darblay was an old-fashioned man,' he said. 'Housekeeper, rectory, in tune with his tombs and his ogee work. Reminded me of Alec Guinness in *Kind Hearts and Coronets* — the Reverend d'Ascoyne, I mean, not all his siblings. Clearly, Mrs Pride was no churchgoer. Your turn.'

She poured the coffee for them both. 'He was battered to death.'

'So the radio said this morning,' he nodded. 'I was hoping for a little more.'

She put the cups down in front of them. 'Max, what I'm about to tell you mustn't go any further. Do you promise?'

'Is the Pope Polish?' he asked her.

'Promise me, Max,' and she reached for his hand.

'I promise,' he said, his voice steady as a church and as deep as her love for him.

'We found him laid out in the nave. I don't mean sprawled on the floor, I mean laid out, arms across his chest.'

'Like Elizabeth Pride,' Maxwell said, the hairs on his neck beginning to crawl like they do when a haunting tune hits home.

Jacquie nodded. 'He was holding a crucifix upside down in his hands.'

'Really?'

'What does that mean?'

'I'm not sure,' he murmured. 'The Templars were accused of that, spitting on the cross, worshipping it upside down.'

'Templars?'

'Monk knights — or knight monks — take your pick. They were an enormously rich and powerful cult until the fourteenth century when they looked funny at the king of France one day and he axed them all — or, more literally, burned them at the stake. They were supposed to worship the severed head of a horned god called Baphomet.'

'A horned god . . . ?'

'The male beast,' Maxwell explained, 'monarch of the glen. It was all to do with ancient fertility rites — the first of Spring and so on. Maypole, dances and kissing the Devil's arse. Most of it was nonsense, dreamed up by frustrated Catholics in hair shirts — not that it's my period, you understand.'

'Of course not,' she said, well used to his encyclopaedic ways.

'Today, most Catholics are quite content to watch Mass of the Day on telly, but in the good old days . . .'

'There were . . . things on the altar.'

'What things?' He looked up from his coffee.

'Black candles. A five pointed star in a circle. A sheep's heart . . .'

'. . . and a cuddly toy,' Maxwell finished the list for her, but neither of them was laughing. 'Are we talking Satanism?' he asked, 'Jacquie, are we talking about black magic? I mean, this is the twenty-first century.'

'I never thought I'd hear you say that,' she tutted. 'I was hoping you'd say something rational, make some sense out of all this.'

'Sorry. Like I said, it's not my period. What about Crispin Foulkes?'

'Crispin?' She sat up. The name still caught her attention, even after all these years. 'What about him?'

'He knows a bit about Satanic abuse. Met it before in his social work. He seemed to think I knew something about it too, what with the calendar and all.'

'Ah, yes, the calendar. He did happen to mention that to me.'

'All right,' he said. 'You're a fair cop. I helped myself to it and I shouldn't have done. I'll hand it over to you or put it back if you like.' And he put his wrists out ready for the bracelets.

'Put it back? Max, where did it come from?'

He blinked at her. 'Well, from Myrtle Cottage, of course, from Elizabeth Pride's place. But you knew that . . .'

'Max.' She was staring at him now, worried, frightened even. 'When did you go to Myrtle Cottage?'

'God, I don't know. Er . . . nine, ten days ago? Why?'

'That would be the day after we went over the place with a fine tooth comb.'

'So?' He didn't follow.

'So, there was no calendar there, then, Max, no calendar at all. Unless . . .'

'Unless?'

She shook her head, rapidly, like a terrier shaking a rat. She was shaking herself free of a sudden thought she couldn't face. 'Nothing,' she said. 'Just forget it. Your coffee's getting cold.'

CHAPTER 9

'Come on, give us a fuckin' fag.'

'I ain't got one.'

'Yes you have, you shit. Cough up!'

Wayne and Darren went back a long way, to the buggies their mothers had wheeled them in down Asda aisles through the nursery years when *Danger Mouse* was still on the telly and Kurt and Courtney were love's young dream. They'd always been there for each other, when Wayne had pinched his first packet of Pickled Onion Flavour Monster Munch and when Darren had had his stomach pumped to get rid of his dad's vodka. It was a case of mi casa su casa where they found Wayne's dad's stack of tasty videos and they'd taken turns keeping watch while the other one went on a rummage of discovery in Jade O'Brien's knickers; it was a well-worn path.

Tonight was Sunday. Skateboarding in the Barlichway. They lived on the edge of the huge sprawling estate that threatened to dwarf sleepy Leighford. No birds sang here, around its wet, windy corners. They just huddled in the angles of the high rise and dropped their contempt on the buggers below.

The rain was driving in from the west, spattering on the graffiti-daubed boarded-up windows that had been the

Raj Tandoori Takeaway before certain racial differences had driven its owners away. Darren fumbled in his jeans and passed a Sovereign to his mate. Out came the cheap lighter that had replaced the one confiscated by that old fart Maxwell on Friday and the boys' hard, cold faces lit up for seconds in the dark.

Wayne inhaled deeply, resting against the wall, his trainered feet expertly rocking the skateboard on the pavement. 'What about that new bit, then?' He was always asking Darren's opinion, especially when it came to women. Darren, the sophisticate, the roué, belched noisily and swigged from his Carling, pondering the matter before giving his days-younger protégé the benefit of his wisdom.

'Great rack,' he nodded.

'Oh, yeah,' Wayne conceded. 'Does she go, though?'

Darren shrugged. 'You can't never tell with them foreigners, can you?'

'Can't you?'

Darren pulled his fleece higher under his chin. 'Don't you listen to nothin' in old bag Byfield's SRS lessons? It's your comparative religions, innit? They're all supposed to be virgins before they get married. Or they can't eat burgers, or summat.'

'Get on!' Wayne guffawed. 'That's only where they come from, though, innit? Not in Leighford.'

'Anyway,' Darren wiped the lager froth from his mouth. 'What about Roxanne, you two-timing git?'

'Nah,' Wayne half-turned. He had loved Roxanne for most of his teenaged life, all fourteen months of it. He'd scratched her name on the underside of his desk in Maths — well, there wasn't much else to do in Maths of a wet January. And last year, he'd broken into his mum's purse and sent the object of his affections a Valentine card — 'Violets are red, Roses are blue, what colour are yours?' it had said. But he already knew the answer to that. They were a virginal white. It had become his favourite colour. He and Darren went back a long way, but he wasn't going to tell him any of this.

'Nah,' he said again, bending to pick up the skateboard. 'Not my type.'

'Right!' chuckled Darren, 'I've seen you . . .' and his voice trailed away in the darkness.

'What?' Wayne followed his friend's gaze. Darren was staring transfixed at something lying huddled in the far corner, next to the battered supermarket trolley. 'What's up?'

Darren was fumbling with the lighter again. Out of the yellow light of the street lamp, that particular corner of the estate was deepest black. The boys made their way forward as an empty beer can rolled noisily across the tarmac. In the flickering light they saw a sight that neither of them would ever forget. It was an old man, sitting in the refuse of a derelict doorway, his white hair plastered to his forehead by the rain, his knees tucked up as though he was sitting by a roaring camp fire. They didn't take in the fact that he was naked, that his white flesh hung like an old wrinkled sheet from his bones. All they saw was his face, looking at them, grinning at them. And he was dead. They, who had never seen death before. They who knew that when you died, pumped full of bullets by Wesley Snipes or John Travolta, you just somersaulted backwards in slow motion and rolled in the dust. Things to do in Barlichway when you're dead.

* * *

Jim Astley had seen death before. Too much of it. Too often. He looked oddly incongruous in his dazzling white hooded suit in the Barlichway night. Coppers in luminous striped coats came and went all around him and the SOCOs were busy erecting a makeshift tent over Astley and a dead man.

The Barlichway crowd had gathered, track-suited, anoraked, a walking ad for Nike and Adidas huddled together in the rain beyond the police cordon stretched across the quadrangle, muttering and jostling. They who never saw a field event.

'This'd never happen if you blokes did your job,' someone called.

'I ain't seen a copper on this estate for years.'

'Who is it? What the fuck's going on?'

Each jeer, each question was echoed by the crowd's dark rhubarb, like some predictable Greek chorus lamenting a hero's woes.

Henry Hall crouched with the police surgeon under the glare of the arc lights. Jacquie Carpenter was behind him, trying not to look at the hideous grin on the dead man's face.

'*Risus sardonicus*,' Astley was prising the dead lips with gloved fingers, tapping the decayed teeth with something metal. 'Your classic *strychnos nux vomica*. It's almost textbook.'

'Bear with me,' Hall said grimly. 'You and I clearly read different textbooks, Jim.'

'We're lucky this is the twenty-first century.' Astley shone his pencil torch into the dead man's bulging eyes. 'Strychnine is a stimulant. It used to be available in patent medicines — Easton's Syrup, for one. It's an alkaloid found in a tree in India — er, I'm not boring you, am I? I mean, no snooker or anything on the telly?'

'I've got a sergeant somewhere,' Hall looked at his watch, 'whose wife's going into labour as we speak. His attention may be elsewhere; mine's here.'

'Makes you almost philosophical, doesn't it?' Astley was going about his business. 'One life begins as another ends.'

'You were talking about strychnine.'

'I was,' the doctor sighed. 'The stuff tastes terrible, so it would need to be administered in something sweet — jam, maybe, or custard. This poor old bugger would have had difficulty breathing and would have gone into convulsions. It's bloody painful. Whoever did this is making a point, Henry.'

'A point?'

'He wants to be noticed. There are more humane ways to take a life. The number of convulsions varies. Each one lasts from one to five minutes. Look at his eyes.'

Hall forced himself to.

'Pupils dilated, eyeballs prominent. What is odd is this.'

'What?' Hall couldn't see what Astley was pointing at.

'His general position, curled up like a bloody armadillo.'

'That's odd?'

'Happens in less than ten per cent of strychnine cases. Usually, the back arches the other way, so that only the head and heels touch the floor — a little acrobatics we in the profession call opisthotonos. This one's emprosthotonos — that's bending forward to you.'

'What sort of dose are we talking?' Hall wanted to know.

'Hundred grams to be certain, but he was an old man . . . what, seventy-five, seventy-six? It probably took less. He'd have died within hours. Who was he?'

Hall shook his head. 'I've got men going door to door,' he said. 'But this is the Barlichway, Jim. The locals'll be as forthcoming as a Trappist monastery.'

'Hello,' Astley's torch beam was playing behind the dead man's head. 'This looks familiar.'

'What?' Hall craned forward. A bloodless wound, about an inch wide, gaping and dark, ran across the nape of the old man's neck, leathery and brown.

'Either I'm having one of my increasingly common attacks of déjà vu,' Astley rested back on his booted heels, 'or this is the same knife thrust wound I saw on the late Elizabeth Pride.' He looked at the chief inspector. You've got a real live one, Henry.' His smile was as sardonic as the dead man's. 'You've found yourself a serial killer.'

* * *

'Are we talking about a serial killer. Chief Inspector?'

It had taken the assorted gentlemen (and ladies) of the press precisely five minutes to get around to that one. Henry Hall was mildly surprised — he'd expected it in two.

'What makes you say that, Mr Barton?'

The cameras were popping and wheezing in the congestion of the press conference room, the two dozen microphones thrust forward to the desk where Hall sat alone. People sat poised with cassettes in their hands, notepads on their laps, ciggies in their mouths. Mobile phones warbled and chattered like demented swallows on a wire. It was the paparazzi in full cry.

'Come on, Chief Inspector,' another voice came back at him. 'Three suspicious deaths inside fifteen days and within a radius of ten miles and you're telling us it's coincidence corner.'

Hall held up his hand to quieten the hubbub. 'We are unaware of any specific connection at the moment.'

'Who was the dead man?'

'I cannot tell you that at this precise moment.'

Fingers were jabbing the air, cassette-filled hands probing forward like the lean and hungry men around Caesar, scenting a rent in his toga.

'What can you tell us?' somebody else wanted to know. 'I mean, you called this bloody press conference.'

Guffaws and 'hear hears!' filled the morning.

Hall was on his feet, waiting for a modicum of silence. He wasn't going to get it. 'When I know anything,' he shouted at them all, 'I'll be in touch.'

Kevin Brand watched him go, white-gilled and rock-jawed. He leaned across to Jacquie Carpenter. 'Longest time I've ever heard it take for anybody to say "No comment". How long d'you think it'll be before he gets a red-hot call from the Chief Constable?'

'As long as it takes for one of these bastards to get through to him,' she shrugged.

'DS Carpenter?' she found herself staring into the cassette-player of a hawk-faced woman from the Telegraph. 'Janet Ruger. Can you tell me, what's the link between the dead man and Elizabeth Pride?'

'No comment.' Jacquie had tangled with the fourth estate before. They had a habit of smashing defences, uncovering secrets and then printing what they damn-well chose. She swept past the woman in the wake of her retreating DCI.

Brand was either less lucky or less nimble on his feet. 'How about you, DC Brand?' Janet Ruger had an NVQ in persistence. 'The link between the Barlichway body and Elizabeth Pride?'

Brand's expression didn't change. He leaned forward and licked his lips with a 'this is for your ears only' wink. 'Siamese twins,' he said darkly and followed Jacquie out.

* * *

The DCI was even greyer when he got off the phone to the Chief Constable than when he'd left the press conference. He was back in the Incident Room at Tottingleigh, the phones jumping, the computer screens flashing messages, the e-mails and faxes coming and going in the communications jungle that was Maxwell's Millennium.

The Chief Constable,' he announced above the row, 'has Social Services and I quote "climbing up his arse". He'd like to see some results. And so would I. What have we got?'

'The dead man was Albert John Walters,' a stocky detective volunteered. 'Lived on the Barlichway . . .'

'And died on the Barlichway,' Hall finished the sentence for him. 'Anything else?'

'He lived alone, guv,' Jacquie was checking her hastily scribbled notes, 'Fourteen A Coniston Court.'

'SOCO are going over the place now,' somebody chipped m. 'Chances are he died there.'

Hall nodded. 'So somebody carried a naked man along a balcony, down two flights of stairs, across a quadrangle and propped him thoughtfully in a corner. Why?' Hall was still standing, his tie-knot loosened, his shirt sleeves rolled, watching every face in front of him, every last member of his team. They'd lost the euphoria of the chase they'd found after the death of Andrew Darblay. Albert Walters had rattled them. They were panicky, jumpy, pressed by the press, leaned on by their guv'nor. People like that made mistakes; missed things. One wrong click on a mouse and Vlad the Impaler could walk free. Worse, it made them desperate for a result, over-zealous. People like that put innocent men in the frame.

There were no answers. Just anxious faces looking back at him, hopeful, eager even. It was that old blind faith. That somehow the guv'nor would have the answers. Because he was the guv'nor.

'Has Astley given us a time of death yet?' Hall asked. It had only been twelve hours since they'd found the body of old Albert Walters. Time enough for the press to get wind of it and for speculation and rumour to be rife. Not time enough for forensic science though — that, and miracles, took a little longer.

The phone shattered the sudden silence and Kevin Brand got there first. 'It's Martin Stone,' he put his hand over the receiver. 'It's a girl.'

There were whoops and applause rippling through the room. Hall looked stern for a moment, then picked up his plastic cup, the one with the lukewarm instant coffee and raised it in salute. 'Give them all our best, Kev,' he said and as the cheering began again, he sat down quietly at the front desk. 'Whoopee-doo,' he muttered.

* * *

'You know why I've sent for you?' Peter Maxwell looked up at the scruffy lads across the desk from him.

'Coursework,' Darren mumbled, avoiding the Great Man's eyes.

'No.' Maxwell shook his head.

'Trainers?' Wayne tried. Both boys were wearing them.

Maxwell shook his head again.

Darren looked at Wayne. He screwed his face up for a moment, then nodded. Sheepishly, Wayne produced a packet of chewing gum from his back pocket and put it down gently on the Head of Sixth Form's desk.

'I was hoping for rather more,' Maxwell said.

'I don't smoke 'em, sir.' Darren passed his cigs over.

'Not without Wayne's lighter, no, I don't suppose you do.'

Wayne's lighter duly saw the light of day.

'Anything else?' Maxwell asked.

The boys shifted uneasily. Then Wayne reached inside his anorak and pulled out a decidedly dog-eared copy of Naughty Neighbours. Maxwell took it and idly flicked through the pages, while the boys stared skyward, awaiting the wrath of Kahn.

'Corker on page sixteen,' the Head of Sixth Form commented, 'but I'd have thought you boys would've got that kind of stuff from the Net these days. Or am I hopelessly new-fangled?'

Whatever Maxwell was talking about had gone straight over Darren's head and didn't remotely impinge on Wayne's world.

'I'm more interested in men,' Maxwell confessed.

Darren did a double take. Then he realised it didn't surprise him. Mad Max was a bachelor, wasn't he? Bound to be gay. Come to think of it, hadn't he seen him hanging around the boys' changing rooms a time or two, after PE?

'Especially dead ones.'

Darren's jaw fell slack. Wasn't there a name for that? Haemophilia or something?

'Sit down, lads.' Maxwell came round from his side of the desk, stuffing the magazine and the ciggies and the lighter and the chewing gum back into the hands of their disreputable owners. He perched on the corner of his desk while they had the comfy seats. 'Word is you found a body last night.'

'Yeah,' said Wayne.

'Well, it's none of my business,' Maxwell told them, 'but I'd like you to tell me about it.'

'Why?' Darren asked. It was a fair question.

'Humour me,' Maxwell shrugged. 'Better still, show me. You free tonight?'

'What?'

'Tonight.' Maxwell was leaning forward, eyes bright. 'At the Barlichway, say, nine o'clock?'

'Where?' Wayne asked.

'You tell me.'

Darren and Wayne looked at each other. They were sitting in Mad Max's office, arranging to go out on a date with the mad old git. What this would do for their street-cred they couldn't imagine.

'Back of the Spar,' Darren suggested, 'and make that ten. Course,' his eyes took on a shrewdness, 'this'll cost yer.'

'Oh, really?' Maxwell lolled back, hands clasped around his knee. 'What are we talking about here? Silk Cut? A year's supply of Men Only? Your combined weights in Wrigleys?'

'No, none of that,' Darren told him, straight-faced. 'Just don't wear that teacher gear, all right?'

* * *

'I don't need it, Count,' Peter Maxwell was hauling the donkey jacket on over his Aran. 'Someone who wears the same fur coat all year round, day after day, is hardly in a position to give me any lectures on sartorial elegance.' He checked himself in the mirror. David Boston's Props and Costumes cupboard in Leighford's Drama Department had done him proud. In this get-up he could easily pass for a middle-aged, middle-class teacher dumbing down and going out on the town with two fourteen-year-olds in search of a murder site. He glanced down at the cat, sitting up with eyes wide and tail lashing — the old bastard smelt like Am-Dram potpourri.

'Don't wait up,' Maxwell said. 'I'll see myself out.' And he ambled down the stairs, humming 'One man went to mow, went to mow Mo Mowlam'.

He didn't take White Surrey. He'd only have to park the beast and find that when he returned he'd have no wheels left. Instead, he clattered through Columbine in his borrowed hoots and caught a cab on the main road.

* * *

The Barlichway was a step into another world, its concrete blocks black and silent in the January night. The rain had stopped but the tyres hissed and spat in the running water as cars purred through the darkness, criss-crossing the hinterland that lay north of Leighford. He was a long way from the sea here, from the brave sweep of Willow Bay and the spur that was the Shingle. The same wind that whipped those dunes hurtled around weed-strewn corners, rattling dark, dead windows and whining in a thousand vortices the architects of high-rise had created, back in the 'sixties when concrete was king.

The Spar was still open, a knot of kids on mountain-bikes lolling with menaces by the door. Puffs of smoke and the odd shout burst from it, obscenities echoing and re-echoing from hostile wall to hostile wall. Maxwell checked his watch. They were late. Idiotic of him to think they'd show at all, really. He stuffed his hands in his pockets and waited. A police car prowled the night, white like a ghost with its headlights illuminating a cuddling couple. Maxwell turned away, just in case. The car's occupants weren't likely to be Henry Hall or Jacquie Carpenter, but there were others who knew him out of Leighford nick and he'd rather not be recognised tonight.

'Psst!' he didn't hear it at first. Then he saw the finger beckoning from the darkness like the Grim Reaper getting hopeful. He crossed the road, pulling up his plastic-lined collar against the cold that nibbled his ears and bit his nose. Two urchins lounged in the shadow of the Spar, both of them checking left and right.

'All right, Mr Maxwell?' Darren asked.

'All the better for seeing you, boys. Thanks for coming. Where?'

Darren led him down the labyrinth that was his home. He knew these graffiti-daubed bricks like the back of his own hand. Maxwell fell into step with his lads, his borrowed boots loud against the velvet tread of their trainers.

'Got a fag, sir?' Wayne asked.

'Gave them up.' Maxwell watched his breath wreathing on the night air. 'People said I smelt.'

'Did you, sir?' Darren was vaguely amazed.

'Here it is.' Wayne stopped the Head of Sixth Form with a tap on the sleeve. It was as touchy-feely as Wayne ever got. He pointed into the shadows. Maxwell noticed that the boys hung back, but he hadn't come to stare into a black hole. He flicked on the torch he carried in his pocket and crept forward. Astley's tent had gone, nearly twenty-four hours on, and the fluttering police sign with its warning not to cross. The torch beam probed the night, the stained pavements, the slimy walls. He half expected to read in chalk the most famous murder clue of them all, from Goulston Street, Whitechapel in the Autumn of Terror — 'The Juwes are not the men that will be blamed for nothing.' But all he got was the assurance, in black spray-can, that 'Angie shags'. He didn't doubt it.

'Ey!' The barked voice made him stand up. Turning, he saw a silhouette the size of a brick shit house standing in the lamp light where the two boys had been moments before. 'What the fuck are you doin'?'

'I dropped a fiver,' Maxwell said, smiling hopefully in the darkness.

'What was you doin' with them kids?'

'What kids?' Maxwell's question was genuine enough. Wayne and Darren had vanished.

The shit house was walking towards him. 'You a pervert or something?'

Maxwell brought his torch up to the level, the beam bouncing off the solid, stubbled face staring accusingly at him, below the shaved head.

'Fuck!' the shit house shouted, flinging his hands up instinctively.

'Barney?'

'Wha? Who's that?'

'Mr Maxwell, Barney. Leighford High.'

'Fuck me,' Barney's saturnine features creased into a grin. 'Mr Maxwell.' A pair of chubby, powerful hands reached out to shake Maxwell's, the torch beam wobbling like some demented searchlight. 'Wot you doin' 'ere? I mistook you for some sort of child molester.'

'Goes with the territory,' Maxwell winked. 'How the hell are you?'

'Oh, you know me, Mr Maxwell. Bit of this, bit of that. How's that Diamond geezer?'

'The Headmaster is very well, thank you, Barney.'

'Bollocks,' Barney snorted. 'He's as much of a tosser now as he was when I left. I know you thought so too.'

'Christ, was I that obvious?'

'Straight up, though, Mr Maxwell. What are you doin' 'ere?'

Maxwell glanced back at the corner. 'The man who died,' he said.

'Old Albert. Yeah, bad shit, that was.'

'Albert? You knew him?'

'Course. Part of the furniture was old Albert. Miserable old bugger, mind. Didn't have a friend in the world. Us kids used to ring his doorbell and do a runner, just to wind him up, you know. Scared the shit out of us every time.'

'Original,' Maxwell observed. 'I hear they found him there.'

'That's right. My Nicole only saw him the other day.'

'Your Nicole?'

'My trouble and strife, you know.'

'You're married, Barney? Jesus, that makes me feel old.'

'Christ no, not married, Mr M. Shacked up wiv, yeah. You remember Nicole Green — she was in Miss Byfield's class.'

Maxwell remembered indeed. Nicole Green was one of the whole fleet of faculty bicycles that Leighford High had produced half a decade ago. 'Where did Nicole see him?'

'Up on his balcony,' Barney pointed up to the black ledge with the uneven, crumbling rim that ran the length of the building behind him. 'He had this habit of looking out on the square. You'd see him there most days, if the weather was fine. Why you involved, anyway?'

'It's a long story, Barney. Look, can you give me Albert's full name? Any other details about him?'

'Yeah, not that I know much.'

'Where's your local, Barney? I'd like to buy you a drink for old time's sake.'

'Yeah, right,' Barney grinned. 'Best years of your life, ain't they, schooldays?'

'You'd better believe it,' Maxwell chuckled. 'And of course, I've had more than most.'

''Ere,' Barney led the way, 'do you remember that old shit Thompson? Taught Maths or something.'

'Arnold? Do I ever,' Maxwell nodded.

'Arnold, was it? Fuck, we thought A stood for arsehole. Tom Ridley's doing time, you know.'

'No? GBH?' Maxwell remembered the boy's knuckles dragging the ground of A block.

'Computer fraud,' Barney told him.

Maxwell had stopped walking and was staring straight ahead. He was watching a figure, rain-coated, collar turned up, standing looking at the pair.

'Who's that Mr Maxwell?' Barney followed his old teacher's gaze.

'Er . . . nobody, Barney, nobody. Just looked like somebody I know, that's all. Where's this hostelry of yours?'

'You what?'

'Pub!'

'Oh, right. The Rat. Just round the corner. They do a fucking brilliant pizza.'

'My favourite flavour,' Maxwell beamed. And he glanced behind him as the rain-coated figure made a dash for the shadows. Now what, Maxwell asked himself as he vanished with Barney into the raucous neon-lit bowels of The Rat, was Willoughby Crown doing on the Barlichway? And why was he in such a hurry?

CHAPTER 10

He was leaning against her doorbell the next night, blond hair a little more dishevelled than usual, leather coat open to the elements. January had taken another turn, this time for the better and the night air struck less cold.

'I do have a workplace,' Jacquie said, holding the door slightly ajar. She'd recognised the silhouette at once; then, when she'd switched on the outside light, the blond curls and the shape of the forehead. She was looking him in the face now. It was a face she'd loved once.

'And you keep anti-social hours,' Foulkes said, straightening. 'We've got to talk.'

'Crispin . . .'

He held up a hand. 'It's business, Jacquie,' he assured her. 'Strictly business.'

'What?'

'Albert Walters.'

She hesitated for a moment, holding the door. Then she relented and let him in. He followed her through into the lounge and she took his coat and scarf.

'Did you jog this time?'

'Drove,' he said. 'I'd kill for a g 'n' t.'

'Scotch,' she told him flatly. 'It's all I've got.'

'Scotch it is.' He helped himself to a chair, and took in his surroundings, the dim lamps, the telly still flickering with the sound off, the gas-effect coal glowing in the twenty-first century twilight. She rummaged in what passed for her wine cellar, a cupboard through in the neon-lit kitchenette and poured him a drink.

'Ice?' she asked. 'I don't remember.'

'No, thanks,' he called. 'Just as it comes. I don't want anything else on the rocks in my life.'

She ignored him and handed him the glass. 'Albert Walters,' she said.

For an instant, their fingers met, then she whirled to her side of the lounge, a world away from the social worker who'd come calling, and switched off the television.

'There are things you should know,' he began, sitting upright and concentrating, watching the lights sparkle in the cut facets of his glass.

'Go on.'

'There's . . . something going on in the Barlichway, Jacquie. Something not right. Not natural.'

She blinked slowly, sitting back in the folds of her armchair, watching his face. She knew that look, that focus, that intensity. It was a look that had frightened her once. But that was then. Before Leighford. Before she was plainclothes. Before Peter Maxwell. She was a different person now. She wasn't going to get involved again.

'How?' she asked. 'Not natural?'

'Tell me how Albert Walters died,' he said.

She shook her head. 'I can't do this, Crispin.'

He tried another tack. 'Who's your DCI?'

'Henry Hall,' she told him.

'Decent bloke?'

'He's a listener,' she nodded. 'Good brain. Not exactly a man you can get close to.'

'Getting close to men was always a bit of a problem for you, wasn't it, Jacquie?'

She sat upright, sighing. 'You said this was business.'

'It is,' Foulkes nodded grimly. 'This is all about your friend Maxwell.'

'We've had this conversation, Crispin,' she stood up, ready to show him the door. The social worker sat tight, looking up at her, the curve of her hips and breasts, remembering. 'Not exactly. You told me he was a Cambridge man?'

'That's right,' she found herself sitting down again, listening. 'Jesus College. Why?'

'And he read History?'

'Yes. Why?'

'You're sure it wasn't Chemistry?'

'Chemistry?' Jacquie frowned. 'Talk sense, Crispin. Why would a Chemistry graduate end up teaching History?'

'Because there's more to Mr Maxwell than meets the eye.'

'Oh, really?' Jacquie was unconvinced. 'Like what?'

'Like the calendar. He told me where he got it.'

Jacquie paused for the first time. 'He did?'

'Foulkes nodded. 'Or at least where he said he'd got it.'

'What are you talking about, Crispin?' Jacquie blurted. 'I don't have a crystal ball, you know.'

'They're linked you know,' Foulkes said darkly. 'Like some demented bloody daisy chain I don't yet understand.'

'What are?' Jacquie asked, but she knew exactly what he was talking about.

'Elizabeth Pride,' he was leaning forward now, fire in his eyes, burning into her soul, 'ends up on Maxwell's doorstep. When did she die?'

'Er . . .' he'd caught her on the hop and she answered despite herself, without thinking; exactly as she used to answer him those years ago. 'December 20th or so the police surgeon thinks.'

'Can he be that accurate?'

'Probably not,' she shrugged, frightened suddenly by where all this was going.

'Let's suppose he's wrong,' Foulkes was in full flight. 'Oh, not by much. By just a few hours, let's say. Let's suppose the old girl died on December 21st — St Thomas's day according to Maxwell's calendar, but in fact the pagan Midwinter Solstice, the shortest and darkest day of the year. This was the time, people once believed, that, ghosts were allowed to walk — witches, bull beggers, hags, pans, kit-with-the-canstick, dwarfs, giants, changelings. Incubus, the spoor, the mare, the hell-wain and the man in the Oak. Tom Thumb, Hob Goblin, Boneless and the firedrake. We are afraid of our own shadows.'

'Crispin . . .' But her voice tailed away. She'd forgotten his voice, how rich it sounded, how deep. 'Those names . . .' She was afraid.

He brightened the moment with a smile. 'Not my names, Jacquie, Reginald Scot's. From his *Discovery of Witchcraft*, that was back in 1584. It's just the idea that's carried down the centuries. And the fear. Let's just suppose that Elizabeth Pride didn't die randomly on December 21st — let's suppose she was a sacrifice.'

'A sacrifice?' Jacquie Carpenter tried to laugh at the hypothesis, but it came out as a whisper.

'How is the vicar connected?' Foulkes asked.

'Darblay?' Jacquie was thrown, flustered, trying to concentrate. 'Who says he is?'

'Journalists various,' Foulkes told her. 'I don't think they were very impressed with the police press conference. They're talking about a serial killer.'

'That's bollocks.' Jacquie's hands were in the air and she was shaking her head vigorously.

'How did he die, this Darblay?' Foulkes wanted to know. 'The telly said he was beaten to death.'

'That's right.'

'What else was there?'

'What do you mean?'

'Jacquie!' Foulkes suddenly thumped her coffee table with his fist and the Scotch glass jumped. 'If you're going to sit there with blinkers on all night, you'll never catch this bastard. I think I know what he's doing, though I don't know why. And if I'm right, he'll make you look like bloody amateurs, believe me.'

'All right!' she shouted, then calmer, 'all right, he was laid out in the church. Somebody arranged him carefully.'

'Like Elizabeth Pride?'

She nodded. 'His feet were towards the altar and he was holding a crucifix in his hands.'

'A crucifix?' Foulkes frowned. 'Which way up?'

'The head towards his feet.'

'Upside down,' Foulkes nodded. 'Inverse magic. The cross upside down. Was there anything else? Any other symbols?'

There was no turning back now. She nodded. 'A pentagram, drawn in blood. We think it was Darblay's. There were black candles, a sheep's heart.'

'Darblay's heart.'

'No . . .'

Foulkes was thinking, shaking his head. 'No, not literally, symbolically. White is the colour of purity, of goodness, of light. So they've used black for the candles. Inverse magic again. They should ideally be made from human fat, by the way. Tell me, was Darblay's throat cut?'

'What? Er . . . no. No, it wasn't. His head . . . his head was smashed in.'

'No mutilations,' Foulkes was thinking, staring into the glass. 'They were disturbed.'

'They?' Jacquie threw back at him. 'Crispin, who are they? Who are you talking about?'

The social worker leaned back in his chair, rubbing his hands through his hair. He looked exhausted, frightened, old. 'There'll be thirteen of them,' he said softly, as though explaining a mental arithmetic problem. 'Twelve plus one. It's a mockery of Christ and his disciples. The One will be the horned god — old Nick, Satan, Lucifer, the light carrier.'

Jacquie sat there with her mouth open.

'They meet in secret at certain times of the year — Beltane, Samhain, Lammas. They hold these times sacred. They are the sabbats, when the witches ride on the backs of their familiars, flying to their ancient appointment with Old Nick. Tell me, have you found any evidence of drugs yet?'

'Drugs?'

'Specifically hemlock. It's an hallucinogenic. Gives the illusion of flight. They rub it on their naked skin and it's absorbed through the pores.'

'No.' She couldn't remember suddenly. 'No, I don't think so.'

'Jacquie,' he broke the spell that bound them both, reaching out and gripping her hands. 'Jacquie, don't you see? I've met all this before in Broxtowe. There it was children. Here? Well, all three victims have been old. But that's not important. It's the same pattern, the same damned circle and the five pointed star.'

'The witches' star,' she remembered.

He nodded solemnly. 'How well are you in with your guv'nor?'

'Hall?' she managed a chuckle. 'Not very at the moment as it happens.'

'Right. Here's what we do. We don't tell him — yet. If those people get wind that you're onto them, they'll clam up and the evidence will be gone. The media had a field day at Broxtowe and we lost whatever credibility we once possessed. I don't want that to happen again.'

'And Maxwell?' she asked him.

He stood up, taking her with him, staring into her eyes. 'Watch him, Jacquie,' he said softly, 'like the proverbial hawk. He's a nice guy. But even nice guys get sucked in to things like this. I know — I've seen it happen.'

And he pulled her to him, kissing her long and hard on the mouth. Then, as he held her at arm's length, the doorbell shattered the silence between them.

* * *

In the hall, she recognised the silhouette again — the shapeless tweed cap, the red and blue of the scarf. An eternal student was standing there in his cycle clips, his eyes watering from the wind in his face as he'd pedalled over the dam, taking the short cut to reach her. His ears burned from the same wind, as he thought, but it could have been the conversation of the social worker, who'd held his fingers to his lips and seen himself out of Jacquie's back door.

'I'm sorry it's late,' Maxwell said, sweeping off his cap and kissing her. 'Got a minute?'

He missed the way she held herself stiffly, uncertain in the whirlwind of Foulkes's information what to think or where to turn. 'Watch Maxwell,' he had told her, 'like a hawk.' And here he was, large as life and twice as sassy.

'You've poured one for me already,' Maxwell threw his scarf and hat down next to the glass on the coffee table. 'Is that spooky or what?'

'That's Scotch, Max,' she swept it up quickly. 'I'm out of Southern Comfort.'

'Tsk, tsk,' he wagged a finger at her. 'When a woman's out of Southern Comfort, she's tired of life — or something like that. I've just come from one of two visits to the Barlichway.'

'The Barlichway?' she sat down on the settee, looking at him.

'Albert Walters.'

'Max, what are you doing?'

He looked at her. 'Murder has a momentum all its own, Jacquie. You know that. I know that. It carries you along, sucks you in.'

'Sucks you in?' Jacquie repeated. Had Maxwell been listening to her conversation with Foulkes? Had he bugged her flat?

'Mixing my metaphors again. Sorry,' and he slapped his own wrist. 'Leighford's a small place, Jacquie. It was two of my kids who found old Walters' body.'

'Yes,' she nodded. 'We've talked to them.'

'Have you talked to Barney?'

'Who?'

'Barney Butler,' Maxwell was in reminiscent mood. 'Class of '91 if my memory serves. Probably hasn't got a GCSE to his name, but he's got a City and Guilds in being a nosey bastard. You should have a chat.'

'What did he tell you?'

'He lives on the floor above Albert Walters. The old boy had been there, on his own, for as long as Barney could remember. They were scared of him as kids. Thought he was a magician.'

'A magician?' the hairs began to crawl along Jacquie Carpenter's neck, her worst nightmare unfolding.

'Wizard, warlock, wicca man, whatever,' he amplified. 'He used to do tricks with coins and marbles. He also used to terrify the local child population.'

'So . . . what are you saying, Max? Somebody killed Walters in retaliation for some childhood fright?'

'I'm not saying anything,' Maxwell lolled back in her armchair, his feet on her coffee table, 'except that he had a visitor the night before he died.'

'Really. Did this Barney tell you this?'

Maxwell nodded. 'And he got it from an old duck who lives next door but one to the dead man.'

'Did you talk to her?'

'That's where I've been tonight,' Maxwell told her. 'And that's why I've come to you, hot foot. She's Adele Atkinson — are you writing this down?'

Jacquie wasn't. 'There'll be time enough,' she said.

'Sharp as a razor, that one,' Maxwell went on, 'for all she's got to be pushing eighty.'

'What did she see?'

'Walters' visitor called about ten p.m. She was putting the rubbish out for the binmen and saw him. He seemed lost, unsure which door to knock.'

'Did this Atkinson give you a description?'

'Medium height, black bomber jacket, white trainers, wavy hair, dark she thinks. Stocky build.'

Jacquie screwed up her face. 'I've heard better,' she said.

'Indeed,' Maxwell nodded, 'but it was dark on that ledge — I've been there.'

'Did Mrs Atkinson hear any conversation?'

'No. She may have a mind like a razor but her hearing's gone home. She does have a hearing aid — the social gave it to her, so I'm told — but she's getting used to it by keeping it on the mantelpiece.'

Jacquie wasn't in the mood to smile.

'Old Walters and his visitor had quite a little chat, that's all she knew.'

'On the doorstep?' Jacquie asked. 'Didn't he go in?'

'Mrs Atkinson went in before that, so she doesn't know. Feels the cold, does Mrs Atkinson — three cardie sort of woman, you know. Haven't your boys talked to anyone yet?'

'Everyone,' Jacquie sighed. 'At least everyone in Coniston Court. But this is the Barlichway, Max. Most of them would eat broken glass rather than talk to coppers. Thanks, though. We'll see this Adele Atkinson and your boy Barney again.'

'Jacquie,' he was frowning at her. 'Are you all right?'

'All right?' She blinked. 'Yes, of course I am, why?'

Maxwell shrugged, smiling. 'I don't know,' he said. 'You seem a little . . . well, distant, preoccupied.'

'Murder, Max,' she said. 'It does that to people. Let me get you a coffee for the long ride home.'

* * *

Martin Stone was running on pure energy. He'd watched as little Sam had been born, holding Alex's hand and wiping the sweat that dotted her forehead. It was gas and air and cold blue lighting and a hideous little pink thing that would become the little sister to Janey. He'd brought his eldest in to the Maternity ward at Leighford General later that day and Janey had stroked and prodded the little bundle wrapped in her mummy's arms. How long it would be before she was trying to gouge its eyes out, only time would tell. He'd left Janey with his mother and left Alex and the baby to the tender mercies of the NHS, with its ice packs and its wholesome institution food.

Now he was back at the crime-face, sifting the mountain of paperwork on his desk, cursing anew the epidemic that had decimated the constabulary's inspectorate with such deadly accuracy that someone had called it Bullshitters' Flu, a sort of mild CJD. He was reading the history of Albert John Walters, the man found in a derelict corner of the Barlichway Estate, grinning forever at the world he had left. Walters had had a multiplicity of jobs. He'd been a farm labourer, motor-mechanic, postman. During the war he'd served in the Western Desert with the 7th Armoured Brigade, which made him, if Stone remembered his O-level History, a Desert Rat. But what interested the detective sergeant more than anything was his place of birth. Albert John Walters had been born and spent the first twelve years of his life in Wetherton, the little village below the Chanctonbury Ring, the little village whose Rector had recently been taken from it.

* * *

They buried Andrew Darblay with appropriate pomp and circumstance that Thursday. In accordance with the fancy of an age yearning to find a grander culture than its own, they'd brought back the grim black stallions that Rudyard Kipling wrote about, with their mane unhogged and flowing and their curious way of going. People who worried about misuse of church funds pointed out loudly under their Sunday hats that it was hardly necessary to hire an expensive horse-drawn hearse to carry a body approximately forty-eight yards. But the Reverend Darblay had not come, cold-foot from his own front door at the rectory, but from the mortuary at Leighford General, where Jim Astley had gone to work on him, via the Swansdown Funeral Home in Tottingleigh.

The great and the good of the diocese of Winchester were there, clergy in their long, black cloaks, the bishop himself, a nice old boy in Imperial purple and, a little way from the rest, two policemen in dark suits and overcoats in the shadow of the darker, towering yews.

'For man that is born of woman,' the priest intoned on the wind that snapped the folds of his surplice, 'hath but a short time to live . . .' The waiting horses snorted and champed their steel bits, the black synthetic ostrich feathers nodding as they tossed their heads.

'See anybody you recognise, Kevin?' Stone asked, thrusting his hands deeper into his pockets to keep out the cold. The sun of mid-January had no warmth in it, for all it flashed on the chrome of the mourning cars and the harness and the hearse.

DC Brand was scanning the crowd of mourners, under the plumed hats. They were mostly over sixty years of age, Darblay's own congregation come to pay their last respects before tucking into Mrs Spooner's baked meats. There wasn't a wet eye in the house, except for Mrs Spooner herself, red-rimmed behind her glasses, blowing her nose copiously into a large, clerical handkerchief.

'Such a one,' the priest's words came in gusts of wind across the sleepers under their slabs, 'was this our brother. . .'

'Church of England,' Brand snorted. 'Any one of them would slit your throat for a penny.' He caught the DS's quizzical glance. 'Baptist, my lot,' he explained. 'Course, that was a long time ago.'

Stone nodded. 'Right,' he said. 'Fancy a trip back in time yourself, Kev? The village school?'

* * *

The village school was once an institution in its own right. When Wetherton School was built in safe, strong Victorian red brick, Mr Disraeli was at Number Ten and Lord Sandon was passing an Act of Parliament to ensure that children not only went to school but stayed there. The Headmaster, with mortarboard and stinging cane and Piccadilly Weepers was a pillar of the community. He stood four square with the

Parson and the Squire, Tories to a man and believers in muscular Christianity.

Now, the Headteacher was Alison Thorn, a bubbly thirtysomething who drove in from Leighford and wore stretch pants and trainers. Her dark hair was bobbed in such a way that someone of Peter Maxwell's generation might mistake her for Christopher Robin. She was certainly as flat-chested, but people like Kevin Brand noticed things like that anyway and made too much of them.

'The school log books?' Ms Thorn's eyes widened. 'Oh, dear.'

'Is that a problem?' Brand was standing head and shoulders and indeed his entire upper body above a wriggling sea of heads.

'No, no,' she smiled broadly. 'It's just that we're a First School now — little ones. All of our current details are on computer.'

'It's the old ones I'm looking for, madam,' Brand said. 'Going back to the 1930s, perhaps 'twenties.'

'Oh, dear,' Ms Thorn was still grinning. 'I'll see what I can do. Children!' And she clapped her hands. The hubbub hardly subsided at all. 'Mr Brand is a policeman. Say "Good afternoon, Mr Brand".'

Thirty plus little mouths intoned the response.

'Er . . . good afternoon, children,' Brand felt decidedly uncomfortable. He wasn't a family man and regarded other people's children with the same dread he might show to an outbreak of E coli.

'Mr Brand is going to tell you all about being a policeman while I go and find some books for him. Now, Mrs Whitemoor is just next door. You'll be good, won't you? Matthew,' she held her hand out to the obvious school psycho in the corner, 'you'd better come with me.' In six or seven years time, a suggestion like that from a teacher would probably result in ABH and a wired jaw. For the moment, however, Matthew was happy to obey.

'Where's your helmet?' a wall-eyed little waif wanted to know.

'He's a detective, stupid,' the class know-all rounded on him. 'They don't wear helmets.'

'No,' said another, smearing the contents of his left nostril all over his cheek, 'they stitch people up.'

'Mr Policeman,' a third piped up, clutching his genitals convulsively, 'I want to go to the toilet.'

No wonder, Brand realised, that society was going to the bloody dogs. He'd wandered into Broadmoor and the loonies were running the asylum.

* * *

'Jesus!'

Willoughby Crown turned to follow Ken Templeton' s gaze. The two men were sitting on the balcony at Beauregard's, staring down at Peter Maxwell who had just come in.

'That bastard's everywhere,' Willoughby hissed.

'No,' muttered Ken, 'just here. I wish I knew who the fuck recommended him. I can't remember who it was.'

'You could have said no.' They watched the Head of Sixth Form engage Sophie Clark in conversation on the floor below them.

'He couldn't be a problem, could he?' Ken asked, swigging from his Evian bottle.

'I don't know . . . I think he saw me on the estate the other night.'

'What?' Ken checked himself in mid-swig. 'You stupid bastard. What was he doing there?'

Willoughby wiped a flabby hand over his dry lips. 'Don't know. He had two boys with him.'

'Boys? You mean children?'

'That's right, Kenneth,' Willoughby patronised. 'Mind like a rapier again. Some local joined them.'

'What were they doing?'

'I told you, I don't know. Oh shit, he's seen us.' Willoughby tried to dive into his mineral glass, as though the bubbles would hide him.

Ken was on his feet, towel around his neck, leaning briefly over the heavier man. 'What do you mean "us", Kemo Sabe?' he hissed and was gone, sprinting along the corridor.

'Was it something I said?' Maxwell's scarf billowed in Ken's slipstream.

'Ah, Mr Maxwell,' Willoughby did his best to radiate all the normal signals.

'Max, please,' Maxwell shook the man's hand. 'Can I get you a drink? Something a little stronger than whatever that is. Sophie said I'd probably find you here.'

'Did she? Well, actually, I've got to be getting along.'

'Oh, really? Time for a snorter, surely?' Maxwell clicked his fingers and a spotty youth shambled over.

'Well,' Willoughby was clearly uncomfortable. 'Just one for the road, then.'

'A Southern Comfort, please,' Maxwell beamed at the lad, 'and whatever Mr Crown is having.'

'Oh, Willoughby, please,' Willoughby's bonhomie was rather less than bon by this stage of a Thursday evening. 'I'll have a g and t, thanks.'

'You know,' Maxwell leaned back in his chair against the rail that ran the length of the balcony, 'I never had a chance to thank you for the party.'

'Oh, there's no need,' Willoughby's grin was painful. 'My wife's affair.'

Maxwell raised an eyebrow. Affairs and Prissy Crown seemed to go hand in hand. 'Quite a little mover, your wife,' he winked.

Willoughby's grin vanished. 'I beg your pardon.'

'On the piste,' Maxwell beamed, waving in the direction of the gym. 'I had the pleasure to cross swords with her the other night. And talking of the other night . . .'

'That'll be three pounds sixty please,' the spotty youth had returned with a tray of drinks.

Maxwell rummaged for his wallet. 'The other night. Didn't I see you on the Barlichway Estate? Keep the change,' he smiled at the lad.

'No,' Willoughby said, a shade too quickly. 'Barlichway? Where's that?'

'You know, over the flyover, Tottingleigh way. Can't miss it. I'm sure it was you.'

'Oh, the Barlichway,' Willoughby snapped his fingers as though forgetfulness was his middle name. 'Yes, I'm sorry. I was checking the place out.'

'Checking it out?' Maxwell sipped the amber nectar. 'What for?'

'Oh, didn't Prissy tell you? I'm a property developer. Always on the lookout on behalf of clients. You know how it is.'

'Yes, indeed,' Maxwell smiled.

'Er . . . and you . . . um . . . Max. What were you doing there?'

'Oh, you know how it is, Willoughby,' Maxwell raised his drink so that the man's fixed features wobbled and rolled in the glass's distortion. 'I was solving a murder.'

CHAPTER 11

Alison Thorn went to school in Salisbury, in the shadow of the tallest spire in England. She was a creative child, who loved painting and music. She got ten O levels, one of almost the last generation in the country to do so. She took Music, Art and Media Studies at A level and then went on to the West Sussex Institute for a B Ed degree. She started teaching in Hove, where the infants loved her and moved on to become deputy at Wetherton four years later. When Mrs Appleton retired the following year, Alison Thorn was a natural to replace her.

Then, in the cold middle January of Maxwell's Millennium, somebody killed her.

Martin Stone stood with Jacquie Carpenter in the first-floor flat where her body was found, looking out of the window that looked out over the park. It was Monday and a leaden sky threatened the outskirts of Leighford, promising snow. SOCO had been all over the place, checking in their meticulous way every inch of the geography of a person's life. The walls, the door handles, the furniture, every bit of it was dusted for prints. They had marked out the place where the dead woman had been found, lying on the floor between the bed and the dressing table.

Stone hadn't been there to see her, but Jacquie had and she turned cold again at the memory of it. Alison Thorn frozen in the hideous stiffness of rigor mortis. Alison Thorn naked. Alison Thorn with her throat cut. Her mouth was slightly parted, with a dribble of blood down her chin and onto her neck. Her stare accused the ceiling, her sightless eyes sunken and dull. Jacquie had watched as Jim Astley had worked his scientific magic, probing with his white-gloved fingers every private place the woman had. Must it always come to this, she wondered, a glittering career cut short by some mad bastard and the results of a rectal temperature?

'Out of my light, dear girl,' Astley had boomed, never one to suffer WDCs gladly. She'd meekly complied.

'Hello, Alison,' Martin Stone had pressed the answerphone button again, now that SOCO had taken their prints and the detectives listened to the disembodied voice. 'Evelyn here. Are you all right? Only, we didn't get a call or a fax or anything. Give us a ring, can you? April's fine for today.'

'That's the school,' Stone said, grim-faced, 'wondering where she is. We only spoke to her last Thursday.'

'What was that about?' Jacquie asked.

'A loose end, really,' Stone sighed. There were no more messages on the machine. 'Albert Walters lived in Wetherton as a kid, went to the local school.'

'So?'

'So, it was my guess that Elizabeth Pride did too. And of course, Jane Cruikshank.'

'Did they?'

Stone shrugged, leafing through Alison Thorn's copies of *Cosmopolitan* and *Red*, piled loosely on her coffee table. 'Kevin Brand drew the short straw and talked to Ms Thorn. I have to confess I had a zizz in the car. Pride of course wasn't the old girl's maiden name, neither was Cruikshank. And Elizabeth and Jane are about as common as you can get in the Christian name stakes back in the 'thirties. Walters was there though; that's definite.'

'How does that help?'

'It doesn't — at the moment. But think of it, Jacquie. Two people from the same village are dead — the rector and the headteacher, two others born in the place are also dead. It doesn't take a DCI to work out the connection.'

'The village,' she nodded.

'The village. Come on,' he sat down on the dead woman's settee. 'We've got papers to sort. Let's see if we can find a reason in this lot why anybody should want to see Alison Thorn dead.'

'Lovely girl,' Jim Astley was feeling unusually poetic for a Monday. 'Puts me in mind of that TV presenter — what's her name?'

Donald peered over his boss's shoulder. 'Carol Vordermann.'

'No.'

Donald peered again. 'Anneka Rice.'

Astley looked at him. 'For Christ's sake, Donald. I can't think of two women less alike than those two.'

Donald had a third look, snapping his fingers. 'Charlie Dimmock,' he said triumphantly.

'Anne Diamond,' Astley growled. 'Just stick to the cocoa, will you?'

Donald pulled a bitch face behind the good doctor's green-gowned back and slid the microscope aside to make room for the coffee tray. 'What's up, doc?' he lapsed into his perennially irritating Bugs Bunny.

'What indeed?' Astley was scooping out the stomach contents on a side table. 'My guess at this stage — and we'll have to wait for confirmation of the tests — is that we are looking at an organic poison, specifically a vegetable irritant as cause of death. Lividity, evidence of convulsions, they all point in that direction. So, what have we, Donald, in your common hedgerow, that's lethal?'

'Aside from old car tyres and used condoms?' Donald queried. 'You've got me there, doctor.'

'I suspected I would have, Donald.' Astley was rummaging in a petri dish. 'We are a different generation, you and I. While you were busy in your formative years discovering how the Starship Enterprise was powered, I was steeped in Nature Study and the lore of the countryside. Which one of us has benefited more, I wonder?'

Bearing in mind that Donald's G-reg Fiesta was parked in the lee of Astley's spanking new state-of-the-art Galaxy, he was forced to concede the good doctor's point.

'Of course, Mr Plod will need to check the Wetherton hedgerows specifically, but it could be yew, white bryony, fool's parsley, laburnum, either of the hemlocks. Time and science will tell us, Donald. Got any digestives?'

* * *

Peter Maxwell was facing the last class of his day, the shell-shocked Year 12, still reeling from their first modular exam, they that rode so well, back from the jaws of death, back from the mouth of hell . . .

'You haven't convinced me, Gary,' Maxwell was saying. 'If William Pitt was simply, as the Whigs complained, a king's friend, why did he trim the civil list, whittle away the Court and Treasury party, officially recognise America? All these things were the eighteenth-century equivalent of kicking George III in the nuts.'

Silence. It was the end of another marathon, in which Mad Max was again doing the impossible, forcing children to think. There was an electronic shattering of the moment.

'Saved, as the boxing metaphor has it, by the bell. Go away, 12B and ponder long and hard the nature of the relationship between the patriot minister and the patriot king. And,' he held up his hand as they started to move, 'when do I want this done by?'

'Yesterday,' they chorused dutifully and trudged out to their waiting buses or the parked cars of their slightly older mates, the hell drivers of Year 13.

Maxwell put his books away in the dingy little cupboard in H4 and sauntered into his office next door. He wasn't quite ready for the visitor who sat there.

'Mr Hall,' he said, closing the door. 'This is becoming something of a habit.'

'I'm sorry,' Hall said, 'and to arrive unannounced. I wanted a word.'

'Coffee?' At the end of a long Monday, it was always Maxwell's first thought.

Hall shook his head. There was a tap on the door and Mrs B. stood there, a halo of ciggie smoke around her head. 'Gawd, it's Monday already, ain't it? Oh, you're busy. I'll call back, shall I? Do that old cow Lessing first. That'd be best.'

'It is indeed, Mrs B.,' Maxwell smiled. 'I am, rather. Please do. Yes, I'm sure Deirdre's bovine needs are greater than mine. It would, I feel certain.' And he closed the door again. 'Heart of gold,' he told Hall. 'Nothing quite like a school cleaner, is there? A breed apart, that's what they are. Oh, you don't mind if I do?' Maxwell waved a coffee cup at him.

Hall shook his head. The DCI was being particularly tight-lipped this afternoon. Maxwell busied himself with the coffee. A gaggle of hysterical sixth formers tottered past his door. He yanked it open. 'Home!' he bellowed and the hysteria stopped. 'To what do I owe the pleasure, Mr Hall?'

'Did you know Alison Thorn, head teacher at Wetherton primary school?'

Maxwell looked blank and sat on the spare chair opposite his visitor, who still dutifully wore the stick-on label given to him by Thingee Too in reception.

'No,' he said. 'Should I?'

'Not really,' Hall said.

'What's Wetherton, four, live miles from here? Not a village I know well.'

'It's three and a half miles as the crow flies,' Hall told him.

Maxwell shrugged. 'Let me explain something to you about teachers, Mr Hall. A primary teacher and a secondary teacher — well, we're chalk-face and cheese, really. One wipes the bastards' bums and mops floors and encourages free expression. The other tells the by-now-much-bigger-bastards to shut up and write this down. We both get results of a sort. But the methods . . . ah, well, the devil's in the detail.'

'It's the devil I wanted to talk to you about.'

Maxwell frowned. 'You're not still looking for poppets, Chief Inspector? Voodoo or whatever.'

Hall shook his head. 'I can't afford to make light of this, Mr Maxwell. The lady I mentioned a moment ago, Alison Thorn, the headteacher at Wetherton, is dead.'

'Dead?' Maxwell looked up. 'Murdered?'

Hall nodded, knowing Maxwell well enough to know the speed with which the man put two and two together. 'Where were you on Sunday?

'Yesterday?' Maxwell got up to fill his coffee mug. 'At home.'

'All day?'

'No,' Maxwell threw caution and his arteries to the winds and threw in three sugars for good measure. 'Not all day. I went walking on the Shingle after lunch.'

'Alone?'

'Alone except for a few hardy perennials exercising their dogs. I didn't see anybody I knew.'

'So, no one can vouch for you?'

'No, Chief Inspector,' Maxwell looked at his man over the rim of his mug, the one that told the world, rather incongruously, that he loved David Essex. Henry Hall looked tired and as grey as his suit. He'd come alone again, as he had the last time, without the usual entourage in tow. As far as anyone could ever tell with Hall, he seemed to Maxwell to be a man on the edge. 'But then, can anyone vouch for you?'

'My wife and kids,' Hall nodded softly.

'Ah, well,' Maxwell smiled. 'There you have the advantage over me. But if you're suggesting I cycled over to Wetherton, killed this poor woman and cycled home again, I'm afraid I'll have to come out with the cliché about straws and methods of grabbing them.'

'Ms Thorn didn't die in Wetherton, Mr Maxwell,' Hall told him. 'She died in her flat in Whitesmith Street. You can almost see it from your window.'

'What killed her?'

'Forensic will tell us that in due course. I'm much more interested in who. Tell me, did you find anything at Myrtle Cottage?'

'Where?'

'Don't be evasive, Mr Maxwell, please. The home of Elizabeth Pride. You went there.'

'You wanted me to.'

'Did I?'

Maxwell chuckled. 'Mr Hall, I could go on fencing with you all day, I really could, but I honestly don't think that would get either of us anywhere, do you?'

'Perhaps not,' Hall said without a trace of a smile. 'You appreciate I had to ask — about Alison Thorn, I mean.'

'On the grounds that you're probably asking everybody else in Leighford, yes, of course. And it's very flattering to have the personal attention of a Detective Chief Inspector.'

Hall stood up suddenly, half turning for the door. 'If I wasn't so damned fond of you, Maxwell,' he said, 'I might take a really personal dislike; know what I mean?'

Maxwell's mouth was still open as the DCI saw himself out. It was an extraordinary thing to hear from Henry Hall.

Extraordinary because it proved the man was human after all.

* * *

'Jacquie?'

'Max?'

The Head of Sixth Form was lolling in his attic, Trumpeter Hugh Crawford sitting this one out while his recreator was busy dappling the flanks of his horse, standing patiently nearby.

'I had a visit from your guv'nor today.'

'Hall? What did he want?'

'Well, that's just it; I'm damned if I know. I suspect a confession would be favourite, but I got the impression he'd have settled for some counselling. He asked about Myrtle Cottage.'

There was a pause. 'What did you tell him?'

'Basically that Queen Anne was dead. What have you told him?'

Another pause. 'How do you mean?'

'The calendar. I seem to be in possession of a pretty important clue and officially your people know nothing about it.'

'I know, Max. I don't know what to do about that. It's a matter for your own conscience.'

'My own . . .' Maxwell hauled his feet off his modelling desk and sat upright, tugging off the forage cap. 'I'm sorry, I must have misdialled. Is this Jacquie Carpenter, companion of a mile, *anima divida mea* or is it the bloody Samaritans?'

'Max,' he heard her sigh, 'we've had this conversation so often. You know I can't tell you things.'

'Alison Thorn,' he said. 'At least tell me that.'

'I can't.'

'It was on the local news tonight. Hall specifically told me she'd been murdered. All you'd be doing is crossing tees and dotting eyes.'

This time the pause was longer. 'What do you want to know?'

'She died on Sunday — am I right?'

'Astley thinks mid to late afternoon.'

'How?'

'Poison. He doesn't know what, yet. Something organic.'

'You mean plants?'

'I suppose so.'

'What do we know about this woman, Jacquie? Alison Thorn?'

'She was a head teacher,' he heard the voice on the end of the phone sounding less and less like the Jacquie he knew.

'We've only just started on this one, Max. I can't tell you any more. Look, I've got to go.'

And she did. There was no love. Not even a goodbye. He didn't notice her throw the phone across the room; didn't see her tired face crumple; didn't hear her start to cry.

'And it's good night from her,' Maxwell said softly. He caught the eye of the great black and white beast in the corner, sitting on the pine chest like the sphinx. 'I don't know, Count, in answer to your unspoken question. What's going on? What do we have here? A hot friend cooling? The hang-up that denotes a hang-up? Something I said? Or didn't say? Christ knows!' And he sat back in his canvas camp chair, staring at the half-finished warrior distorted under the bright light and the magnifying lens. Above him, through the skylight the canopy was a rich velvet studded with stars.

'All right,' he shook himself free of Jacquie, her distance, her coldness. He was old enough to be her father, for God's sake. If it was over, before it had really started, well, perhaps that was how it was meant to be. All part of the grand plan of the Great Timetabler in the Sky, 'back to basics'. For a weak, fleeting moment, he longed for Roger Garret's flipchart, that sad invention dreamed up for captains of industry to handle their presentations. Why use a few well-chosen words when flow diagrams and pie charts were so much more appealing? The infection had snuck itself into schools where Deputy Headmasters were particularly prone to it. Looking at the cat as he was now, however, Maxwell thought the dim creature might appreciate it. Never mind, he'd have to imagine.

'First — and I will be asking questions later, Count, so pin your ears back — Elizabeth Pride is left like an unwanted Christmas present on my doorstep. She has been frozen. Why? Because — yes, you're getting into your stride now, aren't you? Because she was murdered earlier and had to be kept for a while. Now why is that — of course, your next logical question — and I don't know the answer to that one. Which date is significant? The last of the Old Millennium, with its first footers and strange men and long leggety beasties? Or the shortest day — St Thomas Grey, St Thomas Grey? Or both?'

The cat wasn't talking.

'The old girl was poisoned,' Maxwell leaned back, his hands cradling his head, looking at the stars. 'So was Albert Walters; so, allegedly, Alison Thorn. Andrew Darblay is the exception. No poison, just the caving in of his skull.' He slid back the chair and began to pace the attic room, mechanically checking his half-finished Light Brigade for cobwebs. 'Common factors — three of the four died by poisoning. Two of them had wounds in the nape of the neck. One of them — Darblay — with overt symbols of devil worship all around him; right in the middle of his own church. What's the link?'

He crouched suddenly to check the Brigade's line-up — Lord Cardigan with his arm nonchalantly on his hip, Lewis Nolan trotting over to William Morris to ask his permission to ride with the 17th. There was a gap where the Italian observers Govone and Landriani were going to go. For three years, he'd put off modelling them; he hadn't a clue what uniforms they wore. 'The link, Count, is . . . nonexistent!' And he stood upright again. In the end, he succumbed and poured himself a large Southern Comfort, wincing as it hit his tonsils.

'Elizabeth Pride, widow,' he recited to himself from the mental CV he'd put together from his conversations with Jacquie and gleanings from Darblay and the media. 'In her seventies, lived alone, apart from several of your kind — and, no, I don't think any of them are as gorgeous as you, you vain bastard. She was a bit of a dragon, apparently. Had a reputation as a witch. Had the evil eye,' Maxwell shot a glance towards his cat, 'not unlike your good gentleman self. People who wanted her dead? The Cruikshanks in particular, Romanies who bore an ancient grudge. Plus, presumably, anybody else at whom she looked funny. Possibly, even, the Reverend Darblay.'

He sat down again, sipping the spirits that cheered, warming to his theme. 'Andrew Darblay. Nice bloke. Vicar of the old school. On the fence on the idea of women priests and gay clergy. Widower. Lived in Wetherton. Housekeeper came in during the day and said in the *Advertiser* that she didn't think he had an enemy in the world — which, I have to admit, runs counter to every vicar I've ever met. They usually manage to offend somebody. Even Father Ted upset the Craggy Island Chinese Community, if you remember that classic episode, Count.'

Metternich didn't. He'd been out on the tiles at the time, testicles or no testicles. Come to think of it, no testicles.

'His body was found by the police themselves, who'd presumably gone to interview him, as I did, about Elizabeth Pride. Jacquie told me he'd already reported a bogus journalist, namely, moi, provider of vitamin-enriched slime for your delectation and delight. Now, is that why they called back, I wonder? Or had something else occurred to them?' He looked ruefully at the phone. 'No good asking Jacquie as things stand at the moment,' he mused. 'The good clergyman was battered to death with your proverbial blunt instrument at some time on the Thursday morning. There was no poisoning or incision in the neck. But there were the black candles, the pentagram, the sheep's heart. By bell, book and candle, eh, Count? I knew I should have called you Pyewacket. Or Grizzle or Greedigut.' He leaned towards the animal's broad, flat head. Metternich looked at him through one contemptuous eye and sauntered away, tail held high, bum at a rakish angle.

'No need to take offence, Count,' Maxwell called after him as the beast bounded down the attic stairs. 'It's no slur on your character, they're just the names of familiars, witches' imps that worked for the devil.'

No reply.

'Greymalkin!' Maxwell shouted. 'I could go further and call you Paddock! Not,' he saw his reflection in the skylight and raised his glass, 'that I'd be so vituperative.'

He sat down on the chest the cat had just vacated. 'Ah,' he smiled, 'happiness, Count, is a warm bum.'

But Metternich was gone, out through the lounge in its half light, down the stairs to the cat flap in the kitchen and the night's long hunt.

'Albert Walters,' Maxwell was still talking to himself, 'lived and died on the Barlichway. What's that, about five miles from Wetherton? He was of an age with Liz Pride and Jane Cruikshank. Did they know each other? Is that the link? And if it is, where does this Alison Thorn come in? They said Liz Pride was a witch. And Barney Butler told me old Albert was a magician. So who was Alison Thorn — Queen Mab?'

* * *

The little ones had all gone by the time Peter Maxwell opened the classroom door at Wetherton First School. Time was of the essence and he needed to catch someone there before the caretaker shut up shop for the night. He'd dragooned the long-suffering Sylvia Matthews again, assuring her with all his charm and suavity that he didn't just love her for her car, useful though the invention was. A year ago, six months even, Sylvia would have winced at that, but now she was more up-together and could hold Peter Maxwell at arm's length. Even so, she told him, she couldn't handle what he was about to do. She'd wait in the car.

A grey-haired woman was wandering the room, straightening pictures and sticking Blu-Tack onto pieces of paper.

'Can I help you?' she asked.

'I'm Peter Maxwell,' he said, 'from Leighford High.' He'd thought of a dozen aliases on his way over, as the leaden sky prepared for night and the sidelights became headlights on the curve of the A25. Face to face with this woman, he'd abandoned them all. An uncomprehending desolation was etched into every line of her features.

'Yes?'

'Are you a colleague of Alison Thorn's?'

The woman blinked. 'She's dead.'

'That's why I'm here,' he said softly.

'Did you know Alison? Are you a relative or something?'

'No,' he told her, 'to both questions. Mrs . . . er . . . ?'

'Mrs Whitemoor,' she said. 'Look, if you're from the press, I really . . .'

'No, Mrs Whitemoor. Look, your day's over. I'm sure you want to get home, but could I have just five minutes of your time?'

Mrs Whitemoor looked at the man. He was a stranger, barging into her classroom and her life, at a time when she needed it least. But his eyes were kind and his face seemed as sad as her own.

'All day,' she told him, 'all day I've been trying to tell the children where she is, where she's gone. I lied, Mr Maxwell. I told them she was in Heaven, not on a slab somewhere with her throat cut.'

Maxwell blinked. 'Her throat was cut?'

Mrs Whitemoor turned away, suddenly unable to bear the probing questions. 'The police told me she was poisoned, that someone cut her throat afterwards.' She turned back to face him, her eyes brimming with tears. 'She was a lovely person, Mr Maxwell and a great teacher. What kind of monster does that to a person like Alison? To any person?'

'That's what I'd like to find out,' he reached out and squeezed her arm gently.

'Are you . . . a private detective?'

'Unofficial,' he said. 'You see, on New Year's Eve somebody left a body on my doorstep — literally.'

'Good Heavens!'

'I think whoever killed your lady also killed mine. Did you know Elizabeth Pride?'

'I've heard the name,' Mrs Whitemoor nodded, 'and I read about the case. I don't live locally, you see. I live in Littlehampton.'

In other circumstances, Maxwell would have offered his condolences for that, but now didn't seem the time. 'When did you see Alison last?'

Mrs Whitemoor continued sticking her Blu-Tack to her pieces of paper, desperate to keep busy, afraid to sit down. 'On Friday. Nothing out of the ordinary. Nothing all week, except for the visit from the police. That would have been Thursday, I believe.'

'The police?' Maxwell repeated. 'They came on Thursday? Why?'

'They wanted to look at some old school records. Amazingly, we've still got the logbooks from Victorian times.'

'What were they looking for?'

'Some people who were children here in the 'twenties. One, Alison said, was Albert Walters — he was the man found dead on the Barlichway Estate last week. Where a lot of our children come from.'

'They do?'

'Yes. It's the only reason the school's still open. We ship them in from Leighford every day.'

Maxwell nodded. Somewhere, somehow, he heard the ring of a dropping penny. 'And the others were Elizabeth Pride and Jane Cruikshank. I'm sure the boys in blue will have checked their maiden names by now and made the connection. Do you remember the name of the police officer?'

'Er . . . Brand, I think. Alison got him to tell the children all about police work.' Her smile at the memory turned to tears again. 'None of us thought there'd be real police work to be done . . . on Alison herself.'

She began to cry, her face buried in her hands, her shoulders heaving.

Instinctively, he held her to him, stroking her hair, rocking gently with her. Nobody had cried for Elizabeth Pride or for Albert Walters. Only Mrs Spooner had cried for Andrew Darblay. Now, with Alison Thorn it was different. He hadn't known the woman, yet he felt an iron lump in his throat. He felt the world would cry for Alison Thorn.

CHAPTER 12

'Martin,' DCI Hall was cradling a coffee cup. The lights in the Tottingleigh Incident Room weren't burning blue, but they were radiating into another long, dark winter's night. 'Alison Thorn's flat.'

'We've found twelve sets of prints, guv,' Stone told the waiting team as part of the day's recap. 'Hers, of course, a friend from the floor below, a Mrs Whitemoor who was a colleague [illegible] others we're still checking.'

'Men friends?'

'None known. At least, not recently. Her address book has six assorted males other than her father. We're checking them all out.'

'How are the parents taking it?' Hall asked.

Stone shrugged. 'Old man's pretty solid, considering. Mother's a basket case, on sedatives.'

'It's not every day someone poisons your daughter, then slits her throat.'

'That's a post mortem injury, guv,' Kevin Brand said, leaning forward in the hideously uncomfortable seat that had numbed his bum all day.

Hall nodded.

'So, what are we saying?'

'We're saying that whoever administered the poison either stuck around to watch it take effect or came back later. Why, I don't know. Who's got anything on the neighbours?'

Jacquie Carpenter had. 'There was somebody calling door to door on the day in question. Bears some looking at.'

'Any specific reason?' Hall asked.

'Well, according to the two neighbours who saw him, he had a collecting box in hand — Barnardo's, they thought.'

'So?'

'So he didn't call on them. Only on Alison Thorn.'

'There are . . . what. . . four more flats in Alison's block. How do we know he didn't visit them all?' Hall wanted to know.

'Nobody else in that afternoon, guv,' Jacquie told the DCI. 'As far as we know, she was alone in the block.'

'The intercom's not working,' Stone said. 'If she wanted to find out who was ringing her bell, she'd need to get down to the front door.'

'Did anybody see this?'

Jacquie nodded. 'A Mr Ottway, lives at 34 Whitesmith. He was building a new fence at the time.'

'What's his description of the Barnardo's caller?'

Jacquie's face said it all. 'Not helpful, I'm afraid, guv. Mr Ottway suffers from myopia — short sight. He knew it was male, because he heard the voice. Nothing specific. Sounded quite posh, to quote him.'

'Colour hair? Height? Anything?' Hall was hoping.

Jacquie shook her head. 'Sorry, guv. I hoped Mrs Billings might be more useful. Lives at number twenty-six.'

'But?'

'But she didn't get a good look either. Male, certainly, maybe thirty, maybe fifty. She's not — and I quote — good on ages.'

Hall slammed down the coffee cup. This man had the luck of the devil. Like a will o' the wisp no one saw him come, no one saw him go. The only way you knew he'd been there was the body he left in his wake.

'He'd have stayed,' Hall was talking to himself really, tapping his lips with his fingers as though in prayer, 'to wait 'til the poison took effect. For two reasons,' he watched the faces of his team, the trustful eyes that showed less trust by the day. He watched the slipping of faith. It was as visible as the nose on your face. 'First, he couldn't take the chance of calling back. Charity collections are a good reason, but twice the number of visits is twice the risk of being caught, remember.'

'What's the other reason, guv?' Brand asked.

'Because,' Hall's face, like his voice, was ice-cold, 'he enjoys it. How long did Astley give the dead woman from the time the poison was administered? An hour? Two? The sadistic bastard sat in a chair somewhere, perhaps the one in her bedroom and he watched her go into convulsions, then a coma, then death.'

'Then he stripped her naked,' Stone went on, taking up his guv'nor's torch, 'carefully arranging her on her back with her arms by her sides and he calmly cut her throat.'

'One mean son of a bitch,' Kevin Brand grunted. Of all of them in that room, he had been the one to talk to Alison Thorn, to see the sparkling eyes now dull, the radiant smile now gone.

'Her legs were open,' Stone remembered. 'What did Astley make of that, guv?'

Hall sighed, leaning back in his chair, a pencil tapping softly at the end of his fingers to an incessant rhythm that thudded in his brain. 'Nothing,' he said, shaking his head. 'This was no sex attack. No sign of rape or assault, no bruising to thighs, vagina, anus. No semen. But the throat cutting has a significance. Anybody?'

He felt he was back at Bramshill again, with mock scenarios and a class of fast-track climbers, vying with each other to offer the perfect answer. It was like being in school with hands in the air and hissed voices all straining, 'Sir, sir!'

But no one was saying that today. There were no hands in the air. Just a sea of faces, all tired, all nonplussed, all facing the same brick wall. Then he realised they were all looking at him, expecting him to know, to do something. He, who had no answers at all.

'All right,' he slid back his chair. 'Ritual killing.' He crossed to the display boards spread around the old Tottingleigh library, commandeered now as command headquarters in his people's attempt to catch a madman. 'That's what all this is about.' He tapped an index finger on the dead, shrivelled face of Elizabeth Pride. 'Fungal poisoning,' he said, watching the faces in front of him, 'and a wound in the nape of the neck inflicted after death. Ritual. And this,' he paused longer at the shocked, bloodless face of Alison Thorn, her dull eyes wide, the gash in her throat like a second mouth, slightly open like the first. 'An organic poison, perhaps hemlock. The cut throat. Post mortem. Ritual.' Hall walked back along the line, arms locked behind his back like some general reviewing his troops.

'Let's assume,' he said, 'that Darblay was not premeditated. A spur of the moment thing.'

'Somebody was desecrating his church,' Stone cut in, 'and he caught them.'

'Hence the candles and the sheep's heart and the pentagram,' Brand piped up.

'Hence,' Hall rounded the circle, 'no poison. All the others,' he pointed back at the photographs, 'naked. All the others with post mortem wounds.'

'But why, guv?' Brand was frowning, shaking his head. 'Why not kill them that way? A cut throat, stabs through the spinal cord, they're pretty effective methods in their own right. Why the poisoning first?'

'We've checked every chemist on the south coast,' Stone said. 'No one's reported a break-in of any kind in the last three months and there've been no unusual requests on any of their poisons registers.'

'That's not necessary,' Hall thought aloud, 'except in the case of the strychnine for Albert Walters. Death-Cap mushrooms and hemlock can be found in any stretch of woodland in the south. It just takes someone with the knowhow.'

'Witchcraft, guv?' Jacquie Carpenter spoke for the first time. She felt the eyes in the room swivel to look at her. Even the eyes of the dead were turned, it seemed, her way.

'Go on, Jacquie.' Hall sat down, resting his head on one hand, the elbow on the table.

'Elizabeth Pride had a reputation as a witch. Threatened the Cruikshanks on more than one occasion. And there was a poppet in Jane Cruikshank's caravan, the sort of doll witches used to use. And the calendar in Myrtle Cottage . . .' Her words hung like icicles in the artificial heat of the room. She would have given her life to have retracted them, but they were there, as tangible as if someone had written them on the wall in a victim's blood. One by one puzzled heads came up. Frowns creased foreheads. Blank looks were exchanged.

Hall's hand fell away and his head angled to the level. 'Jacquie, Martin, my office.'

They waited until he was sitting comfortably — the work of a second. Then he was looking up at them, the eyes hard and cold behind the neon-lit lenses. 'Calendar?' he asked.

'It's from Myrtle Cottage, sir,' Jacquie said, staring straight ahead. Her own voice was barely audible for the blood rushing in her ears and the blood thudding in her heart.

'Yes, Jacquie,' Hall was nodding, 'you said. Martin,' he turned his chill gaze to his sergeant. 'You fouled up at Myrtle Cottage.'

DS Stone cleared his throat. This was not going to be a comfortable ride. 'Yes, sir,' he thought it best to admit.

'Look at me, dammit!' Jacquie had never seen Hall explode before. It was all the more unnerving for that.

'I went back there, sir,' Stone assured him. 'It's in the file.'

'Just tell me, Martin,' Hall said softly. He sounded like a man on the edge.

'I went back with DC Brand the next day; after we'd discussed the matter. I took samples of cat food and had them analysed. Nothing, sir. Well, I mean, nothing toxic. Just cat food.'

'And the calendar?'

Stone looked uneasy. 'I'm sorry, guv, I don't understand all this about a calendar. I don't remember any calendar at Myrtle Cottage. Not the twice I went there. What's its significance?' He was looking as much at Jacquie now as he was at Hall.

'All right,' the DCI relaxed, leaning back. 'Poisons, Martin. Get back on it. Every chemist, every farm, every outlet you can think of. Again. Do it all again.'

Stone heard the weariness in Hall's voice. The DCI knew the size of the task all too well. He was asking the impossible. And what was worse, he was asking the impossible for a second time.

'Yes sir,' and DS Stone was gone.

'Sit down, Jacquie.' Hall took off his glasses and rubbed his aching eyes. He waited until she had. 'What calendar?' he leaned forward. She'd seen him do that a hundred times in interview rooms without number. But always before, she'd been sitting behind or alongside him, never in front. Now she had an inkling how a suspect felt, watching the large, square, expressionless face as relentless as the tide. She wished it was Peter Maxwell's, dark, smiling, the eyes bright with what she always hoped was love.

To her left was a rock. To her right, a hard place. She felt the walls closing in, the ceiling coming down. She wanted to scream. She, who had never fainted in her life, felt like fainting. What was it then that made her open her mouth?

'Peter Maxwell found it, sir, at Myrtle Cottage.'

Hall leaned back, slowly, the solid face receding, a quizzical expression coming over it. They both knew, in that moment, that Jacquie had been withholding evidence that could be vital. They both knew her job was on the line.

'Tell me,' Hall said.

Jacquie shook her head, feeling oddly better now all this was out in the open. 'Peter Maxwell went there,' she said, 'and found it. It's just an ordinary calendar, nothing special. It's what's written on it that's odd.'

'Oh?'

'Certain dates, ringed, marked. Cryptic rhymes.' She fished in her bag. 'I've written them down.'

Hall took the piece of paper. 'Candlemas Day, plant beans in the clay,' he read for February 2nd. 'Put candles and candlesticks all away.'

'Andrew Darblay,' Jacquie said. 'We haven't found the murder weapon yet, but it seems likely that's what smashed his skull — a brass candlestick.'

Hall read on. 'He shall be a liar and unsteadfast of courage and will take vengeance on his enemies. The Spring Equinox. 1st March.'

Jacquie nodded. 'When the day and night are of equal length. It's the festival of Eostre, the bringer of the light of the day.'

Hall blinked at the girl sitting in front of him. He was entering a strange world which had no relevance to his own time and Jacquie Carpenter was taking him by the hand and leading him through it.

'*A fair maid who*,' Hall read, '*the first of May*
'*Goes to the fields at break of day*
'*And washes in dew from the hawthorn tree*
'*Will ever after handsome be.*'

'Beltane,' Jacquie said, 'the beginning of summer. But it's more than that, sir. It's Alison Thorn, isn't it? Hawthorn, I'll grant you, but it's close. Looking at her in her flat — all right, it's not the fields either — looking at her photograph; wouldn't you say she was handsome for ever? She's not going to age and wither like the rest of us, is she?'

'June 21st' Hall was reading after a pause. 'The Midsummer Solstice, "*and the Gentleman grew lean and pale with the Frights*".'

'Albert Walters,' Jacquie said, leaning forward now. 'If ever a man looked as if he was scared to death by what he'd seen, it was him.'

The DCI had to agree. 'Lammas Day,' he'd found August 1st. 'Fly over moor and fly over mead, Fly over living and fly over dead . . .'

'Witches flew,' Jacquie told him. 'On broomsticks or the backs of their familiars. Or they believed they did.'

But Hall was racing ahead, spellbound by the paper's magic. 'Oh weans, oh weans! The morn's the Fair, Ye may not eat the berries more. This night the Devil goes over them all, To touch them with his poisoned paw.'

'Poison, guv,' Jacquie leaned back again in her chair. 'Death-Cap, strychnine, hemlock. It's all part of the craft . . .'

'Jacquie!' Hall stopped the girl in her tracks. 'That's enough. This is the twenty-first century, for Christ's sake.'

She blinked, suddenly afraid at the turn her life was taking. 'Christ has nothing to do with this case, sir. Nothing in this world.'

'Meaning?'

'Satanic abuse,' she said, looking him straight in the eye. 'It's so fucking obvious and you can't see it! Why did you send Peter Maxwell to Myrtle Cottage?'

'Why didn't you find the calendar when you went there?'

'It wasn't there!' she was shouting louder than he was, her eyes flashing, her knuckles white as she gripped the chair.

Hall leaned back, relenting, letting the calendar details slip from his grasp onto the desk. He was himself again. 'Then we only have his word that was where he found it,' he said.

It was Jacquie's turn to calm down. 'It's a word I trust,' she said.

'Is it, Jacquie?' Hall asked her. 'I hope you're right.'

* * *

The snow came to Leighford that night, a sudden blizzard blowing from the west. John Hammond had missed it on the Met. Office roof, but then the Met. Office roof was not on the south coast of England. By the time Maxwell poked his head out of Beauregard's, the town lay silent under a carpet of white and the wind had gone. Tomorrow the kids would destroy the sparkling beauty by building snowmen and trying to kill each other with snowballs. The cars would prowl the roads and turn the silent silver to sludge, dirty and brown. Tonight, though, as the old clock of All Saints' struck eleven, it was pure magic.

'You can't cycle home in this.' It was Prissy Crown leaning out of the window of her Shogun, her breath like dry ice on the night air. Maxwell had already unshackled White Surrey and was wheeling into the darkness.

'No problem,' he called.

'Look,' Prissy hauled on the hand-brake and killed the engine. 'I'm sorry I missed you inside, Maxwell. You're snooping, aren't you?'

'Sorry?' Maxwell could be extraordinarily stupid if need be.

'You're on the case, aren't you?' She lowered her head, 'For little old me.' Maxwell couldn't believe the woman was actually fluttering her eyelashes at him, like some latter-day Miss Piggy.

'Case, Prissy?'

'Don't be coy, big boy,' she purred. 'You think there's something going on, too, don't you? Ken, Sophie and Willoughby, I mean. You're on to something.'

He got as close to her as he dared while still being out of tongue range. 'As a matter of fact, I think I am . . .'

'Tell me,' she'd grabbed his lapel with a lightning thrust born of years on the piste.

'I can't,' he said, gently releasing her fingers. 'Not yet. Tell you what. Do you think White Surrey would hang on the back?'

'What?'

'The bike.'

'Sure,' she said, jumping out to secure it for him. 'Your place or mine? Willoughby's out.'

'The Barlichway,' he replied, hauling the cold metal into position behind the Shogun. In response to her puzzled expression he said, 'Prissy. There is something going on — you're right. There's something I need to check on.'

'On that disgusting council estate?'

'The same,' Maxwell nodded, feeling as he always did around horsy-setters like Prissy, a little to the Left of Lenin. 'Will you take me? I suspect the roads will be rather treacherous.'

'Of course,' she said, feeling his muscles under his coat, 'By the way, seen much of Jacquie C. lately?' She smiled, licking her lips. 'Because, you see, if you're not,' and she waited until he'd fixed the straps on the bike before taking his hand and plunging it into her blouse. Her nipple was hard, like an acorn, which was hardly surprising bearing in mind the ambient temperature of Maxwell's fingers.

The Head of Sixth Form laughed. 'Prissy, please,' he said. 'Accepting a lift from you like this, I feel enough of a tit as it is.'

* * *

The journey was spent in silence, Prissy's face a mask of fury in the green light of the dashboard. As they reached the High Street, Maxwell began a running commentary of Smalltalk but he may as well have been talking to Harpo Marx. The Shogun screamed to a halt on the edge of the Barlichway as Pussy slammed its gears into reverse.

'This is as far as I go,' she said.

Maxwell was glad to hear it. He leaned across. 'You know, Prissy,' he said, 'if you didn't try so damned hard, I could get quite fond of you.'

She turned to look at him. 'Fuck you,' she snarled and as he stepped down from the Shogun she screamed away into the night, White Surrey still firmly strapped to her back.

'A bike, a bike,' muttered Maxwell into the Barlichway night, 'my kingdom for a bike,' and he trudged, hands in pockets and nose in collar, along the road to the Rat.

Gentrification had not reached this far into the abyss. The Rat was a concrete watering-hole in a concrete desert, the badly painted rodent crouching on its haunches on a piece of Edam — or was it Gruyere? The pub's paintwork was peeling badly and its windows, crisp with the night frost and driven snow, looked dark and dead.

Maxwell tapped on a side door, but it wasn't Bess the landlord's daughter who answered, but the landlord himself.

'We're closed, mate. Blimey, it's been snowing.'

Here was an intellectual, Maxwell realised. 'Barney about?' he asked.

'Barney who?'

'Barney Butler.' Maxwell's crisp fiver spoke more eloquently than a hundred surnames.

The landlord checked right and left, though whether for a police patrol car or a snowplough, Maxwell never knew. All he knew was that the crisp fiver vanished from his grip in less time than it took to say 'Come in.'

'Mr Maxwell,' Barney was lounging in a corner of the snug, an old mate sprawled unconscious on the table next to him.

'Evening, Barney. One for the road?'

'We're closed, mate,' the landlord reminded him.

'Fuck off, Yardley,' Barney shouted. 'I'll have a Smith's and my ol' teacher'll have . . . ?'

'A Southern Comfort please, Yardley. And a small one for yourself.'

Yardley surlied his way around the bar. 'If the filth arrive, you got this ten minutes ago, right?'

'I getcha,' grunted Maxwell as one of Harry Enfield's characters and prodded the snoring lump lying face down across Barney's table.

'That's Bull,' Barney said. 'His wife left him today. He's a bit upset.'

'Yes,' nodded Maxwell, dropping his tweed hat onto Bull's head. 'I can see he is. Ever read any Conan Doyle, Barney?' he asked his man, suddenly unable to remember whether Barney could read at all.

'Who?'

'Sherlock Holmes.'

'Nah,' Barney drew heavily on a wizened roll-up. 'I seen the films, though.'

'Ah,' Maxwell beamed. 'Dear old Basil and even dearer old Nigel Bruce. So you know what a Baker Street irregular is then?'

'No,' Barney looked blank. 'An occasional shit?'

Rather than give his man time to suggest any more possibilities, Maxwell said, 'People employed by the world's greatest detective to watch the streets, finger the undesirables, that sort of thing.'

'Don't think I follow,' Barney muttered.

Maxwell dug into the inside pocket of his coat. 'Seen this bloke before?' he asked.

Barney tried to focus on the photograph. He'd had a few. 'No,' he said. 'Should I?'

Maxwell dug deeper and found his wallet. 'Here's a brand spanking new twenty spot, Barney, keep you in ciggies for a day or two. There's another thirty if you spot this man.'

Barney looked at the photograph again, the dark wavy hair, the limp grin. 'Who is he?'

'That doesn't matter.' Bull stirred and muttered from his position of oblivion on the table. 'If you see this guy on the Barlichway, I want you to follow him. No contact. Just eyeballing. Watch where he goes, what he does. This bloke,' he pulled out a second photograph, 'might be with him.'

'Fair enough, Mr Maxwell.'

Yardley arrived with the drinks tray.

'And Barney,' Maxwell tapped the side of his nose, 'this is our little secret, okay?' And as Yardley stood there, looking down at them in a puzzled sort of way, Maxwell and Barney looked up at him and chorused, 'Yeah?'

* * *

Martin Stone slammed the door of his Peugeot. It sounded oddly muffled in the night. He wasn't a poetic man, but he paused briefly as he reached his front door and looked at the pavement, a powdery Cartland pink under the street light. The heaviness of the snowclouds had gone and the stars were sharp as diamonds overhead, so close you could reach out and touch them.

He put his key in the lock and went into the darkened hall. There was no sound, other than the soft padding of the old spaniel that snuffled out to meet him. Deaf or gaga or too old to care, the animal had not barked at his master's footfalls in the drive or the sound of the lock's rattle. He sniffed and whined as Stone patted him briefly.

'What's the matter, boy? Everybody gone to bed and left you?' He went into the kitchen, switching on lights as he went. He looked in the huge chest freezer, toying with an Indian. Then he looked in the fridge, throwing his coat onto a chair. He pulled out a carton of milk, then thought twice. 'Ah, stuff it,' he said and mechanically put it back, checking that the back door was locked and the central heating set right. He clicked off the light and climbed the stairs.

There was a glow from the nursery and he popped his head round the door. Janey's cot was empty, the little half moon mobile twirling above it glowing luminous in the dim light. His eldest little bundle of joy was with his mother in Littlehampton. He wondered briefly how much grief she was giving her. Little Sam's cot was empty too. Alex had obviously put the baby in with her. He nipped into the bathroom, too tired to wash or clean his teeth. Another bitch of a day. He looked in the mirror before deciding on a pee. That business with Jacquie Carpenter had rattled him. He'd thought he was all right with Jacquie; that she was no threat to him. But now he wasn't so sure. Now he'd have to watch his back.

He switched off the light and fumbled into his own room. The second cot in there was empty and more importantly, so was the bed. He reached the lamp and its light flooded the room. No one had slept here recently. The bed was made and cold. There was no indentation on the pillow. Alex's photo smiled at him from the bookcase.

'Oh, Jesus, no,' he whispered. 'Not again.'

CHAPTER 13

'Good Morning, Count,' Maxwell drifted through from the kitchen, still wearing his dressing-gown. 'Yes, I know,' he could read the feline's astonished whisker movement a hundred yards away, 'it's only half past six and your master is already upright, adopting that unnatural position to which your lot could never hope to aspire. But don't get me on the iniquities of evolution or we'll be here all day.'

Metternich had no intention of talking evolution or anything else philosophical. He intended to lick his armpits and that's precisely what he did.

'The village,' Maxwell had a pad of file paper open on the coffee table and a pen in his hand. 'Not the place where they imprisoned poor old Patrick McGoohan in the good old days of television, but Wetherton. The Saxon scholar in you, Count, realizes the derivation of the place name — the ton or settlement of Wether, some local Wessex warlord, I suspect.'

Metternich slurped loudly on some clump of fur — 'Hunnermuhorkpork.'

'But, to more pressing matters. Here,' he sketched as he spoke, 'is the church. Here, the school. If I remember aright, the hostelry is over this way. There's a post office, I think. Cluster of houses. A green, with or without maypole .

. . and that's it. That's all I can remember. Population? Yes, good question, Count. Two less with the rapid departure of the rector and the headmistress; although, strictly speaking, Ms Thorn didn't live in Wetherton. So, where do we start?' Maxwell tapped his teeth with his Biro. 'Indeed. Mrs Spooner.'

* * *

Wednesday afternoons were a godsend to Peter Maxwell. He had a joyous clump of free periods during which, every early Autumn, he lied on the UCAS forms about the hopefuls applying for university and at other times he marked crap. This Wednesday, however, he'd checked with the sadist who arranged cover lessons and told him he'd be out. 'Peter Maxwell has left the building' echoed around the corridors of Leighford High as the Great Man bundled into Sylvia Matthews' car and they did a runner through the school gate.

'No bike today, Max?' she asked him.

'Having an oil change, Sylv,' he said.

'So how will you get back? You know I can't stay.'

'See this,' he raised his thumb. 'Man's oldest tool. It's wonderful really and so underrated. You just stick it in the air and cars come screeching to a halt, their drivers falling over each other to be of service, only too pleased to help their fellow man.'

'Mad,' she chuckled. 'Stark raving mad.'

He kissed her goodbye at the lych-gate and watched as the Clio snarled away in a cloud of exhaust. Up here on the Weald, the snow had gone overnight but the hoar frost still gripped the hedgerows and looked set to stay all day. As his feet crunched on the gravel drive, he saw the flowers, still a fresh mass of colour on the unsettled grave of Andrew Darblay. No doubt the old man would secretly have liked to be buried inside, with a fine marble canopy overhead and a three-D likeness of himself in alb and stole; but there was probably some EU directive against it.

He knocked on the door of the rectory and a small, dark-haired woman answered it.

'Mrs Spooner?' Maxwell raised his hat.

'Yes.'

'My name is Peter Maxwell. I came here a few days ago to talk to Mr Darblay. Bad time though this must be, can I talk to you?'

She hesitated. 'Are you a reporter?'

'No,' he told her. 'I'm a teacher.'

'You'd better come in.'

They talked for nearly two hours, the lonely housekeeper and the Head of Sixth Form. At the end of it, he was no further forward. From what she told him, the late rector was Jesus and Mother Teresa rolled into one. He'd put the Nice into Mr Nice Guy. He thanked Mrs Spooner for her time and crossed to the Falcon in happy hour. In the pale sun of the January afternoon, Maxwell watched the local Wetherton mums, with buggies and siblings in tow, gathering at the corner to collect their kids. The big yellow and white school bus, its engine snarling in the cold, coughed and waited in the no-parking zone outside the school gates.

'You another of them coppers?' the girl behind the bar asked.

Maxwell tapped the side of his nose. 'Didn't know I was that obvious.'

'Are you blokes supposed to drink on duty?'

'Surveillance,' Maxwell confided, sipping his pint. 'Different rules.'

'Yeah?' the girl's eyes widened. 'Who are you surveying, then?'

'Anybody,' Maxwell's Peter Sellers' Inspector Clouseau was lost on the girl. 'Everybody. Look,' he was Maxwell again, 'is this as happy as the hour gets?' He had already noted the ancient gent dozing in the snug and the two old boys playing shove-ha'penny. Hugger-mugger at the Falcon.

'I told the boss it wasn't going to work. Happy hour's supposed to be early evening — catch the punters. After lunch, it's like a bloody morgue in here.'

'Janet, isn't it?'

'Trisha,' she corrected him.

'Trisha. Right. Can I get you a drink?'

'All right,' the girl beamed. Her face took on a radiance when she smiled. Her bright eyes balanced her enormous breasts. 'I'll have a vodka and blackcurrant.'

'Shrewd choice,' Maxwell smiled.

'You don't mind me saying this, do you,' she poured the drink, 'but aren't you a bit . . . well, old for a copper?'

'This is my last case,' Maxwell said. 'Wanted to go out in style, write my memoirs, grow petunias.'

'You after the bastard that killed the vicar, yeah?'

'Rector,' Maxwell corrected her. 'And the headmistress.'

'Now, that's what I said,' Trisha warmed to her theme, clinking Maxwell's glass and sipping away. 'I said to the boss the same bloke done 'em both. He said bollocks . . .'

'What made you think that?' Maxwell asked.

'What, that the boss talks bollocks?'

'The murders.'

'Stands to reason. All that black magic stuff.'

'Black magic?' Maxwell played the ingénue.

Trisha edged closer, her breasts enveloping yet more of the bar, obliterating the cutting edge of Strongbow. 'Look, I don't know whether you blokes ever talk to each other, but I told your oppo.'

'Oh?' Maxwell was all ears. 'Who's that?'

'Dunno. Some DS or other. Youngish bloke. Stone, was it? Stonewall? Something. Didn't seem all that interested.'

'I am,' Maxwell assured her.

'Well, I read this book once.'

Maxwell could believe that.

'About this village where they was all at it?'

'At it?'

'Devil worship, you dirty old man.' Trisha tapped his arm playfully.

There was a sudden series of grunts from the end of the bar and the ancient gent stood there, coins in his hand, making incomprehensible noises.

'All right, Harold,' Trisha said loudly. 'Same again, is it?' And she poured a frothy pint. 'Thank you, love.'

Harold threw the coins on the bar and grunted again.

'Oh, yeah,' Trisha laughed her tinkling laugh. 'That's what I said, but you know him. Load of bollocks. Bon aperitif,' and she came scurrying back. 'Yeah,' her confidential tone returned, 'the leader was the vicar and everybody else was involved. They all had . . . whatsname . . . cloven hooves.'

'Sort of BSE novel was it?'

'No, cloven hooves. The devil. He's got horns and a tail, he has. And of course,' she giggled, 'a bloody great willy.'

'Really?'

'Oh, yeah,' Trisha grinned broadly. 'There was lots of that going on. Women spread over altars and that. The vicar shagging his way through the congregation. Mind you, try getting any of 'em to buy a bloody raffle ticket . . .'

'And that's how it is in Wetherton?' Maxwell asked.

'Oh, bloody hell,' Trisha pulled a face. 'Don't bear thinking about, does it? I mean, that Darblay bloke was a nice old git, but I can't see the village crumpet lining up for him, know what I mean? Mind you,' she leaned forward, whispering with a snigger, 'Old Harold there'd be up for it.' Maxwell glanced furtively across to where old Harold had clearly gone to sleep over his pint again. 'Always sniffing round, he is. We had a spate of knicker-nicking last year.'

'Harold?' Maxwell was astonished.

'Gives you the creeps, don't it?' Trisha shuddered. 'Thought of his hands in my underwear. Not even my boyfriend gets his hands in there.'

'All right,' Maxwell said. 'So what did you tell my oppo?'

'Just this.' Trisha was serious now, concentrating and staring into Maxwell's dark eyes. 'There's something funny going on. And that Mr Darblay knew something about it.'

'Funny,' Maxwell murmured. 'Mrs Spooner didn't seem to know anything.'

'Well, there you are.' Trisha's point was made. 'She's more his age, ain't she? Got an old man with a face like a swede. I think he may have been slipping her one.'

'The rector and the housekeeper?'

'Unnatural, ain't it?' Trisha bridled, adjusting her breasts around the mixed nuts. 'He didn't get in here often but he was here, funny enough, a day or two before he died. We got talking.'

'Go on.' They both sipped their drinks.

'He asked me if I'd seen any strangers recently. Anybody like yourself, passing through.'

'And had you?'

'Well, of course. Though we don't get many this time of year. It's mostly in the summer. Tourists going up to the Ring, you know. I remembered two or three blokes, couple of women. Vicar said he was looking for a man, though, And,' Trisha winked, 'that wouldn't surprise me neither. You hear such stories, don't you?'

* * *

'Martin, are you all right?' Jacquie Carpenter was on her way through to the Incident Room.

'Hmm? Sorry.' Stone was clipping his pen in his inside pocket. 'I was miles away. What?'

'The guv'nor's back from the Chief Constable's.'

He was. Henry Hall sat behind the long table that ran the length of the old library's west wall, a piece of paper in his hand. 'This,' he said, once the team had settled down, 'is my resignation.'

You could have heard a pen drop.

'The Chief Constable has informed me,' he went on, unblinking, unemotional, 'that I have until the end of the month. If, by that time, there is no breakthrough, nothing tangible, this letter will be on his desk.'

'That's not on, guv.' It was Kevin Brand who broke the silence first.

There were hear hears all round and a hubbub of protestation. Hall's hand was in the air. 'This is not a topic for discussion, lady and gentlemen,' he said. 'Neither do I mean to put any more pressure on you than you are already under. I merely thought you ought to know. On February 1st, barring some developments, DCI Knight will be taking over the case.'

More murmurs. More rhubarb. Geoffrey Knight was about as welcome as a dose of clap. Only Martin Stone's expression hadn't changed. Martin Stone was elsewhere.

* * *

'Serial killers, Count,' Maxwell was lying on his settee, a glass of Southern Comfort perched precariously on his chest, his hands behind his head. 'What do we know about them? According to the best sources, namely the FBI, Federation of Bungling Investigators, seventy-four per cent of them are American — well, yes, they always have more of everything than everybody else, don't they? Most of them are Caucasian, but then, in Leighford, I'd be surprised to find much else. They're between twenty and thirty-five, wet their beds until a depressingly advanced age, and had a fascination with fire and animal torture as kids.' He threw a glance across the room. 'Especially cats, I understand.'

Metternich snored loudly as if to underline his contempt for the whole notion.

'One of the genuinely brilliant experts is Joel Norris. He says serial killers have seven phases — starting with aura. Our man retreats into a solitary, strange world fuelled by fantasies. These get stronger and stronger until he is forced to act. Then — and I will be asking questions later, Count — the trawling phase. Chummy — if I may borrow a hackneyed word from the days of Gideon of the Yard — prowls Leighford and the environs looking for a victim; Elizabeth Pride, Andrew Darblay, Albert Walters, Alison Thorn. It's the wooing phase where he'd have to be at his most charming. Somehow he inveigled himself into Myrtle Cottage, cutting through old lady Pride's natural suspicions of a stranger. Even allowing for the fact that Darblay caught him up to no good in the church, he'd still have had to gain entry to Albert's flat on the Barlichway. With Alison Thorn, what did he do — pose as a charity collector or something? Is that the cover he used throughout, selling the Warcry or a time share in Heaven? The capture phase would be easy enough. Three old people, one relatively small woman. Assuming average strength, that wouldn't be difficult. Only, he doesn't go in for the full frontal assault, does he? He uses poison. The woman's weapon? The coward's weapon?' Maxwell shrugged and nearly toppled his glass, 'I don't know. Then, the totem phase — taking something away to remind him of the glorious moment of killing. Was there anything missing from Myrtle Cottage — apart from the calendar I pinched, of course? The church? The Walters and Thorn flats? I don't know. But maybe I still know a woman who does.'

He sat upright suddenly, slamming the half-filled glass down on the coffee table. 'The point is, Count,' he said as the cat stirred and turned over, 'Joel Norris is talking about your classic serial sexual murder. Is that it?' He got up, pacing his lounge like a father waiting in a Maternity Ward ante-room for word of the birth of his child. 'Is sex the motive? Pride, Walters, Thorn — all naked. Signs of sexual abuse? Nothing in the papers. Nothing from Jacquie or Hall. Then, there's this black magic nonsense. No,' he shook his head and picked up a sixth-form essay, 'it's all too preposterous, Count. What Joel Norris misses out is the "Let's Drop Maxwell In It" phase of the serial killer, when a victim lands on my doorstep.' He read the opening lines of the essay in front of him and his red pen leaped into action.

'The wooing phase, Count,' he decided. 'That's where the key to this one lies. How he gets people to trust him. Who has right of access to your home? Or who would you trust on your doorstep? Boy scout? Barnardo collector? Property developer? Policeman?' His mind wandered away and his voice turned dark gravel, like Alec Guinness's 'Tinker, tailor, soldier, spy?'

* * *

'War Office?' Maxwell was always grateful when he'd finished the reins. Those infuriating bits of stuff that modellers Historex provided for harness were fine and dandy in their own way, but my God, they were fiddly.

'Max. It's Jacquie.'

'Darling.' He put the glue down before it oozed all over his fingers and he spent eternity in close proximity to an MFI desk. 'How the hell are you?'

'Worried,' she said.

'Worried?' he pulled off the forage cap, 'Why?'

There was a sigh.

'All right,' he smiled. 'Why particularly?'

'It's Hall,' she said. 'His job's on the line.'

'Really? Why's that?' Maxwell came from a profession where they only ever fired people for two things — fingers in the till or fingers in the knickers.

'He's not getting results.'

Maxwell's blood ran cold. That of course was the government's agenda. That nice Mr Blunkett was so in touch with education that he wanted to reintroduce payment by results for teachers. That Victorian idea they'd abandoned, along with hanging. Hello starvation. 'Who's piling on the pressure?'

'The Chief Constable. Ever met him?'

'Don't think so.'

'Professional bastard. I feel sorry for the guv'nor, Max. He's a decent bloke. Stood by me often enough.'

'I thought you were off hooks at the moment?'

'That's because I've been letting him down recently. Martin and I both, as it happens.'

'Martin?'

'DS Stone. On the make, but his wife's just had a baby and he's not really holding up his end of the job. Look, Max . . . there's something I've got to tell you.'

'Oh?'

'Hall knows about the calendar.'

'Ah.'

'I told him.'

'You did?'

'I'm sorry.' He could hear the tiredness in her voice. 'It just came out. We had a bit of a slanging match.'

'Was that wise?'

'Probably not. He's got 'til the first of the month. Then he's out. Then he'll be quietly sidelined somewhere, dog-handling or records or some such crap. They won't give him murder again.'

'What did you row about?'

'The calendar. Max, this whole thing is about witchcraft, black magic. I yelled at him, thinking he couldn't see it. How could he not? He's an intelligent bloke. I was being stupid.'

'Perhaps he doesn't want to see it?'

'What?' she asked him. 'What do you mean?'

'Jacquie, do we have any idea about callers to Albert Walters' flat? Or Alison Thorn's?'

There was a pause. 'With Thorn we believe it was someone collecting for Barnardo's.'

'Bingo,' Maxwell said. 'But not, I suspect, on the Barlichway. On the Barlichway, they'd pinch his money and run.'

'Why do you ask?'

'Policemen,' said Maxwell. 'People you trust. Blue murder. Look, Jacquie, where's Hall now?'

She checked her watch. 'Still at the Incident Room, I expect. Why?'

'Nothing,' he said. 'Just sit tight. Let's see if we can't get your guv'nor to hold onto his job. 'Bye, darling. Love you.'

The line went dead. 'Do you, Max?' she asked herself, cradling the receiver in her hand. 'And there again, do I love you?' There were no ways to count. Then an odd thought entered her head. 'People you trust?' She was talking to the air. 'Max, no one on the Barlichway trusts a policeman.'

* * *

When you've remembered where you've left your bike — on the back of the Shogun of the most dangerous man-eater west of Bengal — you catch a taxi. That's what Maxwell did when he'd got off the phone to Jacquie. It was time for some straight talking; time for some sorting out.

Members of the public weren't welcome in Incident Rooms. It was too hands on. There were macabre photos of dead people all over walls and display boards, sensitive information, names and car registration numbers. The fact that the place was manned twenty-four hours a day couldn't screen the openness of all that.

The desk man was mean, shifty, tired. 'Who wants to see him?' he asked.

'Peter Maxwell,' Maxwell said. 'And it's urgent.'

The desk man was reluctant but he did go away and he did come back. 'He's busy,' was the result.

'Fine,' Maxwell beamed. 'It'll take a little while, but I should think in an hour or so I'll be back with a few lads from the media. Meridian won't want to miss this. South Coast Radio'll be along, plus all the nationals of course. I'm lucky, actually. Copper-bashing is quite the trend at the moment, isn't it? What with institutional racism and all?'

'What the fuck are you talking about?' the desk man leaned over his desk.

Maxwell leaned towards him, the echo of his posture reverberating down the corridors of the old Tottingleigh library. 'I'm talking about offering a vital piece of information — evidence, in fact, to DCI Hall in connection with the current spate of murders in and around Leighford. Now, if you're not interested, I'm sure the paparazzi will be.'

'Mr Maxwell,' Henry Hall's voice carried across the open space from his office. 'That's all, Bob. You'd better show Mr Maxwell in.'

The desk man lifted the counter top and the Head of Sixth Form swept past. 'Helpful isn't the word,' he said.

Hall's office was a converted corner of the old library Maxwell remembered well, with bolted on walls of cardboard and spit. The DCI offered the Head of Sixth Form a chair. 'I think it's time I gave you this,' Maxwell said. He threw the calendar down onto the table. 'I think you know what it is.'

'It's a calendar from Elizabeth Pride's house, Myrtle Cottage.' Hall was in his shirt sleeves, his tie gone, his glasses perched on top of his head. He looked terrible as he closed the office door and most of the building shook, 'and it contains key dates.'

'In the year of Wicca, yes. Except I'm not sure it's as harmless as all that.'

'Harmless?' Hall sat down on the spare chair against the wall. He couldn't look at the paperwork on his desk any more. There was just too much of it and the words weren't making any sense.

'Wicca is modern witchcraft and not, as I once believed, a trendy name for the WI . . . although I don't know, though! It's not much more than holistic medicine viewed from one angle.'

'And the other angle?'

'Wiccans have a code, a creed if you like,' Maxwell told him. 'It's called the Rede, a sort of "love thy neighbour". "An it harm none, do what wilt".'

'That's it?'

'An it harm none,' Maxwell repeated. 'If you're talking about Elizabeth Pride, Andrew Darblay, Albert Walters and Alison Thorn, I'd say that's quite a lot of harm, wouldn't you?'

'I don't follow.'

Maxwell looked at Hall. He'd crossed swords with the man before. It wasn't all cosy chats in Maxwell's office and Hall's Volvo. He'd faced him across the table of an interview room, briefless, friendless, the tape recorder turning to his right. For all his blandness and his immobility of expression, Hall wasn't a man to cross; Maxwell knew that. But tonight, he'd lost it. The life seemed to have drained out of DCI Hall.

'The Wiccan Rede reminds me of someone,' Maxwell said patiently. 'Aleister Crowley, the great beast. I won't bore you with the man's dates because I can't remember them, but he liked to think he was the Devil's anointed. Had a phone number Purgatory 666, that sort of thing.'

'What's your point?'

'Crowley had a creed, too — "*Do what thou wilt is all of the law*". In other words, the master-magician didn't give a rat's arse whom he hurt. The more harm done the better. That's what you've got here, Mr Hall. Somebody's twisting the Wiccan tradition for good and using it to frighten the bejesus out of people. How long will it be, do you think, before the media really hits top gear? Are you ready for the locust pack? Because, believe me, there won't be a decent man left standing when they're finished.'

'Why did you take the calendar?' Hall asked.

'Why did you send me to Myrtle Cottage?' Maxwell snapped back.

'I didn't.'

'Jesus, Henry! You don't mind if I call you Henry, do you? Because right now, as all the best B movies had it, I'm the only friend you've got.'

Hall just sat there, blinking.

Maxwell got to his feet and leaned down to the man. 'I know from Jacquie that you've been given a yellow card,' he said. 'Six days, isn't it, 'til you're given the red one?'

Hall opened his mouth to say something, then changed his mind and nodded.

'Well, the day after that it won't matter.'

'What won't?'

'Why did you tell me Elizabeth Pride's address?' Maxwell persisted.

'Because . . .' Hall wavered, looking up into the man's face, 'because there's someone here I can't trust. Mr Maxwell, I've been working on murder cases now, man and boy, for nearly twenty years. I'm good at them. I get results. And this one . . .' He slumped against the wall, 'This one's getting nowhere because somebody here is involved. They know every turn, every twist.'

'Who?' Maxwell asked.

'If I knew that,' Hall said, 'do you think for one moment I'd have given you Myrtle Cottage? Or even the time of day? Who put the calendar there, Mr Maxwell? Because whoever did that is playing some twisted, sick game — with you and me.'

Maxwell sighed and crossed back to Hall's desk.

'I was hoping you'd find some answers. Something we'd overlooked,' Hall said. 'With that bloody calendar, all you've done is confirm my worst suspicions.'

Maxwell looked at the DCI and swept to the door. 'There's an end to all this, you know,' he said.

'Yes,' Hall chuckled weakly, 'February 1st.'

'No,' Maxwell shook his head. 'Read your calendar. February 2nd — Candlemas, St Mary's Feast of candles. "*Candlemas Day, plant beans in the clay, Put candles and candlesticks all away.*" That's the next sabbat, Mr Hall, the next time the witches ride. You go and see your boss. Have a word with the Chief Constable. Get him to give you one more day. I've got some beans to plant.'

* * *

It was nearly Friday when the phone rang in Leighford nick. Jock Haswell was on the desk, his tea curdling by his elbow, his illicit fag smouldering between his brown fingers. 'Leighford Police station.'

'Hello?'

'Yes, madam. Can I help you?'

'Yes, yes, I rather hope you can. My daughter has gone missing. She and her baby.'

'Right, madam,' Haswell reached across for his pen. 'Name, please?'

'My name?'

'Please, madam. And your address.'

'Saunders. Veronica Saunders. Mrs. Fifty-one, Wainwright Avenue, Windsor.'

'Windsor?' Haswell checked. 'May I suggest, madam, that you contact your local station there?'

'Pointless,' the woman told him. 'You see, my daughter and her baby have gone missing from your area, not mine.'

'I see. Could I have your daughter's name, please?'

'Yes, it's Stone. Alexandra Stone. And the baby's name is Samantha.'

'Stone? Er . . . Madam, would this be any relation to DS Martin Stone at all?'

'It's precisely because of that relationship that I'm ringing you,' the voice said. 'Somebody has to do something about this situation.'

CHAPTER 14

'Mr Maxwell? I'm Janet Ruger. *Daily Telegraph*.'

The woman standing on the path outside 38 Columbine was wiry, with short dark hair and slightly bulging eyes behind her glasses. Her scrawny hand was firm in Maxwell's and spoke volumes for the go-getting sort of woman who was smashing through the glass ceiling these days.

'Can I come in?'

'Be my guest.' He held the door open for her. 'Are you the forlorn hope?'

'I beg your pardon?'

'Skirmishers,' Maxwell explained. 'You find them in civil war armies and rather later, a tiny band of masochists prepared to draw enemy fire.'

'I don't think I have those tendencies,' she told him.

'But you are an advance guard, I suspect,' he said, 'the first of many.'

'Surely the media have been on to you already?'

He closed the door, checking up and down sleepy Columbine first. 'For a while,' he nodded, 'they formed an orderly picquet on my lawn. I'm geared up for suing for the price of a packet of bulbs — I think my croci are a no-no. After you.'

She led the way up the stairs to Maxwell's lounge, glad, with a man behind her, she was wearing a long skirt and coat. 'What a charming place,' she cooed, dutifully.

'Barratt,' he shrugged. 'I think on balance I'd have preferred Wimpole Street. Can I get you a drink?'

'Perhaps a sherry.'

There was a hurtle of black and white fur and the rattle of claws on wood.

'My cat, Metternich,' Maxwell explained. 'Misogynist, I'm afraid,' and he clanked in his drinks cabinet for a glass. 'Doesn't care for women, either,' he beamed. 'Old Particular?'

'Fine. It's good of you to see me.'

'I shall probably regret it, Ms . . .'

'Janet, please.'

He waved her to a cosy seat by the fire, sweeping a pile of dog-eared exercise books to the rug.

'I'm doing an extended piece for the *Telegraph* on the murder-fest in Leighford. This is where they found the first body.'

'Well, out there, yes,' he passed her the glass and topped up his own Southern Comfort. 'And for "they" read "me".'

'Indeed,' she sipped the sherry. 'That must have been quite an experience.'

'I've had better,' he told her.

Janet Ruger opened her coat and pulled out a notepad from her handbag. 'I understand you have something of a reputation around here, Mr Maxwell.'

'Max, please,' he said. 'Wit, raconteur, film buff extraordinaire, lady-killer . . . oops! Perhaps you'd better scrub that last bit.'

She smiled, arching an eyebrow. 'I was thinking,' she said, 'of your reputation as a sleuth.'

'Overrated,' he scowled, shaking his head. 'Right now I couldn't detect a nuclear explosion in my kitchen.'

'May I?' she'd whipped out a packet of cigs.

'Please,' and he hauled out the only ashtray he possessed, the one marking the wedding of Charles and Diana.

'But you are involved?' she pressed him, lighting up. Her shrewd, all-knowing features glowed orange for an instant and then she was framed in soft lamplight again.

'I don't know to whom you've been talking . . . ?'

'Sheer poetry,' she held up her hand, ciggie aloft, 'Forgive me, Max, but there can't be many with your sense of grammar.'

'None, madam,' he boomed. 'I am a dodo, a velociraptor, the last auk. When I depart this life, there will be no one left who does not split an infinitive or mix a metaphor.'

'Or do so brilliantly at changing the subject.'

'Touché,' he laughed, 'although I believe it was you who did that.'

'Elizabeth Pride,' she brought him back with a jolt to the straight and narrow. 'What have you found out?'

'Somebody left her on my doorstep,' he said, cradling his glass. 'She'd been poisoned and frozen, presumably in that order.'

'I read that in the pile of wombat's do they call the *Leighford Advertiser*,' she said flatly. '*Telegraph* readers will want a bit more. You can give me a bit more.'

'Can I?' Maxwell leaned back, wondering what kind of bitch he'd invited into his home.

Janet Ruger leaned back as well. 'Peter Maxwell,' she said, 'known as Mad Max. First-class degree in History from Jesus College, Cambridge. PGCE at Distinction level.'

'That was a typo,' he told her. 'A computer error before they invented computers.'

'You helped solve the murder of Jennifer Hyde some years back and that Eight Counties television business. Then there was Charts . . .'

'I'd love to stroll with you down felony lane, Janet,' he smiled. 'And I'm flattered — and not a little disturbed — that you have so much on me. But this time, I really can't help.'

She dragged on her cigarette, then impulsively stubbed it out. 'All right,' she said, putting her notebook away and standing up suddenly, 'if you can't help me, perhaps I can help you. What are you doing Monday morning, ten thirty?'

'Monday,' he said, standing up with her. 'Ah, that'll be 7C4. The lesson I'm preparing for Ofsted — "Tying up our Shoelaces".'

'Shame,' she said. 'I think you might have enjoyed an alternative.'

'Oh?'

'Have you heard of Dr Zarina Liebowitz?'

'Not Dr Ruth's replacement on the telly, is she? For people with, you know,' he slipped into his excruciatingly shy routine, 'hang-ups about their . . . you know . . . personal thingies.'

'No,' said the journalist. 'Dr Liebowitz is an expert on satanic indicators and multi-generational incest.'

'Like you do,' nodded Maxwell, manifestly impressed.

'She's heard of your little problem here in dear old Leighford, Max, all the way from the West Coast, USA. She's taking it all rather more seriously than you are. She's called a press conference in the town hall at half past ten, Monday 29th January. Here.' She thrust a laminated card into his hand.

'What's this?'

'It's a Press pass. Just for half an hour on Monday, you can be a member of the fourth estate.'

'Goody!' he smiled. 'Will you be there?'

'I wouldn't miss it for the world,' she said. 'And then, Max, we'll talk again.'

* * *

Now Paul Moss owed Maxwell a favour or five. He was a curly-headed lad with a broad smiling face and boundless optimism. One of those Thatcher's children who was actually far too nice to teach. He'd bought himself a pair of heavy-rimmed specs to help his gravitas and some incompetent — actually James Diamond BSc, mEd — had appointed him Head of History. It was Maxwell who'd written out his schemes of work, explained to him the complexities of the Corn Laws and had a quiet word in the ear of Quentin Shovell, the one-time school psychopath who'd temporarily had it in for Mr Moss. After that Quentin risked the howling opprobrium of his peers by carrying Mr Moss's books for him.

So Maxwell had no qualms at all about shunting 7C4 in with Moss's 7A2 for a quiet hour of Kevin Costner running rings around Alan Rickman (or was it the other way around?) in *Robin Hood, Prince of Thieves*. Still bikeless, he'd hot-footed it through the morning shoppers and the January sunshine to the great, grey edifice of civic pride that was Leighford Town Hall.

There were people everywhere, milling paparazzi with reassuringly expensive cameras, lung cancer and attitude, wallowing in cynicism and waiting for the pubs to open. Maxwell flashed his card and as though it was a blank cheque, he was in, carried on the tide of journalese.

He found a seat near the back and beyond the mass of craning heads and arching sound booms saw Crispin Foulkes and a senior policeman flashing silver from every orifice thanking a huge, opulent-looking woman in a headscarf.

'Ladies and gentlemen,' the top brass copper opened the ball right on cue. 'I am Chief Constable Leonard Dickinson and this is Mr Crispin Foulkes of Leighford Social Services. We've called you here today in view of the series of related deaths in the area and to introduce Dr Zarina Liebowitz who is an international expert in the field of psychotherapy.'

The large woman smiled, turning first in one direction, then another as the cameras popped and flashed.

'Dr Liebowitz,' the Chief Constable announced. It was a while before the hubbub died down. Maxwell was impressed. Like Hitler used to do in the Sportspalast, the good doctor was waiting, arms folded, for the kiddies to behave themselves. Psychotherapy at its best.

'When your social services contacted me,' she said, the accent thick and pure LA, 'I'd already picked up some vibes on the Internet. Clearly, I'm an outsider here. I don't know Leighford and I've yet to involve myself fully in the case, but this much I will say. What you have here — and sadly, those of us in social services have seen this before — is clear evidence of multi-generational incest and institutionalised sadism. Physical and sexual abuse is manifest. And, given the evidence as it stands, I would not rule out the sacrificial element of satanic abuse also.'

There was a roar from the paparazzi. Maxwell recognised it at once. It was the sound of locusts rubbing their legs together before the off. Questions were being hurled at the trio on the top table, but especially directed towards our American cousin, who calmly and cryptically fielded the lot. Newsmen came and went, ears glued to mobile phones, pens in hand, camcorders whirring. The circus of sound bites went on until Maxwell caught sight of Jacquie Carpenter and fought his way to her.

'Jacquie,' he caught her arm and yelled above the row. 'What are you doing in this madhouse? Is this Hall's idea?'

She shook her head. 'That silly bastard Dickinson,' she told him. 'This is the last straw, Max.' He could see tears in her eyes. 'Four bloody corpses on our hands and now this. It's as if he wants us to foul up. We won't be able to move for this lot now. He's finished us, you mark my words. But why are you here?'

'I was invited,' he shouted. 'By a journalist, Janet Ruger? Do you know her? Is she here?'

* * *

Janet Ruger wasn't there. The way the chambermaid at the Brougham told it to DCI Hall that afternoon, she was lying naked in Room 22, her arms trailing each side of the narrow bed, her legs spread wide and an ugly knife buried up to the hilt in her throat. Her mouth gaped open, as it would for ever in the chambermaid's dreams and her eyes were wide with terror.

Someone had dabbled his or her fingers in the journalist's blood and written above the head the single word 'Maleficarum' Her epitaph. Her obituary.

'Martin?'

'Jock.' DS Stone didn't look up from his paperwork. The word had come in from the Brougham that a body had been found there, but there were no details yet and the DCI was on his way. He'd told Stone to stay put. He and DC Brand could handle things and a call was put out to Dr Astley.

'Look, er . . . can I have a word?'

'Sure.' Stone was still lost in concentration, trying to make sense of eyewitness reports of Albert Walters' last known movements on the Barlichway.

'Look, I should have said something first thing this morning, but, well, it's a bit difficult . . .' Haswell stood in the doorway of the DI's office, its owner still down with the flu that had decimated Leighford CID since Christmas. The old git should never have joined the police. Not unless he could have been granted a posting to Dock Green along with dear old Jack Warner.

'What is it, Jock?' Stone sighed, looking up for the first time.

'I had this phone call,' he said. 'Last Thursday night, late.'

'You on the double shift?' Stone asked.

'Tell me about it,' Haswell grumbled. 'A woman called to report her daughter missing. Something about a baby. I should have told you sooner, but I was off at the weekend. Touch of flu.'

Stone's expression didn't change. 'This woman have a name?' he asked.

'Saunders,' Haswell told him. 'Veronica Saunders.'

Stone's nose wrinkled, his jaw flexed for the briefest of seconds. 'The mother-in-law,' he said, straight faced. 'Mad as a snake.'

'Really? She sounded all right.'

'I have no doubt, Jock,' Stone said, putting his pen away, 'that when we catch this ghoul who's going around poisoning people, he'll sound all right, too. Did she give any details?'

'Just the basics, address and so on. She said somebody had to do something. She's waiting for my call.'

Stone turned a page and got back to his reading. 'Forget it,' he said.

'What?' Haswell frowned. 'No, look, Martin, it's a logged call . . .'

'Jock,' Stone leaned back, placing a pencil horizontally on the page to remind him where he'd got to, 'She told you Alex had gone, right?'

'Yeah,' Haswell nodded.

'And taken Sam with her?'

'That's right.'

'Did she mention my eldest? Janey?'

'Er . . . no, I don't think so.'

'Right, then.'

'But . . .'

'Alzheimer's, Jock,' Stone said patiently. 'We've been here before. She did exactly the same when Janey was born. Then — as now — they're staying with my mother. Veronica knows that. Except she can't remember it. She's forgotten about Janey completely. You know Alex had a rough time, with the baby being late and everything?'

Haswell did.

'Well, we thought it made sense for someone to look after them all. I'm up to my bollocks in these murders and we're still short-staffed despite the Incident Room set-up. I don't have the time at the moment. You haven't sent anybody out on this, have you?'

'No, not yet. I wanted to talk to you first.'

'Quite right, Jock.' Stone nodded. 'Look, I'll sort it, all right? When she rings again — and chances are she will just play along, okay? Usual thing. Posters have gone up. Patrols out. Door to door. You know the drill.'

'Sure, Martin, sure,' Haswell said. 'Anything you say.'

* * *

'Who's this one, then?' Donald wanted to know for the record.

'Well, it's not bloody Anneka Rice or bloody Charlie Dimmock,' Jim Astley assured him. 'According to her NUJ card, she was Janet Desiree Ruger.'

'Desiree? That's a potato, isn't it?'

Jim Astley approved of gallows humour. Sometimes it was all that kept you sane in this business, of trying to glean lost secrets from dead souls. But gallows humour at Donald's level he could do without. He looked up at his rotund assistant with a basilisk stare that would have shrivelled a more sensitive man. 'You should get out more,' he said softly and bent to work.

Janet Ruger was a martyr to the menopause. Her once pert breasts sagged now and the tonnes of Oil of Olay her erratically inflated salary sometimes afforded her were to no avail. She lay without her face on Astley's steel draining board, her short brown hair resembling the mode à la guillotine that French aristos wore in the tumbrils on their last trip to the Place de Grève. Her eyes, that had sparkled in Peter Maxwell's sitting-room the night before, were sunken and dull and dead. Her lips, deprived of their carmine coating, were thin and pale, peeled back from her large, regular teeth.

Astley jabbed a metal spatula against her tongue. She did not say 'ah'. Then he got to the nitty-gritty, speaking, for the record, into the microphone he'd lowered from the ceiling. 'The throat wound is approximately,' and he felt, first with a gloved finger, then with a probe, 'five inches deep, breaking the skin at the nape of the neck. Lividity indicates that she haemorrhaged internally. I expect to find the lungs awash. There was, I remember, a great deal of blood soaked into the mattress. Massive damage to throat tissues. It's likely the epiglottis is smashed and the trachea split. Cause of death was a single, very violent blow to the throat, the knife slicing through the spinal cord between the second and third vertebrae.' He angled the neck. 'Smartly done.'

His eyes wandered through the powerful lens strapped to his forehead. 'Considerable bruising to the forearms and stomach. The woman protested too much, methinks and tried to fight her attacker off. He may well be bruised too, but,' he checked the fingernails carefully, 'no obvious signs of debris here. I shall take scrapings later. Donald, time for the gingernuts, I think.'

* * *

Jacquie Carpenter sat that night in a corner of the Incident Room. The DCI's door was shut, his blinds drawn. Martin Stone had long gone and most of the others. Kevin Brand was still there, dosing himself with Lemsip in an attempt to shake off the flu he felt creeping up his spine.

'Penny for them?' he said to Jacquie.

She came to with a start. She'd been miles away, remembering the first time she'd met Peter Maxwell, the first time he'd kissed her. How warm and strong and safe she'd felt, ready to take on the world. Now, she didn't know. A man she'd loved once had put doubt in her mind. Doubt about the man she loved now. Thought she loved now. She felt frightened and lonely and ashamed all at the same time, desolation in a converted library where a team of people were trying to catch a madman.

She looked at Brand, square, solid, dependable. Nothing much got to Kevin Brand. At the end of his shift he'd put on his coat and go home to his wife and have a beer and watch some telly. She envied him. 'Talk me through the Brougham, Kev,' she said.

'All right,' he shrugged and rolled his swivel chair closer. 'Not your state-of-the-art south coast hotel.'

'No CCTV.'

'Exactly.' He blew copiously into his handkerchief. 'And that's the bugger of it. If this Ms Ruger had been staying at the Grand, we'd have all her visitors on video loop. At the Brougham, you've got a desk girl who, if you ask me, is a few sandwiches short of a picnic.'

'Astley gives an approximate time of death at twelve to half one Sunday night/Monday morning.'

'That covers the entire shift of Miss Dozy. Didn't see a bloody thing.'

'Isn't it a bit unusual,' Jacquie was wondering aloud, 'having a woman on night duty?'

'She wasn't alone. There was a male oppo having a kip in the inner office. In an emergency, she could wake him.'

'Like a murder in the hotel, you mean?'

'Yeah,' chuckled Brand. 'The guv'nor said something along those lines.'

'What time did Janet Ruger get back to the hotel?' she asked, crossing to pour herself one last cup of stewed coffee.

Brand checked his notes. 'Nearly eight thirty. She had a night cap in the bar. They closed at eleven and the barman remembers saying goodnight to her. She drank . . . er . . . two Martinis on the rocks and smoked maybe half the state of Virginia. Seemed, the barman said, to be waiting for somebody.'

'Oh?'

'Kept looking at her watch. The barman noticed because he was doing the same, hoping she'd go to bed.'

'So, her room was on the first floor?'

'That's right. From the bar, she'd have had to go through the lobby and up two sets of stairs. There's a sort of landing halfway up.'

'This room of hers,' Jacquie was looking at the plan on the wall that the police artist had compiled, 'looks standard.'

'It is,' Brand said. 'One bed, two chairs, wardrobes, sideboards various. Usual tea and coffee facilities. Hospitality bar — she'd made inroads into that, by the way.'

'What had gone?'

'A couple of Scotches.'

Jacquie shrugged. 'So she liked a drink.'

'You could say that.'

'And the body?'

'Spreadeagled on the bed. I tell you, Jacquie,' Brand's solid face said it all, 'I've seen some sights in my time, but Jesus Christ. Know what it reminded me of? The Sharon Tate murder.'

'Charles Manson?' she frowned. 'Bit before my time, Kev.'

'Yeah, but the blood on the wall. Manson's family wrote "Kill the pigs". Our boy wrote "Maleficarum", whatever that is. There was a fuck of a lot of blood.'

'And that's not like him,' Jacquie nodded.

'What isn't?'

'The others — Pride, Walters, Thorn. All the wounds have been post mortem. No blood. But Darblay and Ruger,' she shuddered inside at the memory of the red-daubed church, 'enough to drown in. Why is that?'

'Jacquie,' Brand shifted uneasily, looking at the photograph of the dead journalist's face, 'you don't think we're talking about two killers, do you? What do the shrinks call it — folie a deux?'

'I don't know, Kev.' She shook her head. But she knew a man who might.

* * *

The man who might slumped in a darkened corner of his classroom. He'd been listening to the collective wisdom of Year 13, attempting a seminar on Disraeli's New Imperialism. About half past three he'd contemplated throwing himself through the window. At least the social ramifications of the defenestration of Maxwell would make a change from Dizzy. For the umpteenth time he pronounced the name Bartle Frere for the verbally challenged and then the bell saved his life.

He packed up his encyclopaedic historical knowledge and stumbled next door to his office. A young man sat there, with dark wavy hair and an earnest expression, made more so by the bruise on his jaw.

'Mr Maxwell?'

'Detective Sergeant Stone,' the Head of Sixth Form said. It was only then he noticed the second man half hidden by the door.

'This is Detective Constable Grimshaw.' The second man flashed his warrant card.

Maxwell nodded briefly to him and took his seat behind his desk. 'If you're going to snoop into a man's private life, sergeant,' he said with a smile, 'at least have the wit, if not the grace, to put his desk diary back straight.' Stone's jaw flexed and his eyes narrowed. He'd heard rumours about Maxwell. Down the nick he was legendary; for a pain in the arse, that is. Rumour had it he was slipping Jacquie Carpenter one, that he'd got something on the guv'nor, that he was an ex-Yard man put out to grass.

The question now was — was he the Devil himself?

'I'd like to ask you about Janet Ruger,' Stone said.

'Journalist,' said Maxwell. 'Writes for the *Telegraph*. Sorry . . . wrote.'

'You know what's happened, then?'

Maxwell got up to close the door and noticed the constable scribbling in his notepad. 'At four o six,' he said, 'Mr Maxwell rose and closed his office door, not as an admission of guilt, but simply because a conversation about a murder is hardly a suitable one for young ears. This is a school,' he sat back down again. 'Children everywhere!'

'How did you find out about Ms Ruger's death?' Stone asked.

'*Meridian News*,' Maxwell told him. 'That nice Sally Taylor. It did, I confess, come as a bit of a shock.'

'Really?' Stone crossed one leg casually over the other. 'Why was that?'

'I'd only talked to her the other night.'

'Friday?'

'That's right. She came to my house at about nine, nine thirty.'

'Oh?' Stone's expression hadn't changed. 'Why would that be?'

'She wanted to pump me,' Maxwell shrugged. 'Find out what I know.'

'And what do you know?'

'In general terms?' Maxwell asked. 'Or specifically?'

Stone uncrossed his legs and leaned forward. 'Specifically, Mr Maxwell, we're getting jerked around by people like you. In case quantitative history isn't your particular bag, five people have died in and around Leighford in the last month. And before you come out with Joe Public's usual cry "What are you blokes doing about it?" the answer is pratting around with people like you. There is such a thing as wasting police time, you know.'

Maxwell nodded. 'Indeed,' he said. 'And you're doing most of it, Mr Stone. Impressive, though, about quantitative history. What board did you do?'

'Cambridge . . .' Stone was caught off guard by that one. 'That's hardly the point,' he went on. 'Specifically what did this Ruger woman want?'

'She wanted to pick my brains,' Maxwell told him. 'I couldn't help.'

Stone looked at the young DC who looked back at him. 'See, what I find a little more than a coincidence,' he said, 'is that of those five deaths, two of them can be laid, if you'll excuse the pun, at your door. Now that does strain credulity somewhat, doesn't it? How well do you know the Brougham?'

'The hotel? Not very,' Maxwell said. 'I've had the odd dinner there. Nothing special, I seem to remember. Quite nice uplit wall decorations, sort of Klimt meets Bauhaus.'

'What time did Ms Ruger leave?' Stone asked.

'She didn't stay long,' Maxwell remembered. 'Perhaps ten, a little after.'

'She drove away?'

'I didn't notice.'

'Did she tell you anything?' Stone changed tack.

'I don't understand.'

'Think back. Did she give you any information?'

Maxwell sat upright in his chair. 'As a matter of fact, she did,' he said. 'She gave me a press pass and invited me to Monday's press conference — Dr Liebowitz.'

'The shrink?' Stone checked.

'To put it in the vernacular, yes.'

'Now that is interesting,' nodded Stone as Grimshaw wrote furiously.

'Is it?' Maxwell was all innocence.

'Oh, yes,' Stone assured him. 'It's very interesting that a woman who was going to die a little more than forty-eight hours after she left you should think you'd be interested in the services of a shrink. You see, Mr Maxwell, you're one of those fascinating people we police officers have a special place in our hearts for.'

'Oh?' Maxwell bit his tongue to stop himself from commenting on the prepositionary faux pas.

'The person we call,' Stone smiled, 'the last person to see someone alive.'

'You mean no one saw Janet Ruger for forty-eight hours? The entire weekend?' Maxwell was incredulous.

'No one, Mr Maxwell,' Stone assured him. 'No one at all.'

CHAPTER 15

Mark Ruger arrived in Leighford that Wednesday. He wasn't exactly the distraught husband. In fact he'd stopped being Janet's husband eight years ago, after it was clear that she was more in love with her career than she was with him. He went through the motions, identified his ex-wife's body for the record and talked to the police.

Jacquie Carpenter got the short straw, sifting through the remains of another person's life. The dead woman had graduated from Essex University (well, somebody had to) and had worked on a whole variety of local papers before reaching Fleet Street. A spell on the *Guardian* had been the high-water mark in the early 'nineties and then, on a whim, she'd retired to rural Wiltshire with hubby to write the great British novel.

Instead, she'd drifted, dabbling here and there, freelancing as she went. She was never at home, Mark told Jacquie, never there for anybody but herself. Oh, she was a clever woman certainly, but there was no heart, no soul. Why would anyone want her dead? Well, that was a different question. Not Mark Ruger certainly. He'd taken the coward's way out years ago with letters to solicitors and amicable settlements. They'd metaphorically divided the sofa and the bed in half. Janet had the PC and Mark the Sheltie — it seemed a fair deal.

And Jacquie was still typing up the report at Leighford nick when Jock Haswell announced a visitor. Zarina Liebowitz loomed larger in a confined space than she had at the press conference. Her earrings dangled onto her ample shoulders and the dress she was wearing seemed to be made of several miles of batik.

'I was hoping for Henry Hall,' she said in her Californian drawl.

'Sorry,' said Jacquie. 'The DCI isn't available at the moment. You've got me.'

'DCI?' Dr Liebowitz replied. 'That's a kind of lieutenant, isn't it?'

'Kind of.' Jacquie shrugged. She really had no idea.

'Is there somewhere where we can go, my dear?'

Jacquie drew herself up to her full five feet six. 'Let's get one thing straight, Dr Liebowitz. I am a detective constable. I'm not anybody's dear.'

'Oh, now,' the psychotherapist said. 'I find that very hard to believe. I was assured every co-operation by your Chief Constable.'

Jacquie Carpenter caught Jock Haswell's eye across the corridor and the kindly desk man suddenly found something fascinating in the filing cabinet to check on. Jacquie led the way to Interview Room Two, with its desk, its chairs, its tape recorder.

'Sorry this is a little . . . basic,' she said.

'This'll do fine,' Dr Liebowitz replied. 'Murder is a pretty basic business, after all.'

'Can I get you some coffee?'

'No, thanks, honey — or aren't you anybody's honey either?'

'Let's get another thing straight,' Jacquie offered the woman a seat and took the other one, across the desk from her. 'The Chief Constable may have promised you every co-operation, but to be absolutely frank, I don't know how helpful I can be.'

'That's all right,' the doctor nodded, pulling out a packet of Marlboro. 'Oh, do you mind?'

'Be my guest,' Jacquie said; she who hadn't touched the weed this century.

'Perhaps I can help you.'

'Oh?' Jacquie's tone may have sounded hopeful but her face said it all.

'The murder weapon,' Dr Liebowitz said. 'Can I see it?'

Jacquie shook her head. 'I'm afraid not. It's at the lab undergoing tests.'

'No matter,' the psychotherapist lit up with the age-old skill of one who can puff on a cigarette while in full flow. 'Let me tell you. The dagger that killed Janet Ruger has a double-edged blade, which is five or six inches long. The hilt is made of obsidian, probably with some kind of shamanistic motif. Am I right?'

Jacquie remembered to close her mouth. 'How did you . . . ?'

'I've been here before, DC Carpenter, not once, but many times. The dagger is called an athame. The hilt is black, the colour of death and it would have to be consecrated, like any sacred tool, before use.'

'Consecrated?'

'Sure, to remove any traces of negative or psychic energy. In the hands of a white witch, it can never be used to draw blood. It corresponds to the element of the Air.'

'In the hands of a white witch?' Jacquie repeated.

'What you guys used to call a wise or cunning woman. Somebody who works for good. In the hands of a black witch now . . .'

'And that's what we have here?' Jacquie asked. 'Black witchcraft?'

'Oh, yes,' Dr Liebowitz nodded, staring hard at Jacquie.

'Look,' Jacquie twisted in her chair. 'Can we get something else straight? I mean, this is the twenty-first century.' She was trying to sound like the DCI.

'So?' Dr Liebowitz shrugged. 'I won't bore you with the pedigree of witchcraft. Endor, Pendle, Loudon, Salem — it goes back a long way. And it's too late in the day to start debating whether the Dark One is for real or a dimension of our own psyche. The situation as I see it — the reality in Leighford today — is that there are folks round here for whom he's real enough.'

'What are you talking about?' Jacquie asked, drifting, increasingly, in a sea of psychosis she didn't understand. 'Some kind of organisation?'

'A coven,' Dr Liebowitz said. 'Thirteen people, maybe more. They meet regularly in each other's houses at esbats. On high days and holidays, it's the sabbat — Halloween, Walpurgis. And it's a lot more trick than treat, believe me.'

'Nobody believes in this nonsense,' Jacquie said, wishing Peter Maxwell was there to back her up.

'Oh, but they do,' Dr Liebowitz told her. 'Janet Ruger, for one.'

Jacquie blinked. 'Janet Ruger was a believer?'

'If you mean did she dance skyclad, widdershins around a maypole, I've no idea. But I met this woman. Believe me, she's involved.'

'You met her where?'

'Nottingham, ten years ago.'

'Nottingham?' Jacquie repeated.

'A housing estate called Broxtowe.'

'Had you met Crispin before?' Jacquie asked.

'Crispin Foulkes? No.' Dr Liebowitz blew smoke rings to the ceiling. 'He's quite a dish, isn't he? No, we kept missing each other at Broxtowe, though it's because of him I'm here.'

'Really?'

'Well, him and the local social services. He knew my work, of course. I wrote my PhD on satanic abuse. It's flattering he remembered.'

'And Janet Ruger?'

'Well,' the good doctor became cosy, wriggling nearer on her plump elbows, 'Janet came to see me on the night she died.'

'She did? What time was this?'

'This is the Sunday night. The day before my press conference. It would have been about half eleven.'

'Where?'

'At the Barlichway Estate.'

'The Barlichway? What were you doing there?'

'I wanted to see the place for myself. It's on estates like that the trouble often starts. It did at Broxtowe, Rochdale.'

'You were there alone, just the two of you?'

'Sure. Listen, honey . . . er, detective, I was brought up on the West Coast and believe me, you ain't seen nothing 'til you've sampled the delights of downtown LA.'

'What did you do?' Jacquie asked.

'At the Barlichway?' Dr Liebowitz leaned back as far as her proportions and the police furniture would allow. 'Visited the spot where Albert Walters was found. Bad karma.'

'And?'

'And then I went back to my hotel and she to hers, I guess.'

'What time was this?'

'This would be soon after twelve. I had the press conference the next day and there were some notes I needed to check.'

'Did Janet Ruger say she was meeting somebody else, back at the Brougham?'

'No,' Dr Liebowitz said. 'I can't say that she did.' She looked at her watch, glittering gold on the chubby arm. 'Jesus, look at the time. Sorry, Detective, I've got to run. Listen, we'll talk again, huh?'

Jacquie was still in her chair as the big woman reached the door, 'Oh, yes,' she said. 'I'm sure we will.'

* * *

Metternich looked up at Maxwell with his usual 'And where have you been?' kind of stare. It was always the same. Regular as clockwork when the old bastard was out, that plastic thing in the corner of the lounge would ring and bleep and then start talking to him as if he was standing there. Then it would flash like an alien and every time Maxwell would press a button and the voice would come again, from nowhere.

'Hello, Mr Maxwell, it's Barney. Barney Butler. Look, I think I've got something for you. That bloke' and there was a gap, 'around. And I think I know what. . .' another gap. 'But the reception round here on the old mobile isn't. . . So if you don't get this message, give me a bell, yeah?'

'Thank you, Barney,' Maxwell cancelled the missive, 'Irish as always. I suppose I should be grateful you didn't send me an e-mail in that I haven't got a computer and all.' He noticed the cat looking at him in the corner. 'I've been meaning to ask you, Count — you are, after all, a cat of the world; do you think if dear old Herman Melville had been alive today, he'd have started Moby Dick with "Call me e-mail"? No?'

He rang Barney's mobile. It was switched off. Wasn't it odd, he thought as he changed into the Drama department's donkey jacket and his old gardening boots, how in the days of super-efficient communication and a world gone mad with gadgetry, it was actually more difficult to talk to somebody than ever.

He took a cab in the wet Wednesday to the Barlichway and paid his fare at its edge. His boots squelched on the mud of the grassy rise the mountain bikers had made their own and he padded past the estate map that someone had can-sprayed with that immortal battle cry and mission statement rolled into one 'Fuck off'. It was a far cry from the one Maxwell had painted, by hand, on a bridge near his home when he was a kid — 'Marples Must Go'. He was never quite sure, at the confused age of thirteen, whether Marples was a particularly unpopular transport minister or an ancient lady detective: he'd just liked the ring of the phrase.

Even in the desultory rain that drove from the west and bitter cold, a couple of sad-eyed skateboarders rattled round the windy corners of the Barlichway. A dog barked and, here and there, babies cried, cold and damp and abandoned, while mums got engrossed in Brookside and dads snored over the Tandoori takeaway they'd picked up on the way home.

The Rat was lively as ever that Wednesday night and the rush of heat was welcome as Maxwell opened the door. At the far end, three of the great unwashed calling themselves Dogbreath were psyching up with a sound check, that utterly unnecessary precursor to live music. Electronic crap hurt Maxwell's eardrums and he had to yell to make himself heard by the barman.

'Barney about?'

The barman looked up, froth trickling over his tattooed hand. 'Barney Butler?'

Maxwell nodded.

'He's in hospital, mate.'

'Hospital?' Maxwell frowned. 'What happened?'

'Dunno. Intensive care is all I heard. Fell out of a fucking window, they say.'

Maxwell was out of the door like a bat out of hell, sprinting through the rain for the edge of the estate where he could hail a cab. Men like Barney Butler had grown up on the Barlichway. Even pissed as a fart they didn't miss their footing or fall out of windows. He thought of poor sad Junot, Bonaparte's old buddy, last seen wandering the streets of Madrid stark naked except for sword and epaulettes. He had jumped from a window. But then, Junot was mad. And Berthier, the little Corsican's chief of staff, who had suffered a similar fate. But he was pushed. Barney Butler was no general. He wasn't even a friend of Napoleon's. Yet, he was in intensive care.

* * *

'No, I'm sorry,' the sister was adamant. 'You can't see him now.' Maxwell looked through into the dimly lit room at Leighford General. Barney lay on his back, his head swathed in bandages, tubes trailing from his body to great, grey machines.

'What happened to him?'

The sister had had a long day and was already into a longer night. 'We don't know. Except that he was found in an alleyway with severe head and internal injuries.'

'Will he be all right?'

The sister shrugged. 'Time's the best healer,' she said. 'We're doing all we can.'

'He has a . . . partner,' Maxwell said, struggling even now to be PC to this cold, starched woman. 'Has she been to visit yet?'

'You're the first one,' she told him. 'Shame, isn't it?'

'Nurse,' Maxwell took the woman's arm. 'Had he been drinking?'

'Drinking?' she frowned. 'No, I don't think so. Does that make a difference?'

'Oh, yes,' Maxwell nodded. 'All the difference in the world.'

* * *

'Who's there?' It was an old woman's voice, weak, hesitant.

'My name is Peter Maxwell, Mrs Cruikshank. I'd like to talk to you.'

There was a pause and the rattling of bolts. The door opened an inch or two, no more and Maxwell could see a lined old head peering out. 'What do you want?'

'Just a chat,' Maxwell said. 'About Elizabeth Pride.'

He heard the scrapings of the old girl's throat and heard her spit.

'There are some people,' he said, 'who say you killed her.'

'Fuck 'em,' the old girl growled.

'Well, yes,' said Maxwell, 'that's one solution. Look, it's about forty below out here, Mrs Cruikshank. May I come in?'

The door creaked wider until its hinges gave up the ghost and swung open. Maxwell climbed the steps and stood inside the caravan. He was ankle deep in rubbish.

'Who are you?' Jane Cruikshank looked ill and old. She huddled by a paraffin stove that gave off the old familiar smell that Maxwell remembered from his childhood, when his bedroom was lit by a solitary lamp. For a moment he was there in that terrifying room, his wardrobe a gigantic shadow, its twin knobs the evil eyes of a monster just waiting for darkness to swallow him whole.

'Peter Maxwell,' he told her again. 'Somebody left Elizabeth Pride's body on my doorstep.'

The old girl's eyes widened for a second. 'My boys'll be back soon,' she warned him, suddenly feeling very afraid, very alone. 'They're just out walking the dogs.'

Maxwell had expected the Cruikshank boys. The taxi ride from the hospital all this way out here had cost him an arm and a leg and it was after midnight. But he hadn't been able to wait any longer. People were dying all around him — Liz Pride on his garden path; Andrew Darblay having talked to him; Janet Ruger having sampled his sherry. Somebody had pushed Barney Butler out of a window because he'd talked to and was doing a favour for Peter Maxwell. Mad Max wanted some answers and he wanted them now, tonight.

'Your grandsons,' Maxwell nodded. 'Joe and Ben.'

'That's right,' she said. 'How do you know 'em?'

'We met at Myrtle Cottage,' he told her.

'You got any tobacco?' she asked.

'No,' he said. 'I don't smoke. Tell me about the poppet.'

'The what?' Jane Cruikshank's eyes were suddenly sharp, her mind alert. She was looking at the shadows that filled the room.

'The police have talked to you, haven't they? About a poppet, a doll used in witchcraft.'

''T'ain't me,' the old girl mumbled. 'I told that copper it weren't me. Have you seen it?'

Maxwell nodded.

'You haven't . . . You haven't seen another, have you? Another doll?'

'No,' Maxwell eased himself down on the edge of the battered old chair nearest the door. 'Why?'

'Nothing,' the old girl looked away quickly. 'No reason.' Her voice was thick and rasping and her scrawny chest rose and fell under the shawl she clawed at convulsively. 'My boys'll be back soon, Joe and Ben.'

'Why are they afraid of Myrtle Cottage?' Maxwell asked. 'And why is garlic hanging at the front door?'

'That's a blind,' Jane Cruikshank hissed. 'Beth Pride had the evil eye, she did. Killed my old dog. Drove my lad away and his missus. She'd have got my boys too, if'n I hadn't stopped her.'

'Stopped her, Mrs Cruikshank?' Maxwell raised an eyebrow. 'How? By killing her?'

'I didn't kill her,' the old girl growled. 'Oh, I wished her dead often enough, the old besom. We've got our ways, us Romanies.'

'Poppets?' Maxwell urged. 'The evil eye?'

'Binding,' the old girl croaked. 'That's all. Just binding.'

'By which you mean . . . ?'

Jane Cruikshank fumbled behind her and produced a piece of grey string with knots along its length. 'Binding,' she said. 'It's a spell against the wicked. A curse. It stops the mouths of gossips and prevents disasters.'

'A pity the Reverend Darblay didn't have one of those,' Maxwell said.

Jane Cruikshank tried to chuckle. 'He followed the New Religion, he did. Jumped the wrong way, so to speak. He had no chance.'

'And who killed him, Mrs Cruikshank? Who battered the rector to death in his own church? And the schoolteacher, Ms Thorn, who killed her? They all lived a few miles away from your caravan here. Tell me, is binding,' he tapped the string, .is harmless as it gets? Got any other charms?' He was on his feet, his voice loud, his eyes burning. 'Any other poppets with their heads bashed in or their throats cut?'

The old girl looked up at him, terrified, her hands like claws shaking on the shawl. 'I told you,' she said, 'I don't know nothing about no poppets. No spells. No curses. You leave me alone. My boys'll be back soon.'

Maxwell relented. He was a public schoolboy, for God's sake. And here he was, haranguing an old lady. He crouched down in front of her as she pulled away, a terrified look on her face. 'Can I get you anything, Mrs Cruikshank?' he asked.

'Tobacco,' she said, lip trembling. 'You can get me some tobacco.'

* * *

'Max?' Jacquie Carpenter was still in her dressing-gown, staring at her morning caller, trying to focus.

'Jacquie, I'm sorry it's so early. Can I come in?'

Everything within her screamed no. Her doubts. Her fears. Her utter, total confusion. About who he was. About who she was. Then she saw his face.

'God, Max, you look like shit.'

'I haven't been to bed,' he told her.

'You'd better come in. No bike?'

'Surrey's rest day. You?'

'I'm not on 'til lunchtime. Come into the kitchen. I'm cooking you the full English.'

'Ah, you temptress,' and he pecked her on the cheek. Part of Jacquie Carpenter wanted to hold him, to fold him in her arms and hear him say it was all right. The other half told her to run. But it was too late to run.

'What do you know about Barney Butler?' he asked, grateful for the hot coffee and the warmth of her kitchen-diner.

'Nothing.' Jacquie looked blank, rooting around in her fridge. 'Who he?'

'He's an ex-pupil of mine. Fell out of a window on the Barlichway last night.'

'My God, how awful.'

'More awful than you think. He was pushed.'

Jacquie cracked three eggs on the edge of a bowl. 'You saw this?'

'I saw the results of it. He's in a coma. The hospital are worried.'

'Why do you think he was pushed?'

'Because he was working for me,' he said.

'What?' The next words were out of her mouth before she could help herself. 'A sort of sorcerer's apprentice, you mean?' She bit her lip and turned her back, dealing with the sausages.

'Something like that.' Tired as he was, Maxwell had a nose for nuance. Archness wasn't like Jacquie. That's what he loved about her. Her honesty. That and Heaven in her face. 'He was trailing Willoughby and Ken.'

She turned back to him. 'Why?' Her eyes were wide.

'Because they're up to something. Or at least Willoughby is. I saw him on the Barlichway the night I followed up Albert Walters's murder.'

'Max . .

'I know.' He raised a hand as if in admission. 'I shouldn't be following up murder at all. But you know me, Jacquie. Just can't keep a mad man down.'

She hoped, no, she prayed, that that was all it was; the intellectual curiosity of a man who had lost his way some time ago. When they'd asked him what he wanted to be, he'd said 'teacher' when really he meant 'copper'. It was an easy slip of the tongue to make.

'I asked Willoughby about it. He said he was there on business.' She looked blank. 'A property developer, Jacquie,' he spelt it out, 'on business on a council estate. Pull the other one.'

'Well, you were there innocently enough,' Jacquie hoped as she said it. 'Why shouldn't he be?'

'Because he lied about why he was there,' Maxwell told her. 'I didn't. How well do you know the Crowns — and Ken Templeton too, come to that?'

'Not very,' she shrugged. 'Before they opened Beauregard's, I used to play tennis with Prissy. There was a time, according to Sophie Clark at least, when she and Willoughby were very much in love.'

'And now?'

Jacquie shrugged as the delicious smell of sizzling bacon wafted across the room. 'People change,' she said. 'You've been on the receiving end of Prissy, Max, you know what I'm talking about.'

'Have I?' Maxwell chuckled. 'Who's been talking?'

'Crispin Foulkes.' Again, she could have bitten off her tongue.

'Crispin?' Maxwell frowned. 'Where does he fit into all this?'

'He's another friend of the Crowns. He was at the party, remember?'

'Of course. What about Templeton?'

'Ken?' She took a swig from her coffee as breakfast began to bubble and seethe in the form of scrambled eggs. 'Bit of a non-event, really. Pleasant enough bloke. Miserable little wife, Josie. I think probably he and Prissy were at it like knives at one time.'

'Or swords,' Maxwell said.

'Max?' Jacquie sat down while the toast was browning. 'I hate to ask you this . . . I mean, it's not as if . . . well, what is the state of play between you and Prissy?'

'The state of play?' Maxwell asked, eyebrows raised. 'Well, I can't quite remember the score before she broke free of her electric cord and tried to cut my gonads off, but I think it was two nil. Just her idea of foreplay, really. Jacquie, I know the difficulty you're under, but tell me, give me an inkling — do you have anything in your files on Crown or Templeton?'

'Well,' she responded to the ping of the toaster, 'I don't think so. I'd have to check. But Max, even if there were . . .'

'. . . You couldn't tell me,' he finished off the sentence for her. 'Yes, I know. I've been walking the Barlichway all night, trying to figure it out. The answer's there, somewhere. I know it is.'

'What answer, Max?' Jacquie was afraid to hear herself say it.

'No, no,' Maxwell shook his head. 'It's not about answers yet, Jacquie. It's about questions. Am I asking the right questions? I went to see old Jane Cruikshank too.'

'You did?' She was serving out breakfast.

'What with her and poor old Barney, I had to remortgage for the taxi fare, but hey? How did she strike you? When you interviewed her, I mean?'

'Martin Stone did most of that, but she's hard as nails,' Jacquie remembered, handing Maxwell his plate. 'Pointed a shotgun at us.'

'A shotgun?' Maxwell was appalled. 'Jesus, Jacquie, you didn't tell me that.'

'There's a lot I haven't told you, Max,' she said softly. 'Can't tell you. Ever.'

He looked into her eyes and nodded. 'I know,' he said. Then he sprinkled salt over his meal and got stuck in. 'Mmm, full English to die for.'

'Cholesterolly speaking,' she said, 'very likely.'

'Don't tell me,' he looked at her empty plate. 'You're going to do the whole guilt trip by eating budgie food?'

'Ryvita,' she told him.

'That's what I said,' he said.

'What did Jane Cruikshank tell you? Anything?' Jacquie asked.

'Oh, yes,' said Maxwell, between sausages. 'She's not the same Jane Cruikshank spitting fire and brimstone over you boys. She's a sick, tired old lady. And she's very afraid.'

'Of what?' Jacquie asked.

'The witchfinder,' Maxwell said. 'The witchfinder.'

CHAPTER 16

'Who are you?' the elderly woman with the battleship-grey hair wanted to know.

'I'm Constable Haswell, madam. Can I help . . .'

She looked him up and down, what was visible of him above the counter at the entrance to Leighford nick. 'I doubt it. Who's in charge?'

'In charge, madam? May I ask what it's in connection with?' Jock Haswell had seen the lot in his years on the force. This was one of those 'go to the top' people, don't bother with the hoi-polloi beneath.

'It's in connection with Detective Sergeant Stone.'

'Really?' alarm bells were sounding in the desk man's ears. 'And why . . . ?'

'You!' The old lady was clearly tired of the monkey and bounded across as well as her arthritic hip would allow to try the organ grinder.

'Yes?' Jacquie Carpenter had drawn the short straw again. It was her bad luck to be on her way to the car park just then.

'Possibly in these enlightened times, you do more than make the tea around here.'

Jacquie caught Haswell's eye. How many more mad-women would she be called upon to handle? 'Yes,' she leaned against the doorframe and folded her arms, 'I am a detective constable.'

'Hm,' the old lady snorted. 'Well, that's one up from that, anyway,' she was pointing at Jock Haswell. 'Do you have a private room where we can talk?'

'Madam,' Jacquie said, 'I'm afraid I'm rather busy. Perhaps Constable Haswell . . . ?'

Jock was flapping his arms wildly in the background.

'It's about Martin Stone,' she said. 'I am his mother-in-law and he has kidnapped my daughter and grandchild.'

Jacquie's arms unfolded and she found herself standing upright. 'Interview Room Three, Jock,' she said. 'Get a message to the Incident Room I'll be a few minutes late, would you?'

* * *

Veronica Saunders didn't look like a madwoman. She didn't sound like one either. It was what she said that made Jacquie Carpenter sit up and take notice.

'This has happened before,' the old woman said. 'When Janey was born. It's as if he can't bear the competition.'

'The competition?' Jacquie was trying to be sympathetic. Her own world had turned upside down and the bodies lay head to toe in Jim Astley's morgue in some insane danse macabre. Normally, Jacquie wouldn't have given Veronica Saunders the time of day. But she was talking about her immediate boss, a man Jacquie had shared murder with. You didn't just walk away from colleagues like that. Or colleagues' mothers-in-law.

'He's a child, you see. I saw it from day one. Alex's father was just the same. They have to come first. Anthony once told me, "I'm the only child in this house." He was never quite the same after Alex was born.'

'Alex is an only child, Mrs Saunders?'

'Oh, yes,' the woman said. 'She took enough of a toll on Anthony's fragile mind. A second would have tipped him over the edge. Now I'm not enough of a psychologist to know whether Alex chose Martin because he reminded her deep down of her father — that's all rather Freudian, isn't it? I do know that when Janey was born, he took her away.'

'The baby?'

'Yes. I had this distraught phone call from Alex to say the little one had gone — been taken from her cot. This time, it's both of them.'

'Both?' Jacquie was confused. 'Where's Janey?'

'With Dorothy, Martin's mother, in Littlehampton. I can just about see the sense of that. In fact, I offered to have the little mite myself, just until Alex gets fully back on her feet, you know.'

'Have you talked to Martin about this?' Jacquie asked.

'Please, my dear,' Veronica growled. 'Give me some credit. That was how I found out they'd gone in the first place. When Alex didn't ring at the usual time I went round there. He'd been evasive on the phone, telling me she was out, at his mother's, anywhere. I didn't believe it. When I rang Dorothy, sure enough, she hadn't seen either of them for days. In the end I rang the police.'

'Which station?'

'This one. That was two days ago. Got some idiot, I suspect that ancient chappie on the desk out there. He assured me every avenue was being explored. I didn't believe that either.'

'Mrs Saunders,' Jacquie reached out and patted the old woman's veiny hands, 'I don't want you to worry. We are exploring every avenue, believe me. I'm going to send a WPC in now to take a written statement from you. I expect you could do with a cuppa, too, couldn't you?'

'I could do with some action, my dear,' Veronica said.

Jacquie stood up. 'You'll get it,' she said and the smile hadn't left her face before she'd left the room.

'Jock,' Jacquie stood head to head with the man, even though she only reached his tie-knot. 'I want to see all the calls logged on that machine within the last forty-eight hours — no, make that seventy-two.'

'Seventy-two hours?' Haswell chuckled. 'Come on, Jacquie.'

'And while I'm checking that, get Brenda into Room Three. You make that woman a cup of tea, but don't you dare take it in yourself. She'll have your throat out. And do you know, I might just lend her the razor to do it with.'

* * *

Peter Maxwell remembered Nicole Green. She'd been slimmer then, with too much make-up, hanging round the bike sheds with the boys. Now she was pale, sitting in the long watches of the night holding the hand of the man she loved. She looked at him under his bandages, at the trailing tubes and the thumping green lines on the screen that told her he was still alive. She couldn't take this in, not any of it. She just felt cold and numb, not even embarrassed by her old History teacher who sat across the bed from her, leaning forward, as if he was willing the young man in the bed to get up, to stir, something.

'This is my fault, Nicole,' she heard him say. 'All of it.'

'How's that, Mr Maxwell?' Her eyes never left Barney's.

'He was doing some work for me.'

'What, DIY you mean?'

Maxwell shook his head. 'No. Snooping. On the Barlichway. I asked him to keep an eye out for two blokes.'

'Everybody knows Barney on the Barlichway, Mr Maxwell. And he knows everybody. Nobody would do this to him.'

'Do you think he fell?' Maxwell asked.

Beyond the glass partition, nurses in green and white dresses came and went, Milburn's angels flitting around the antiseptic corridors like moths in the half light.

'Nicole,' Maxwell reached out and took the girl's hand. 'Do you think he fell?'

She turned to face him, her cheeks running with tears, her nose and eyes red. She was shaking her head. 'No, Mr

Maxwell, I don't.' Without any warning, she got up and ran to him, he who'd put her in detention for not doing her homework, who'd warned her mum that work had to come before boys. She ran to him and as he stood up, she threw her arms around his neck, burying her face in his scarf. She smelt of cigarette smoke and the interior of the Rat, but her cheek was wet against his.

'He'll be all right, Mr Maxwell, won't he? My Barney — he'll be all right?'

He stroked the long, damp hair and snuggled briefly against her. Five years ago he'd have been struck off for doing this. Now he was her dad, her best mate, the last lonely raft in a sea of pain and fear and despair. 'Of course he will, darling,' he said, softly. 'He'll be fine.' Then he held her limp body at arm's length, his hands strong, his smile firm. 'In all the years you've known him,' he said, 'did Mad Max ever tell you a lie?'

She smiled back through the tears. 'Yeah,' she sniffed. 'Just once. You told me I could get Grade C GCSE History,' and they laughed together in the silence of Barney's room.

* * *

The spotty youth on the desk was just about to go off duty when Maxwell arrived at Beauregard's. It was late and the place would close in an hour. He was grateful not to be on the graveyard shift itself. The place was getting him down.

'Mr Crown in tonight?' Maxwell called through the Perspex.

'In the pool, I think,' the spotty youth said. 'Er . . . did I ask you about your veruccas?'

'They're coming on a treat,' Maxwell called back, striding clown the atrium. 'John Innes Number Two is the answer. I'm exhibiting them come spring.'

He cut through the side door and crossed the corridor, following the signs to the pool. To his left the changing rooms echoed to the sounds of the last punters spraying their armpits prior to going home. A solitary figure stood on the high diving board at the far end of the pool. Sophie Clark looked positively mouthwatering in her black bikini as she soared skyward before jack-knifing and twisting in mid-air to hit the water like an arrow.

Maxwell was impressed. The last time he'd done that, the water had slapped him so hard he'd nearly passed out and carried the red reminder of it for days.

'Well, well,' a cold voice echoed as Sophie's ripples died away. 'Maxwell.'

He hadn't seen her there before, but lolling at the water's edge, in a fittingly scarlet swimsuit which left little to the imagination, sat Prissy Crown. She wasn't smiling. In that get-up, she didn't have to.

Sophie bobbed to the surface and swam to her.

'Well, well,' said Maxwell in return. 'The ladies who lunge.'

'That's Prissy,' Sophie said, reaching the side and running both hands back through her long, blonde hair. 'I dive.'

'And plunge. Very sporty, both of you.' Maxwell crouched above her. He gave Prissy his best John Wayne. 'I've come for my bike.'

'It's at home,' she said, stretching back to reveal as much of her body as possible.

'Let's get it, then,' he stood up. 'Willoughby won't be there, will he? The surly little zit on the door told me he was here. Clearly not.'

'Why, clearly not?' Prissy asked.

'When two or three are gathered together,' Maxwell said, 'you can guess they won't be Mr and Mrs Willoughby Crown. Going to join us, Sophie?'

The blonde girl looked at Prissy, her mouth slightly open, her eyes unsure. 'Three's a bit of a crowd in this case, isn't it?' And she threw herself backwards to crash through the dappling water.

'Give me five,' said Prissy, standing up and wrapping a towel around her bare neck. 'You know,' she purred, stroking the curve of Maxwell's cheek, 'you'll have to work for that bike, don't you?'

'What is it the good book says?' Maxwell asked her. 'Men must work and women must weep?'

'Now don't tell me you've suddenly got religion?' she laughed.

'Oh, I've always had religion,' Maxwell said. 'The question is, is it Old or New?'

* * *

The Crown house looked different in darkness. True, the security light came on as the Shogun snarled onto the gravel, but the last time Maxwell had seen it, it was party time. All the lights had been blazing and the poppers were popping and the bucks were fizzing. It looked quite dead now with its windows dark in the ivy.

She let them both in and threw her keys onto a table.

'Not the mat?' Maxwell asked.

Prissy snorted her horsy laugh. 'I think you need a drink, Maxwell. Scotch?'

'Southern Comfort if you've got it.'

'Sure,' she shrugged, hauling off her coat and tossing it over an armchair. 'Make yourself at home.'

He did. He placed his hat, scarf and coat carefully in a neat pile beside hers and plonked himself down in an armchair.

'Now, now,' she growled, coming back with two large ones. 'Don't tell me you're afraid to sit on the settee.'

'This is comfy,' Maxwell said, snuggling down.

'Good.' Prissy handed him his drink. 'It's good to see you again, Maxwell.'

He raised his glass to her. 'Here's to corruption in low places.'

She didn't always understand Maxwell's conversation, but Prissy Crown never let a little thing like incomprehension stand in her way. She sat opposite him on the long velvet settee, her breasts jutting out of her blouse, her legs crossed and swinging slightly. Maxwell wondered how many come-on positions the woman had. At least she hadn't got her tongue down his throat — yet.

'So where *is* Willoughby then?' he asked.

'Who cares?' she asked. 'He leads his life. I lead mine.'

'I was hoping to have a word,' Maxwell told her.

A thought occurred to Prissy and she sat up. 'You're not into that, are you? A threesome, I mean? Of course, I couldn't contemplate it with Willoughby, but Ken might oblige.'

'Really?' Maxwell enthused. 'Do you think so?'

'Oh, yes,' she smirked. 'Ken's all right, actually. Oh, he's a bit . . . inhibited at first, but once he's warmed up . . .'

'He and his wife . . .' Maxwell probed.

'Josie? She's a mouse. And about as exciting in bed, apparently. No, Ken comes to me if he wants a woman.'

'And you go . . . ?'

'My, my,' Prissy purred, 'but aren't you the naughty one? I bet you'd like that, wouldn't you? Me and Sophie perhaps? It's every man's dream, isn't it? A ménage with me and Sophie? Well, I'd have to ask her. She needs a bit of coaxing, does Sophie.'

'You've got over your fear, then?' Maxwell asked.

'What?' Prissy blinked.

'When we last met, you were convinced there was something going on. It involved Willoughby and Ken and Sophie. "Sinister" I think was the word you used. It's Latin for left-handed.'

Prissy put down her drink and swayed across the room. Before Maxwell could move, she'd ripped off her blouse and unhooked her black lacy bra. Her breasts bounced free, her nipples taut in the dim light of the lounge. 'I've asked you this before,' she growled, standing in front of him. 'Are you fucking Jacquie Carpenter?'

He clambered wearily to his feet. 'Talking of fucking,' he put his drink down and held her cheek with his right hand, his face dangerously close to hers. Already her eyes were closing, her mouth opening for his kiss. 'That's none of your fucking business, is it? Where's my bike?'

Prissy stood there for a moment, shaking with rage, her face a livid mask of anger. Then she snaked out with her right hand, but Maxwell was faster. He caught her wrist and held it in mid-air. 'Tsk, tsk,' he said. 'You really must work on that riposte of yours. Never mind, I'll find the bike myself.' He walked away from her and turned back at the hall door, 'And put some clothes on, Prissy, my love. You'll catch your death.'

* * *

It didn't exactly take an MA in History to find White Surrey. Intuitively perhaps, he tried the garage first, cutting through the kitchen and there the thing was, leaning nonchalantly against a wall. His MA in History was less useful however when he tried to open the garage door. Risking a hernia by tugging at various metal projections, he finally saw the electric button and pushed it. There was a click and a drone and the gravel drive came into view. Maxwell wheeled Surrey out into the cold night, his breath wreathing ahead of him.

It was only then that he happened to glance up at a bedroom window. Prissy was standing there, a housecoat round her nakedness, clearly screaming at someone across the room. Even through the double glazing, Maxwell could hear the raised voices. Something made him wait, pull back into the shadows, the gleaming white of Surrey's frame hidden in the bushes. Doors were slamming through the house, lights flashing on and off. He almost broke his cover when he heard the shattering of glass, but checked himself and still he waited.

He saw a figure dart into the garage and he ducked behind the wall, flattening himself as best he could between it and the bushes. The BMW inside snarled into life as the headlight beams lit the gravel and the tail end of Prissy's Shogun. He noted the number as it crunched away across the drive, sending showers of pebbles in its wake. No need to chase the car, he mused. He knew who it was and he knew where he was going.

* * *

By the time Maxwell got there, the Barlichway was like a scene from the French revolution. Ugly mobs roamed the streets, baying for blood. He kept White Surrey with him for a fast getaway. Knots of lads, not much older than the ones he taught, were prowling the darkness, chanting and singing. He heard the metallic ping of kicked cans and the shattering of glass. Not a good night to be a stranger on the Barlichway.

He crossed Lion Square with the wind at his back, wheeling Surrey when he could into the shadows. It was here, he remembered, they'd found the body of Albert Walters, sitting upright, grinning horribly at the world he'd just left. The wailing sirens and flashing blue lights told him the law had arrived. From nowhere, mattresses and furniture were being hurled into the street, anti-establishment hands twisting and piling the debris into makeshift barricades. It was Madame Da Farge and Victor Hugo all over again. He expected the street prowlers to break into songs from *Les Mis* any minute.

But no one was singing, not anything he could recognize anyway. They were roaring taunts at the line of dark blue coppers forming up beyond the square. An explosion of flame ripped through the darkness as someone torched a car. In seconds, it was a blazing wreck, columns of flame illuminating the tawdry flats overhead. Now the mob were throwing bricks, supermarket baskets, anything, at the lengthening line of plastic shields. People were lighting torches from the burning cars, whirling them around their heads like Napalm.

Maxwell couldn't make out faces. Many of the yobs had wrapped scarves round their mouths, others wore balaclavas. It was Derry and the Falls Road. Bloody Sunday had come to the Barlichway. There were kids in the crowd now, hurling abuse and debris along with their elders. Tarts in tight jeans psyched up their men. But Maxwell was close enough to see .in older element in the throng, tight-lipped with hatred, their faces gaunt with anger and defiance.

This kind of thing happened in summer, when the heat and the flies and the hose-pipe ban combined to distress an already tetchy people, depressed by long-term unemployment and endless repeats on the telly. It never happened in the bleak midwinter when the cold and the rain kept people indoors. And it had never ever happened on the Barlichway until now.

Maxwell's line of retreat was cut off. Unwilling to abandon his bike to the mercies of the mob, he couldn't with safety cut across the open square to the line of riot shields. To his right the braver or more foolhardy of the mob were edging closer. It would only be a matter of time before they edged around his corner, for the shelter of the darkness. And then he'd be part of them.

Scenting blood, television camera crews were circling the edge of the police lines, cameramen with that wonderful facility for walking backwards carrying heavy and expensive loads. A police van was braying out the same message over a tannoy, over and over again, but much of it was lost in the wind and the roaring of the crowd.

The crowd were black beetles crawling against a sea of fire behind them where three, now four cars blazed. The riot shields answered them, flames leaping in their reflectors and on the visors of the police. Maxwell prayed that Jacquie wasn't somewhere in that lot. Or that Nicole wasn't one of the harpy characters among the sans-culottes to his right. He could feel the heat now from the nearest blaze licking his eyebrows and scorching his scarf. He flattened himself further into the shadows and saw with horror the line of horses splaying out in the darkness at the edge of the square.

The historian in him remembered Peterloo. When the local police chief in Manchester nearly two centuries ago, had been unable to move the crowd, they sent in the Manchester and Salford Yeomanry, who hacked about them, right and left. It was slaughter.

'Not the horses!' He broke his cover, leaping onto Surrey's saddle and pedalling like a demon. 'For God's sake, you don't need that!'

Nobody heard him. Three shields came up to the level as he desperately swerved trying to avoid them. He felt something hard and sharp hit him full in the back and then Surrey's front wheel locked and he slithered across the tarmac, feeling rather than hearing his trousers rip and tear and his leg along with them. There was a night stick under his chin, two powerful arms gripping him and he was hauled upright. Before he had time to gain his balance, there was an almighty roar and the mob burst forward. He barely had time to turn when the horses clattered into the centre, the shield wall breaking as the cavalry smashed through. Their timing was off however and the thin blue line wavered and shook as the Barlichway Light Infantry crashed into the shields.

Maxwell was suddenly free of his captors. The night stick had gone, swung round in defence of its owner. His right arm was free as the man who had held it was carried struggling backwards thirty or forty feet.

'Don't take this personally,' Maxwell said to the constable still clinging to his left arm and he brought his knee up sharply in the man's groin.

'Brilliant, mate!' a yob shouted alongside him. 'But next time, use this,' and he thrust a length of lead pipe into Maxwell's fist. The Head of Sixth Form looked at it, unsure whether to go for the next policeman or the bloke who'd just given it to him. In the event, he threw it away.

'Enough of this dithering, Maxwell,' he said to himself. 'Time to come off the fence.'

He dragged the horizontal bike out from under a fallen rioter and steadied the man before wheeling away into the night. He'd done the valour bit. Time now for a spot of discretion.

'Where the fuck are you going?' somebody asked him.

'Getting another chain,' Maxwell screeched to a halt. A huge man, all tattoos and attitude had straddled his handlebars, so Maxwell gave him the equivalent of a Barlichway kiss.

He jabbed his fingers into the idiot's eyes and pushed him aside, hauling the bike around and pedalling over the grassy rise to freedom.

On the mountain-bikers' ridge he halted, out of breath, his back in half and a throbbing in his jaw where a night stick had caught him. The battle was all but over now as the boys in blue had retaliated, their well-organized baton charge driving the black beetles back, across their own square through the blazing vehicles. Fire engines were edging forward behind the police line, ready to throw their power-hoses on flames or people alike. The tide of war had ebbed as quickly as it had swelled and the mob was limping home to lick its wounds and hide behind locked doors and deny all knowledge.

Maxwell, too, had had enough. He eased Surrey's gears into position and felt the wind in his face as he turned to the sea. As he pedalled past an abandoned car, all its windows smashed and its paintwork scraped, he recognized the registration number. A battered BMW. Police aware.

* * *

There was, as he expected, no reply from Jacquie's place. She hadn't switched on her answerphone and the hour was late. With difficulty, Maxwell stripped off his shirt and twisted in the bathroom mirror to check his back. A stone or something like it had caught him high on the left shoulder blade and the bruise was purple and spreading. Somehow he had gashed his forehead in the clash of arms and he was still patching himself up when the phone rang. Going to answer it, he left a small trail of blood across the bedroom carpet.

'War Office,' he winced as the Savlon stung.

'Max, is that you?'

'Yes. Who's this?'

'It's Crispin Foulkes, Max. I'm sorry to ring you at this hour, but we have to talk.'

'All right, Crispin,' Maxwell said. 'I couldn't sleep anyway.'

'No, I mean, face to face, Max. Columbine, isn't it?'

'Thirty-eight,' Maxwell told him.

'A bientôt,' and the social worker hung up.

* * *

But it wasn't Crispin Foulkes hanging on Maxwell's doorbell in the wee hours. Not at first. It was a large, brassy-looking woman in a sheepskin coat and dangly earrings.

'Mr Maxwell. I'm Zarina Leibowitz.' Her handshake was firm, her accent West Coast. 'You bump your head?'

'From time to time,' Maxwell smiled and noticed Foulkes hovering like a male sun fish by the large woman's shoulder. 'You didn't tell me we were having female company, Crispin; I'd have rinsed my smalls.'

'Max, Zarina is . . .'

'An expert on multi-generational incest. Yes, I know. I was at her press conference.'

'There'll be another one tomorrow,' the social worker said. 'There's been trouble on the Barlichway.'

'Do tell,' Maxwell replied, opening the door for them. 'I've just come from there.'

'You have?' Foulkes looked concerned. 'God, Max . . . the bump on your head . . .'

'All part of my riotous lifestyle,' the Head of Sixth Form clicked his tongue. 'I'd show you my other bruises, only it might embarrass the good doctor.'

'Honey,' she turned on Maxwell's stairs. 'You ain't got nothing I haven't seen before,' and she plodded on up to his lounge.

'Just what I need after a good beating,' Maxwell said to Foulkes. 'A homespun shrink with a couchside manner to die for. I take it this isn't a social call by social services?'

'I'm afraid not, Max,' Crispin said solemnly, 'it's all gone way beyond friendly.'

CHAPTER 17

'What were you doing on the Barlichway, Max?' Foulkes sat in the Great Man's lounge, sipping the Great Man's Southern Comfort. 'If you don't mind my asking.'

'Or even if you do,' Dr Leibowitz added. 'I'm sorry to be so blunt, Mr Maxwell, but we're past the niceties now.'

Maxwell nodded. 'Trying to make sense of what I saw,' he said. 'I still am.'

'Let me help you,' Foulkes put his glass down on the coffee table. 'Someone has leaked allegations about the late Alison Thorn.'

'Allegations?'

Foulkes looked at Zarina Leibowitz. 'Well, it's common knowledge now, I suppose. It'll be all over tabloid land tomorrow.'

'Not to mention your quality press,' the psychotherapist added.

'You've got to remember, Max, the kids at Wetherton School come from the Barlichway. They're only five or six. And . . . well, various things have been going on.'

'Things?' Maxwell blinked. 'At the school?'

'Have a look at this,' Foulkes pulled a dog-eared piece of paper from his coat pocket.

'Jesus,' Maxwell whistled through his teeth.

'Not the first name that sprang to my mind,' Zarina said.

A devil's face leered at Maxwell from the bright yellow A5 sheet, its tongue protruding obscenely in the direction of a little girl, spread-eagled on an altar.

'Where did you get this?' he asked.

'They're all over the Barlichway,' Foulkes told him. 'Somebody delivered them, door to door earlier tonight. Look at the back.'

Maxwell did. '"*Grey, grey, devil's day; white, white, hide from light.*" What does that mean?'

Foulkes looked at Zarina again. 'Doctor?' he said.

'We think it's some sort of mantra,' she leaned forward, cradling her left knee in her hands. 'Exactly what, we don't know. Grey witchcraft, white witchcraft. It's only a guess.'

'Thomas Grey, Thomas Grey,' Maxwell remembered.

'What?'

'God, yes,' Foulkes clicked his fingers. 'Your calendar. I'd forgotten that, Max.'

'Calendar?' Zarina raised an eyebrow. 'Somebody mind filling me in here?'

'The first in our little ol' series of murders,' Maxwell said, freshening everybody's glass. 'I found a calendar in the dead woman's house. Myrtle Cottage.'

'Myrtle?' Zarina echoed. 'That's quaint.'

'What is?'

'Myrtle was used in the old days to ward off evil,' she told him. 'The evil eye specifically.'

'The calendar was marked with various dates . . .'

'Occult dates,' Foulkes butted in. 'Samhain, Beltane . . .'

'And December 21st, the shortest day. "*Thomas Grey, Thomas Grey*".'

'So this woman . . . er . . . Pride, was it? She was a practising witch?'

'Yes,' Maxwell mused. 'And I'm Beelzebub.'

'Baal,' Zarina murmured. 'Lord of the Flies, Prince of devils, next in crime to Satan. Now, why should you mention him, Mr Maxwell?'

‘It was a sort of joke, Dr Leibowitz,’ Maxwell said.

Zarina was shaking her large head, the chins wobbling, the earrings swinging.

‘There’s nothing funny about this, Max,’ Foulkes was solemnity itself. ‘What happened on the Barlichway tonight proved that.’

‘It happens on estates,’ Zarina said, her eyes never leaving Maxwell’s. ‘Rochdale, Broxtowe . . .’

‘What happens?’ Maxwell shouted. He shook the crumpled piece of paper. ‘This sick nonsense? Where does it come from?’

Zarina leaned back, taking a calm sip from her amber class. ‘Mr Maxwell, Crispin suggested we come to you in your position as a teacher.’

‘Oh?’

‘Leighford High, isn’t it?’ she checked. ‘Where you teach?’

He nodded. ‘So rumour has it.’

‘You’ll have to forgive me,’ she smiled. ‘I’m not familiar with British High Schools. How old are your kids?’

‘Eleven to eighteen,’ he said.

‘Okay. You . . . er . . . picked up any vibes from them, oh, I don’t know, scraps of conversations, parties, swimming pools maybe? Dead babies?’

‘Dead babies?’ Maxwell repeated. ‘I’m sorry, Dr Leibowitz, I don’t have the time to eavesdrop on the children I teach. But if I catch any conversation at all, it’s about last night’s match or who’s groping whom. I don’t tend to get complete recitals of the Black Mass.’

‘Please don’t joke, Mr Maxwell,’ Zarina was stone-faced. ‘I don’t think you realise how much trouble you’re in.’

‘Really?’ Maxwell leaned back now, trying to make this woman out. ‘How?’

She looked at Foulkes, who nodded. ‘Elizabeth Pride’s body is found on your doorstep. You go to her house and find an occult calendar — you say.’

‘That’s right,’ Maxwell said. ‘I do.’

'You talk to Andrew Darblay, the rector, who dies next. We haven't been able to establish a contact with Arthur Walters . . . except you were at the Barlichway tonight, for example, where the old guy was found dead. Janet Ruger comes to your house . . . this house, before she dies. And it wouldn't be beyond the realms of possibility that you and Alison Thorn knew each other — I mean, two teachers in a small neck of the woods . . .'

'Wait a minute,' Maxwell said. 'You're forgetting I've got a blackish cat and live alone. Sorry, I can't help with the broomstick; would a Hoover do?'

Zarina was shaking her head again. 'I'm afraid flippancy won't save you, Mr Maxwell,' she said.

'Save me?' Maxwell repeated. 'From what?'

'Life imprisonment,' she told him. 'Or a padded cell — I can't decide which.'

'So,' Maxwell raised both his hands. 'Let's see if I've got this right? I'm some sort of black magician, a sort of Agrippa-cum-John-Dee-cum-David-Copperfield. I decide to kill people, starting with one I leave cunningly on my own doorstep to belay suspicion. That's so fiendishly clever, I frighten myself sometimes.'

'Mr Maxwell,' Zarina was calmness itself, focused, in control. 'We've got to let you in on a teeny white lie.'

'Really?' Maxwell couldn't wait to hear what else the woman was going to charge him with.

'I've been in Leighford, staying at the Grand, for a few weeks now, ever since Elizabeth Pride died, in fact. Crispin wired me the moment it became public knowledge. I recognised all the symptoms on the Barlichway. He did absolutely right to call me. I've interviewed all of Ms Thorn's little class at Wetherton School. And I think we've got hard evidence of ritual Satanic abuse.'

Maxwell remembered to close his mouth. 'Such as?' he asked.

'Witch parties,' she sighed, appalled by the litany she was about to recite. 'Dead babies. Specifically abortion, infants with their heads bashed in, animal sacrifice, transportation. Murdered children hanging around the necks of adults. Talk of a monster, urine, faeces, a mysterious church, the drinking of human blood.'

Maxwell shrugged. 'Could be a storyboard for Home and Away,' he nodded.

'For Christ's sake, Max!' Foulkes snapped. 'This isn't make believe. It's happening. Here. In Leighford. On the Barlichway. In the twenty-first century.'

Maxwell looked at them both. 'Dr Leibowitz,' he said softly. 'I assume, perhaps because I'm impressed by qualifications, that you are an intelligent woman. You're familiar with that late great countryman of yours, Senator Joseph McCarthy, one of the sickest, most bigoted men the world has produced. And, no doubt, you're familiar with another countryman of yours, John Hawthorne of Massachusetts. Different era, same sickness. What was it Arthur Miller said in *The Crucible* "the devil's loose in Salem, Mr Proctor"? Well,' he leaned forward, 'the devil's not loose in Leighford. Nor on the Barlichway, take my word for it. Whoever killed these people is flesh and blood, like you and me. And, Dr Leibowitz, I don't know where you got that nonsense from, but it's not from any kids I ever knew.'

Zarina Leibowitz hauled herself to her feet. 'That's a pretty speech, Mr Maxwell. I would imagine Father Urbain Grandier said something not dissimilar in the market place at Loudun before they burned him alive. Just look at the evidence.' She snatched up the leaflet from his coffee table. 'You're supposed to be a historian, dammit. Witch parties — you been to a party recently, Mr Maxwell?'

He was standing with her now, remembering the first time he'd met Prissy and Willoughby Crown.

'What about a mysterious church? That — and the pun'll no doubt kill you — ring any bells?'

The Gothic tomb of Sir John Viney crept into his vision, dark with Andrew Darblay's blood.

'How about swimming pools? Had a dip the other day?'

He saw Sophie Clark hit the water like an arrow and heard Prissy laughing at him from her corner of the Beauregard pool.

'Satanic indicators, Mr Maxwell,' Zarina was saying, staring into his eyes. 'Crispin and I, we've been there. And what you saw on the Barlichway tonight, that was just the beginning, believe me.'

'What are you going to do?' he asked as they made their way to his stairs.

'We're bringing in the full weight of the law. Police, the courts, child protection agencies. There'll be arrests, a full public inquiry of course, we need to do some rooting out here. There's a nest at the Barlichway. But you should be grateful, Mr Maxwell; John Hawthorne would have burnt the place down. Oh, by the way,' Zarina paused at the top of Maxwell's stairs with Foulkes at her elbow, 'you might be able to interpret this one for me. A little girl, right here on the Barlichway, told me she'd seen a naughty policeman killing babies. You got any ideas about that, Beelzebub?'

* * *

It was sixth-form assembly that Monday, when the cream of Leighford's youth shambled into their Common Room for ten minutes of uplifting haranguing from Mr Maxwell. Except Mr Maxwell wasn't there. And Helen Maitland, aka the Fridge, did the honours instead.

Peter Maxwell was helping the police with their inquiries.

'Everything all right, Max?' Legs Diamond, the Headmaster, had asked as he saw Maxwell escorting a pretty plainclothes woman he thought he knew towards his office.

'Sweet,' Maxwell grunted, winking at him, leaving Diamond wondering which of his many personae Maxwell was being this morning.

'You heard about the Barlichway?' had been the question on everybody's lips in the staffroom that morning. James Diamond had moved among his staff, reminding them not to gossip with the kids, but to keep their ears open. Careless talk costs lives. Be like dad — keep mum etc, etc.

'Not a social call, then?' Maxwell read Jacquie's body language like an open book.

She stood, arms folded in his office, facing a fanatical James Cagney in *Shake Hands With the Devil*, I left the uniformed copper in the car,' she said, 'because I wanted to say things I can't say while he's around.'

'Won't you at least sit down?' He did, trying to ease the moment.

Jacquie ignored the offer and crossed to the window. A leaden sky promised rain beyond Leighford High's boundaries. An old man walked his dog and a sudden shaft of sunlight caught the flat line of the sea. 'Max, what were you doing at the Barlichway last Friday?'

'Ah,' he turned to her, looking up at the back of her head.

'Who's been talking? The Mr Plod whose gonads I crushed or the one intent on strangling me with his nightstick?'

'We've got you on CCTV,' she said. 'You and lots of others. But the scarf was kind of distinctive.'

'Curses!' Maxwell clicked his fingers, 'it took you a while to recognise it.'

'Well?' It had been a long weekend, one way or another.

He stood up and took her shoulders in his hands, spinning her round. 'Jacquie,' he said softly, his dark eyes burning into her soul. 'Are you asking me as Detective Constable Carpenter of Leighford CID or as Jacquie Carpenter, the woman I love?'

'The woman you . . . ?' and her voice tailed away. For a second she looked away. Had to look away. Then her head was up again, her eyes on a level with his. 'Why were you there?'

He dropped his hands, his question answered. 'I was following Willoughby Crown,' he said.

'Willoughby?' she frowned. 'Why?'

'Because he was at the Barlichway that night and I need to know why. Did you pick him up on your tellies?'

She shook her head. 'No, but we found his car, wrecked and abandoned.'

'So did I,' he nodded. 'Have you talked to him?'

'We're making inquiries,' she said.

Maxwell smiled. 'Cryptic as ever,' he winked. 'How's young Hall?'

'You gave him the calendar, Max. Thank you for that.'

'That's all right,' he shrugged, wandering alongside her and gazing out of the window. Leighford's hapless Under-14 rugger team were going through their paces, fumbling badly in midfield and using weak tackles as an excuse to wrestle. 'Wouldn't know a maul from a pear tree,' he muttered. Then he turned back to Jacquie. 'I duly await my summons to the Tower for withholding vital evidence,' he said. 'What's he got now before the Chief Constable pulls the plug? A day? Two?'

'It got to him, Max,' Jacquie was leaning against the windowsill. 'He sat in his office, either at the Incident Room or the nick. God knows how many hours he put in. He said it was flu that was making him just sit there. I think he's cracked. He went on Friday. The last bit of news he got was the riot on the Barlichway. The irony was, he asked for those two days you suggested — I told him to. He had until February the 2nd. Then that . . .'

'I'm sorry,' Maxwell said. 'Talking of cracking, have you met the witch queen of New Orleans?'

'Who?' Jacquie frowned.

'Zarina Leibowitz?'

Jacquie's face said it all. 'Pretty in your face, isn't she?'

'In your face, yes. Pretty? Well, it's in the eye of the beholder, really, that one, isn't it? What do you know about naughty policemen?'

'What?' Jacquie blinked.

'Just a phrase I picked up. Something about naughty policemen killing babies.'

Jacquie's mouth opened, but no sound came out. She looked at him oddly, then cleared her throat. 'Where did you hear this, Max?'

'Leibowitz,' he said. 'She made a point of it. It was the last thing she said as she and Crispin left my house on Friday night. Or should I say Saturday morning?'

'What did they want?'

'Ah, well, there you have me. On the one hand she seemed to want to pick my brains, me being a teacher and all; on the other, she seemed to imply I was the anti-Christ doomed to spend eternity stoking the fires. She was obviously confusing me with dear old Betty Martin, our caretaker.'

'Max, I've got to go.'

'And the Barlichway?' he turned to face her.

'We'll need a statement,' she said. 'I don't know what will happen. We're slowly rounding people up.'

'I know what triggered the Barlichway riot,' he said.

'The leaflets,' she nodded. 'So do we.'

'Found the source yet?'

She shrugged. 'Anybody with access to a computer and a printer,' she told him.

'Well, that narrows the field. Jacquie,' he caught her by the hand. 'Promise me,' he said, holding her as close as she'd let him, 'promise me that when this is all over, you'll be Jacquie Carpenter again.'

She felt an iron lump in her throat and a pain in her heart. He watched her shake her head and go, a silhouette down the corridor to the light.

* * *

Prissy Crown answered the door that night. At least she was dressed this time, in a heavy jumper and jeans. She hadn't put her face on and Maxwell didn't recognise her at first.

'What do you want?' she lolled on the doorframe, a large Scotch in her fist.

'To leap into your arms, you wanton witch,' Maxwell smiled.

'Fuck you!' she snarled, but Maxwell's foot was faster as he held the door and stepped inside. 'Get out or I'm fucking calling the police.'

He saw the phone on the hall table and picked it up for her. 'I forget the number just now,' he said. 'Got lots of nines in it.'

He flicked the door closed with his heel and they stood looking at each other. 'Now, what position do you hold in the coven?' he asked, dropping the phone on to its cradle again. 'You and Sophie. What do you call yourselves, the wicked witches of the east or west? Or is it something altogether more sophisticated? Astaroth or Asmodeus or something? Well, yes, they were male devils, but hey, this is the twenty-first century and it's pretty obvious who wears the trousers in this family, isn't it?'

'What are you talking about?' she slurred, trying to focus through the haze of the drink.

'Where's Agrippa?'

'Who?'

Maxwell closed to her. 'Willoughby. Where is he?'

'He's not here.'

'No,' Maxwell nodded, 'But he hasn't gone to the Barlichway again, surely? Not after last Friday?'

'Someone stole his car,' Prissy said. 'From right outside here.'

'And it was found abandoned on a council estate not a million miles away.'

'How did you . . . ?'

'Have the police talked to him?' Maxwell asked.

'Well, he talked to them.'

'Prissy!' Maxwell shouted, gripping the woman's shoulders. 'Stop it, will you? Stop the lying. Willoughby's car wasn't stolen. He drove it to the Barlichway himself. I saw him do it. And I found the car. What was he posing as last Friday? A Barnardo's collector?'

'This is crap.' She tried to break away, but Maxwell was stronger.

'You were afraid of it yourself,' he yelled, shaking her. 'Willoughby and Ken and Sophie. They were involved, you said, in something sinister. Well, you were right. One of them, two of them, all three, killed Liz Pride and dumped her on my doorstep. Then they vandalised Andrew Darblay's church with their sick paraphernalia. When he caught them in the act, they killed him, smashing his skull. Albert Walters, Alison Thorn, Janet Ruger — sacrifices to the Lord of Darkness.'

'No,' said Prissy, shaking her head.

'Yes, you were right, Prissy. No, Willoughby isn't at the Barlichway. He's at Leighford nick, helping the boys in blue with their inquiries. You know he'll get life, don't you?'

'That's not true!' she blurted.

'Prissy, face it,' Maxwell shouted, still holding her fast.

Your husband's up to his property-dealing bollocks in devil worship. Ritual Satanic abuse. There's no law against witchcraft, of course; not any more. But there sure as Hell is against murder.'

'He's fucking a slapper on the Barlichway!' Prissy screamed.

'What?' Maxwell asked quietly.

'Her name is Natasha Jones. She's sixteen and she lives in Coniston Court. He and Ken, they're both inadequate. Can't function with a real woman.' She held herself erect, the Scotch defiant in her hand. 'They have to run to some little tart barely out of gym knickers. Makes them feel like studs again, I suppose. It's their dirty little secret.'

'And Sophie?'

Prissy shook her head. 'She's got nothing to do with it,' she said, her lips trembling and the tears trickling down her cheeks.

'So it was all bullshit?' Maxwell asked. 'Just so much hot air?'

She looked at him, her lips curled with crying. 'I made it up. I . . . I wanted you. To keep you interested. I knew the only way was to keep you on a hook, concoct some intrigue, some daft bloody story. Why should that little bitch Jacquie Carpenter have you?'

Maxwell let the woman go. 'Because, Prissy,' he said softly, 'she asked me nicely.'

He spun on his heel.

'Wait,' she shouted, on the verge of hysteria. 'Is it true? Are the police interviewing Willoughby?'

'The police,' he told her, 'are chasing their own shadows.' He turned and became instantly, darkly, Jack Nicholson. 'Hocus, pocus,' he growled.

CHAPTER 18

The days were noticeably lengthening by that Tuesday. Helen Hall sat at the wheel of her husband's Volvo, listening to something banal on South Coast Radio. In fact, she wasn't really listening at all; she was thinking about Henry, mooning around at home. She was worried about him desperately worried, although she didn't want either him or the boys to know.

He'd come home on the Friday with news of the Barlichway. There had been rioting, petrol bombs, the whole bit. The lads had gone out, riot gear, CS gas at the ready, horses imported from Brighton along the coast. And after the smoke of battle had cleared, Henry Hall retired hurt. Geoff Knight was the new DCI at Tottingleigh now, the new man on the ritual case. Helen had expected Henry to fume, to rail at the man's incompetence. He hadn't. He just sat in the new conservatory, reading the paper. Most of Saturday, he'd stayed in bed, feeling low with the flu. On Sunday, he'd pottered in the shed for a while, but he was no gardener and on Monday he'd rung in sick to say he couldn't start in Records for a couple of days.

She was worrying, tapping the steering wheel to the mindless bubble-gum music, watching the doors across the school car park for the first surge at the end of another long day. It came soon enough, but before it did, she saw Jeremy, her youngest, marching smartly along the path by the Science labs, his back pack trailing, his anorak undone. Alongside him, a grey-haired teacher with a college scarf flapping in the wind. For a moment, her heart missed a beat. They didn't seem to be in idle conversation, master and pupil. She was not a classical woman or she might have been reminded of Aristotle and Alexander, wandering the plains of ancient Greece in search of education.

Suddenly Aristotle was at her passenger door, tapping on the glass, as Jeremy bundled himself into the back.

'Mum . . .' he began, but Aristotle was faster as Helen Hall lowered her electric windows. 'Mrs Hall, I'm Peter Maxwell. I'd like to talk to your husband.'

* * *

Helen Hall's husband sat in the conservatory. His slippered feet were up on a pouffé, his bum ensconced on the cushions that hideous conservatory furniture makes de rigeur. His eyes were closed, his glasses on top of the novel that lay unread on the table beside him.

'Henry.' He opened his eyes at the sound of his wife's voice. They opened still wider when he saw Maxwell.

'God,' he muttered.

'Now, that's someone we could use about now,' Maxwell said. 'And if he doesn't exist, we shall have to invent him. How are you, Henry?'

'Mr Maxwell . . . I don't understand.'

'Your wife tells me you aren't well,' Maxwell took the police papers off another chair and sat down, plonking his tweed hat on a rubber plant and draping his scarf around its branches.

'Just a touch of flu,' Hall said. 'There's a lot of it about.'

'There's a lot of murder about, too.'

'Mr Maxwell, I really don't think . . .'

'You're out of a job, Mr Hall,' Maxwell reverted to formalities, realizing that cosiness wasn't getting him anywhere. 'On the scrapheap at . . . what . . . forty? What a waste.'

Hall was sitting up now, putting his glasses back on, trying to be professional, trying not to fall apart. 'Perhaps you could tell me why you're here,' he said.

'DCI Knight,' Maxwell replied. 'Any good?'

Hall was taken aback. 'Mr Maxwell, you can't seriously expect me . . .'

'Is he any good?' Maxwell shouted.

In the kitchen, Helen Hall caught the look on Jeremy's face. She bit her lip and clashed about with the dishwasher, glancing whenever she thought Jeremy wasn't looking to the conservatory.

'No,' Hall shouted back. 'He's average to useless.'

Maxwell smiled. At last, some honesty from this man. It was a breakthrough. 'You know,' the Head of Sixth Form stretched out. 'I've got used to our sparring over the last couple of years. It wouldn't be the same with somebody else. How about if we get your job back?'

Hall laughed in spite of himself. 'That's not quite how it works,' he said.

'That's because you've played by the rules,' Maxwell told him. 'Well, in these days of FACE and PC and the McPherson report, you have to, don't you? But me? Well, I've got an altogether freer hand.'

'Mr Maxwell . . .' Hall was shaking his head. 'You don't have any jurisdiction.'

'Oh, but I do,' Maxwell told him. in the good old days, it was called the Hue and Cry. Now it's called citizen's arrest. It's the same thing.'

'Too risky.' Hall was still shaking his head.

'Yes, it's risky,' Maxwell nodded. 'In the good old days, chummy might reach a church and plead sanctuary — though I can't exactly see the man we're after doing that, can you?'

'I'm talking about suing for wrongful arrest. I'm talking about you getting hurt. Whatever you think you've got, Mr Maxwell, you can't go it alone.'

'Oh, I don't intend to. I intend to get by with a little help from my friends. And I intend to start with you. Now, do you think your good lady could be persuaded to put the kettle on and make us a nice cup of tea?'

* * *

DCI Geoff Knight had spent his first two days on the case closeted away with the officers who had worked the ground. The flu had devastated Hall's unit and the draftees from elsewhere to the Incident Room had to learn the ropes anew, rather as Knight was learning them now. He had photographs, depositions, witness statements, SOCO reports, forensic analyses cluttering his filing cabinets and coming out of his ears. He couldn't see his desk.

The phone was ringing non-stop. Demands from the press and Joe Public alike. What happened on the Barlichway? Why was nothing being done? Where was the paedophile ring responsible? And in the middle of it all, Zarina Leibowitz and Crispin Foulkes were issuing press releases, answering questions. Much to Maxwell's amusement that night, the American bitch was quoting him, with no acknowledgement or apology to Arthur Miller — 'The devil's loose on the Barlichway.'

And Knight knew the score. As long as it turned on his own men, the ugliness, it was containable. Riot shields, brick bats, petrol bombs, a few bloody noses and torched cars. Bad, but containable. Even, in a sad sort of way, predictable. But if it turned out on itself, looking for individual targets; if once the mob, fanned by hysteria, decided to turn vigilante, then no one was safe. DCI Knight knew the score and in the instant he knew it, he knew, too, that he was out of his depth.

It was the Meridian Newsdesk that got hold of it first, but it was networked at once and the solemn-toned Michael Buerk told a waiting world at nine o'clock that a baby had been abducted from Leighford, only a stone's throw from the scene of rioting last Friday night.

'Mrs Alexandra Stone,' Buerk read from the autocue, 'and her baby Samantha, went missing last Wednesday or Thursday from their home in Leighford. Mrs Stone's mother, Mrs Veronica Saunders, is worried there is some connection with the Satanic abuse allegedly going on in the notorious Barlichway Estate. John Pienaar reports.'

Mrs Stone's mother duly appeared on the screen, like a latter-day Mary Whitehouse. 'What concerns me most is that the police are doing nothing about this. My granddaughter is only weeks old and someone has abducted her.'

John Pienaar faced the camera from a corner Maxwell knew well. 'Behind me is the Barlichway Estate, the scene last Friday of the worst violence Leighford has ever known. Little Samantha Stone and her mother Alexandra were last seen in the garden of their house two miles west of here twelve days ago. Alexandra's husband is a serving police officer with Leighford CID and has refused to give us an interview. A police spokesman says that everything is being done to find Mrs Stone and there is no cause for alarm. Given the allegations of Satanic abuse made by American expert Dr Zarina Leibowitz yesterday, that will not calm the fears of the local community who are said to be expecting more rioting. This is John Pienaar, for the BBC News, Leighford, West Sussex.'

* * *

The Ka skirted the rise and disappeared briefly in the dip by the park. Then it swung left and purred to a halt close to the waiting cluster of paparazzi cars and vans.

As one, the waiting newsmen scented the arrival and swept, like a shock of sharks along the pavement, jabbering and chattering, poking their microphones and sound booms at the couple who stood before them.

'Who are you?' was the general consensus question.

'I am Tom Cruise,' Peter Maxwell lied with great aplomb, sweeping off his hat as though to accentuate the point. 'And this is Nicole Kidman.' His accent was impeccable. 'We're here to offer Mr Stone the rights for his story. I shall of course be playing the detective sergeant and Nicole here, will be my wife. We haven't signed the kid yet, but there's probably a very young Barrymore around somewhere. Y'all come back now, y'hear?' And he and Jacquie were gone down the dark path alongside the house.

The paparazzi broke up, looking at each other.

'Well, it did sound like him,' one of them said.

* * *

Martin Stone wasn't in the mood for visitors. It had been a helluva day, closeted with Knight at Tottingleigh. And now this.

'My fucking mother-in-law shooting her fucking mouth off to the fucking media!' He threw a glass at the fireplace. Maxwell was a little surprised at the old Cossack tradition, but let it pass. The sentiment surprised him rather less. 'What's he doing here?'

Jacquie wished she knew. All she did know was that Peter Maxwell had rung her out of the blue hard on the heels of the *Nine O'Clock News*. In fact, John Prescott was just explaining his latest transport fiasco when the phone rang.

'Stone,' was all Maxwell had said. 'If you want to see your DCI back on the job,' he'd lapsed into his underworld croak, 'come round to my place. No cops. No funny business. Or the DCI gets it. Savvy?'

Jacquie was all in too. She wasn't in the mood for Maxwell's humour tonight. But she'd caught the news as well. It had hit her like a bombshell and she was still reeling from the blast when his call came through. Too numb to understand and too tired to fight it, she'd got the car out and driven over to Columbine. And here they were.

'Once upon a time,' said Maxwell, hands on hips facing Martin Stone, 'there was an ambitious young copper. He was new on the patch and he wanted to impress. He was good at his job, but there was a problem, you see,' Maxwell looked around for a chair, found one and filled it. 'This young copper — let's call him Stone, shall we? He was a Satanist, one of those perverted sickoes who worships the devil and sacrifices people.'

Stone and Jacquie looked at each other.

'And of course,' Maxwell was in full flight, 'it was perfect for him, wasn't it? A man on the inside. All he had to do was to cover his tracks. He knew all about forensics anyway, so there was no fingerprint problem. As a copper, he had a statutory right of entry to people's houses, so even nasty old besoms like Liz Pride let him in. And if he'd missed anything when committing the crime, well, that didn't matter; all he had to do was go round removing the evidence.'

'What the fuck,' Stone faced him, 'are you talking about?'

'Tell him, Jacquie.' Maxwell waved a hand nonchalantly in the air.

'I . . .' But Jacquie was as gobsmacked as Stone.

'You found Andrew Darblay, the pair of you, didn't you? He was very good, Jacquie, wasn't he? His description of what happened, his blow by blow account. And why was he so good? Because he was there. He did it.'

The police officers just stared at each other, open-mouthed.

'I've read the reports,' Maxwell said.

Stone looked at Jacquie, who shook her head violently.

'No, I . . .'

'I haven't got to put up with this,' Stone snapped. 'Least of all now.' He grabbed Maxwell by the lapels and hauled him upright. 'Get the fuck out of my house!'

Maxwell forced the man's wrists away and stood nose to nose with him. 'Stone,' he growled. 'The way I see it, you've got one chance to get out of the mess you're in and that's to listen to me.'

Jacquie watched them, the man she loved and the man she worked with, head to head, toe to toe. Stone's jaw was flexing and he was blinking, angry, bewildered, confused. Maxwell was immobile. He'd been facing down dangerous young men for years. It was in his blood. She saw Stone's concentration break, his shoulders relax. He spun away from Maxwell and threw himself heavily into a chair.

Maxwell sat down again, slowly. 'Let's get to cases,' he said. 'You killed Liz Pride on December 21 — some ritual significance of the Winter Solstice. For some reason you didn't want her body found then, so you stashed the old duck in your freezer,' he half turned to the kitchen, 'through there, I would guess and waited 'til the next half-baked Wicca date — for auld lang syne, you might say. You dumped her on my doorstep — thanks for that, by the way — and then made sure it was you who was first on the scene. Stop me, if I'm losing the plot, by the way.'

'You're talking bollocks, Maxwell,' Stone said, trying to keep his temper.

'But then you loused up big time at Myrtle Cottage.'

Jacquie sat down, mesmerised by the story that Maxwell was unfolding.

'You missed the calendar — the one with all the key dates, the one that threw one helluva spotlight on what you were up to. What was the matter? Liz Pride going to kiss and tell, was she?'

'This is unbelievable.' Stone was shaking his head.

'Then, of course, you overplayed your hand, didn't you? Desecrating Wetherton church. Darblay caught you. So there was no time for all that eye of newt and toe of frog bollocks you'd used on Liz Pride. You just smacked the poor old rector a few times and walked away with the proverbial blunt instrument in your pocket. What could be simpler? Then you went back to the church with Jacquie on some pretext, so what would be more natural than your fingerprints and boot prints being all over the place? Perfect.'

'Crap,' Stone muttered. 'Utter bloody crap.'

'You had more time with Albert Walters, didn't you? Time to poison the old bugger and time to put him on display like some demented tailor's dummy in a shop window. What was he? Another whistle blower? You realized though that he and Liz Pride had been at school together — and in the interests of leaving no stone (no pun intended) unturned, you went to check the records at Wetherton School. Alison Thorn sussed you, didn't she? That's why she had to be silenced — all of course, in time-honoured ritual manner; naked, with her legs open, like a sexual sacrifice on the altar of your own psychosis.'

'If this wasn't so bloody disgusting, it'd be laughable,' Stone commented. Jacquie just sat staring, open-mouthed.

'It's my bet you weren't ready for Janet Ruger, though. She was a crafty old bird, knowledgeable and streetwise. She was on to you, wasn't she? And here, of course, you made the biggest mistake of all — you left your sacrificial knife in the woman's throat. What a giveaway.'

Stone was staring straight ahead, not looking at Maxwell, not saying anything now.

'You've got two little girls, Stone,' the Head of Sixth Form said. The DS turned to him slowly, the look on his face sending a shiver down Jacquie's spine. 'And, ironically, it was a little girl who put me onto you. One of Alison Thorn's little girls — talking about a nasty policeman killing babies. Is that what you've done, Stone?' The silence was audible. 'Have you killed your own baby?'

Jacquie wasn't ready for what followed. Martin Stone threw himself across the space between himself and Maxwell, the Head of Sixth Form and his chair crashing backwards. The sergeant's hands were around Maxwell's throat and he was squeezing with his thumbs. In desperation. Maxwell brought both feet up and smashed his ankles against Stone's ears. The copper jack-knifed in pain and fell away, rolling backwards as Jacquie jumped between them, a spray can in her hand.

'Martin!' she screamed at him. Stone took one look at the mace and subsided, his head throbbing, his blood thumping. He knelt on his rug, glowering at Maxwell, who rolled from behind the upturned chair, freeing his jaw from the lock it was in.

'All right,' the Head of Sixth Form rasped, his throat bruised and closing down. 'Now, you tell us, Martin; you tell us where they are.'

'I don't know,' Stone mumbled. 'As God is my witness, I don't know. Alex gets terrible post-natal depression. She was the same with Janey. She went off for days the week after she was born. She came back again, of course, but I was scared shitless. And she made me promise, made me swear, not to tell anyone about it. Not even her mother.'

Maxwell crouched down in front of him, nodding. 'You loused up at Myrtle Cottage,' he said, 'because you didn't do your job. When you checked for chemists that had had strychnine stolen, you missed one, in Littlehampton. When Trisha, the barmaid at the Falcon in Wetherton told you about devil worship, you didn't seem interested. For a while I thought it was because you were guilty as Hell. Then I realised it was just because your mind was elsewhere, wasn't it? First the baby was late, delaying the inevitable. Then came the inevitable. Your family vanished.'

Stone nodded. 'That's why I told Jock Haswell to ignore Alex's mother. I didn't think it would get tangled up in all this other mess.'

'No,' Maxwell said. 'I don't suppose you did.' And he stood up. 'Mr Stone,' Maxwell looked down at the man, the upset chair, the rucked mat. 'Promise me that when your wife does return, you'll get her the help she needs.'

Stone nodded. And Jacquie and Maxwell saw themselves out.

* * *

They sat in the Ka. She looked at him. Then she reached out and stroked his cheek. 'Are you all right?' she asked.

He returned her gaze and smiled. 'I'm fine, Jacquie,' he said. She took in the face, with the gash over the forehead, the bruising around the jaw.

'It was probably that scarf of yours that saved you. Max, what possessed you to do that? To accuse Martin of all those terrible things? I know him. He couldn't possibly do anything like that. Kill his own kid?'

'Henry Hall wasn't so sure,' Maxwell told her.

'What?'

'I spent the latter part of the afternoon with your boss today, Jacquie. He let his hair down a little, for Hall, I mean.'

'What did he tell you?' She was wide-eyed.

'The reason he sent me to Myrtle Cottage in the first place.'

'Which was?'

'There was someone on his team he couldn't trust. He'd felt it intuitively. An insider, somebody who knew the score. That's why he wasn't getting anywhere, wasn't making progress.'

'Stone,' she said.

Maxwell nodded. 'It all fitted. Except that Hall, increasingly paranoid and at sea, misread incompetence for guilt. Stone's mind just wasn't sufficiently on the job.'

'Max,' Jacquie said. 'I can't believe Hall told you this.'

Maxwell sighed and shrugged. 'You're right, Jacquie. He's not well. But it's not flu. It's something else. Has he cracked?' He tried to answer his own question. 'Well, if he hasn't, he's that close.'

'What happens now, Max?' she asked him. 'No more surprises, surely?'

'Just one,' Maxwell nodded. 'But first, we've got a little tail to lose.' He was looking in her wing mirror.

'Oh, shit!' Jacquie murmured. Behind her the paparazzi were mounting up. They'd stayed back when the pair had come out of Stone's house, but now they wanted answers. It was Diana and Dodi all over again. 'Got your seat belt on, Max?'

He nodded. 'Be gentle with me.'

And she slammed into gear, screaming away from the kerb and snarling down the road, rubber burning in her wake. At Tinker's Rise, they left the ground and came to earth again with a thud that jarred Maxwell's spine. It was *Bullitt*, it was *Hell-Drivers*, it was *Speed* all rolled into one. But then, he was Mad Max. He bit the bullet, shut his eyes, grabbed the dashboard and prayed.

They lost them on the flyover, Jacquie breaking every rule in the book, undertaking whether it was safe or not, cutting up the sluggish evening traffic on the coast road. All the time the thought was roaring through her head with the snarl of the engine — this was how Maxwell's family had died, all those years ago; his wife and child. She couldn't look at him, knowing what he was going through. And she was praying too. Then she was out beyond Tottingleigh, swinging west on the slip roads of her mind. Suddenly she knew where she was going. She knew and it frightened her.

She switched off the engine outside the gates of the large Victorian house. He unhooked his seat belt and saw her face. 'You can sit this one out if you like.'

She shook her head. 'No,' she said. I'll be all right.' And they crossed the gravel where the dark Peugeot was parked.

'Maxwell? Jacquie? This is an unexpected pleasure.' Crispin Foulkes was standing at the front door of his flat.

'Crispin.' Maxwell was looking furtively from side to side in the well-lit porch. 'Can we come in? I think we've got him.'

'Who?' Foulkes asked.

'The murderer,' Maxwell said. 'The mad bastard who's been going round killing people. You see, Zarina was right.'

'She was?'

Maxwell closed to him. 'Naughty policeman,' he whispered.

Foulkes looked at them both, his forehead frowning under the lion's mane of hair. 'You'd better come in,' he said.

He led them through a passageway and on up a half flight of stairs, past a study crammed with paper. Then, they were in his lounge under a large mirror over an even larger fireplace. It seemed an eternity since the two men had munched their way through a Chinese takeaway when Foulkes's life was all plastic bags and packing cases.

'This has come on no end,' Maxwell nodded, looking around.

'It was rather a tip when you came last. Max, do you mind if I say you look dreadful?'

'Ah,' Maxwell took the proffered seat next to Jacquie. 'Fortunes of war. We needed to pick your brains, Crispin.'

'Go on.'

'Well,' Maxwell settled himself down. 'At first my money was on Willoughby and Ken.'

'I'm sorry?'

'Sorry,' Maxwell said. 'I'm racing ahead again. The murders. You'll agree they're all about Satanic worship — ritual sacrifice?'

'Very much so,' Foulkes nodded.

'Well, I thought we were all looking for a coven. Thirteen people with a secret.'

'And a common faith.'

'Indeed,' Maxwell agreed. 'Prissy Crown put me on to it.'

'Prissy?' Foulkes looked at Jacquie. 'How?'

'She told me something was going on at Beauregard's. "Something sinister", she said.'

'I see.'

'And that Willoughby was involved. And Ken. And Sophie. Well, that was three. If you include the possibility of Prissy herself, that was four. I even began to tot up the people I'd seen at the club — the spotty lad who takes your money; Dr Astley, the pathologist; those two huge blokes in the bar; the bar lad himself; whoever hit me over the head. But then I knew that was ridiculous.'

'You did?'

'Of course. I mean that only made ten. And it only made eleven if I included you. Preposterous!'

'Exactly!' laughed Foulkes.

'Anyway, Prissy eventually explained the whole thing. Seems Willoughby and Ken take it in turns — or perhaps not, bearing in mind an old Crown family custom — to shaft a tart on the Barlichway. When I thought Willoughby was there administering strychnine to Albert Walters, he was just having a bit of rough — reprehensible of course, but human.'

'Of course,' Foulkes agreed.

'Various descriptions of men on the Barlichway — solid build, dark wavy hair — they fitted Willoughby like a glove. Ken was obviously more elusive.'

'I see.'

'So the . . . and this is where it gets interesting, Crispin,' Maxwell leaned towards him, 'Zarina dropped her bombshell — about the naughty policeman, I mean.'

'You know who it is?' Foulkes asked, eyes wide.

'I had DS Stone in the frame,' Maxwell leaned back. 'All very plausible, all very pat. But no.'

'No?'

Maxwell shook his head. 'Not clever enough. It had to be someone quite brilliant to plan the way our man did and get away with it.'

'So, who . . . ?'

'Then,' Maxwell was folding his fingers across his chest, 'I thought Zarina.'

'Zarina?' Foulkes exploded. 'Oh, come on, Max.'

'You're right. Without wishing to be ungallant, the good doctor is a tad on the gargantuan side, isn't she? Even allowing for a certain dumbing down on the clothes front and a possible ability to sublimate her accent, she's, and I'm quoting someone here, "pretty in your face".'

Jacquie smiled despite herself.

'Someone would have seen her. In Wetherton church, on the Barlichway, outside Alison Thorn's flat, somewhere. Nobody did. In any case, she was in California, the good ol' sunshine state, when Liz Pride died, so it can't have been her.'

'Exactly,' Foulkes said.

'Unless, of course,' Maxwell was wrestling with it, 'she had an accomplice. And that brings me inexorably to you, Crispin.'

'Me?' Foulkes laughed. 'Max, you never cease to amaze me. What are you going to do, run through all the inhabitants of Leighford until somebody confesses?'

'Oh, there's no need for that, is there? You know old Bob Cameron?'

'The educational psychologist? Of course.'

'Good bloke, Bob. He and I go back a long way.'

'Happy for you,' said Foulkes.

'Thank you. I got old Bob to call in a few favours earlier today. Make a few phone calls.'

'Really? Look, Max, I don't see . . .'

'He made one to Erdington. It was Erdington where you said you worked, wasn't it?'

'I may have done,' Foulkes said.

'Well, you didn't. Not in social services, anyway. So I got Bob to make a few more phone calls. And one came up trumps.'

Foulkes said nothing. He was looking at Jacquie. And she was looking at Maxwell.

'It was the one to the Marshgrove Clinic. You were a psychiatric patient there for three years.'

'I had a nervous breakdown,' Foulkes said.

'Brought on by events at Broxtowe,' Maxwell nodded. He'd seen Jacquie's mouth open silently at Foulkes's admission. 'Now there, you *were* in the social services. There the whole experience tipped you over the edge, didn't it, Crispin? So that after Erdington, when you conned everybody, maybe even yourself, into thinking you were cured, you wanted revenge. Oh, not in Broxtowe; that was all played out. Psychotics and hysterics like you were exposed there, weren't you? Discredited, shut down. But Leighford, now. Well, we're all pretty green down here; never experienced this madness before. What would you call yourself, Crispin, some sort of *agent provocateur*?'

'You're mad,' Foulkes growled.

'No,' Maxwell shook his head, 'but I know a man who is. You found that delicious, malicious piece of nonsense about Liz Pride being a witch and you played on it. You used country lore, herbal magic, to kill her. Magic mushrooms they certainly were. But you wanted to advertise, didn't you? Make it crystal clear that the devil was in this work. So you killed her on the Midwinter Solstice with all its connotations. But you weren't ready, were you? Something wasn't prepared, so you kept her in a deep-freeze — the one downstairs if I'm any judge. And you made her death public by dropping her on a doorstep. Anybody's would do; but it happened to be mine. And that, Crispin, me ol' fanatic, was the worst mistake you could possibly have made.'

'Really?' Foulkes was unimpressed.

'Max . . . ?' Jacquie tried to break in, but the Great Man's hand was in the air, still looking, as he watched the social worker.

'You drove a knife into the old girl's neck to make the whole thing look like a ritual killing which is precisely what it was. And cashing in on the well known feud between the Prides and the Cruikshanks, you slipped a poppet into old Jane's caravan, careful of course to make the neck wound for posterity. Darblay was next.'

'Darblay was an accident,' Foulkes blurted. 'The old fool got in the way.'

Jacquie blinked.

Maxwell nodded. 'So, no poison. Just a heavy object. Candlestick?'

It was Foulkes's turn to nod. 'Don't you see, Maxwell?' he said. 'Both of you? Don't you see? They're out there, these Satanic worshippers, on the Barlichway, in Wetherton, right here in the nice end of Leighford. They're all around us.'

Maxwell leaned forward again. 'No, Crispin,' he said softly. 'They're in there,' he tapped the man's forehead. 'Only in there. But,' he leaned back, 'I've got to hand it to you. You blazed quite a trail. Quite the Matthew Hopkins, quite the Witchfinder General. You got hold of some strychnine — where from, I wonder? The pharmacy, at Marshgrove? The burgled chemists at Littlehampton? And you killed Albert Walters. Knife through the neck again. It took some nerve, carrying a naked body through the Barlichway. With Pride, you could always pretend it was a pile of rubbish, a practical New Year's Eve joke. But luck, I guess, was on your side.'

'God,' Foulkes shouted. 'God is on my side,' then quieter, 'Elizabeth Pride was a virgin. Can you imagine that? A virgin and married all those years. She told me on the night I killed her — isn't it odd what old people will tell you, once they trust you. Married and a virgin — it has magic significance.'

Maxwell looked at Jacquie, sitting ever more uneasily on the settee.

'You were getting into your stride, now. You'd brought it to the Barlichway, but you didn't want the finger pointing in your direction as a social worker there, so you moved back to Wetherton for Alison Thorn. She was inspired, wasn't she? Not some old nobody now, but a sexually active young woman. You went to town on the whole ritual bit. First you posed as a collector for Barnardo's, then you killed her with hemlock. You stripped her naked and cut her throat. Black candles, sheep's hearts, pentagrams and neo-virgins. And you brought in children — always the Satanist's trump card.'

'I'm no Satanist!' Foulkes screamed, making Jacquie jump.

'Aren't you, Crispin?' Maxwell asked him.

'I had to expose them, don't you see? Force them to show their hand. Well, we've got them now.'

'Ah, yes. But first, Mrs Ruger. What was that all about?'

'She was one of them, Max,' Foulkes said. 'I remembered her from Broxtowe. She was covering the situation there, pretending to be a journalist, but I knew better. She said she knew what was going on. Came to see me that weekend. I kept her here, then I took her back to the hotel and stabbed the bitch.'

'Leaving your ritual knife, your athame, just in case there was anyone left who didn't believe that all this Satanic mumbo-jumbo was real.'

'It is real, Max,' Foulkes shouted. 'How can you, an intelligent man, doubt it?'

'You printed the leaflets — in the study downstairs, I would think and you scattered them in the darkness at the Barlichway. I've got to hand it to you again, Crispin. Your timing was immaculate. I thought you'd kill again on February 2nd — Candlemas, another of your Wiccan dates. You put the calendar in Myrtle Cottage, didn't you? As another pointer. You must have been shitting yourself when you realised I had it and not the police.'

'It worked in my favour,' Foulkes said. 'I had Jacquie here believing you were the devil incarnate.'

Maxwell looked at her. She shook her head, then looked away.

'But on Candlemas, you went one better, didn't you? Your sick leaflets stirred up the Barlichway.'

'They all carried candles that night all right,' Foulkes was triumphant. 'We'll root them out now.'

'You see, it was your cleverness that spoiled it all,' Maxwell shook his head.

'How?'

'On the headboard, above Janet Ruger's hotel bed — the bed on which you killed her, you wrote "Maleficarum".'

'So?' Foulkes sneered.

'What does it mean, Jacquie?' Maxwell asked her.

'Er . . . witch?' she said.

'Not exactly.' Maxwell was shaking his head. '"Malefica" is one witch. "Maleficae" is more than one witch. But "Maleficarum" means of the witches. And that got me thinking. As soon as dear old DCI Hall told me about it, bells began to ring. It was part of the title of a book written a long time ago by two Catholic monks who were probably as rabid as you are, Crispin. It was called *Malleus Maleficarum* — the hammer of the Witches. And that's what you are, isn't it? Witchfinder, avenging angel, servant of the Lord, psychopathic killer. You couldn't, in the end, avoid advertising, not just your cause, but yourself.'

Nobody was ready for the next move. Foulkes was across the floor, Jacquie gripped in his left arm, an ugly blade glittering at her throat, firm in his right hand.

Maxwell was on his feet too. 'Well, well,' he said softly. 'You've got quite a collection of these things, I see.'

'The athame?' Foulkes's eyes danced with the knife's blade in the half light. 'Oh, yes,' he said. 'They come in handy.'

'What now?' Maxwell asked. Jacquie's head was tilted back at a crazy angle, Foulkes's forearm compressing her windpipe.

'Another, regrettable, ritual killing,' the social worker replied. 'This time of one of the police officers involved in the case. A police officer who is having an affair with someone who is clearly . . . Beelzebub.'

Foulkes was in mid-slash as Jacquie's elbow hit him in the stomach and he dropped back. In a second, she was squirting her deadly can in his face and Foulkes staggered backwards, the knife gone, screaming in agony. The door crashed back and Henry Hall stood there, a sheet of yellow A5 paper in his hand.

Foulkes was sobbing on the floor, his temporarily sightless eyes a wilderness of pain.

'Timing could have been a threat better, Chief Inspector,' Maxwell felt obliged to tell him.

'Sorry, Mr Maxwell,' the DCI said. 'But you were right. And for once it doesn't pain me to admit it. I had quite a time rummaging around in your study, Mr Foulkes. I think this paper will match those distributed on the Barlichway Estate. Forensics will have a field day with his computer and deep-freeze. Jacquie, are you all right?'

Maxwell held his arms out as the girl ran to him, the mace still in her hand, her eyes wet with tears.

'I'm fine, guv,' she said. 'Now.'

'By the way, in rummaging around downstairs — and before you ask, Mr Foulkes, I do have a search warrant — I found this.'

He held up a poppet, a little doll in his own image, with a grey suit and wire glasses. Hall smiled at them both. 'And do you know, I think I'm over the flu now. Mr Foulkes, my lads are on their way. You and I are going to take a little drive to Leighford police station. And I'm going to say some time-honoured words to you. After which,' he looked at Jacquie and Maxwell, 'I'm going to the Tottingleigh Incident Room, have a word with Geoff Knight.'

* * *

'Mr Maxwell?' He didn't recognise the excited voice over the phone.

'Yes?'

'It's Nicole, Mr Maxwell. Nicole Green. I just wanted to tell you. Barney's okay. He came to last night. Opens his eyes and says he wants a Chinese takeaway. Innit wonderful, Mr Maxwell?'

'It certainly is, Nicole.' Maxwell said. 'Thank you for telling me. Was he able to tell you what happened?'

'Yeah, silly bugger slipped and fell, didn't he?'

'Trailing those men for me?'

'Nah. Playing silly buggers for a bet. Trying to cheer up old Bull. D'you know old Bull? His wife left him. Well, ta ta, Mr Maxwell.'

'Bye, Nicole. And give my love to Barney, will you? Tell him I owe him a pint.'

And she hung up. Peter Maxwell sat in his attic, Trumpeter Hugh Crawford sitting astride his grey, patiently waiting with his old comrades for orders from the front. Maxwell pushed the chair back and looked up at the stars in their velvet sky.

'There's one thing, Count, I haven't covered.'

The cat snored obliviously in the far corner.

'Who was it swiped me round the head at Beauregard's?'

On an impulse, he pulled a book from the bookcase to his right. Not just any book, one in particular. Alex Stone had come home that day, safe and well, if a little confused and a little sorry, with baby Samantha in her arms. Henry Hall was back in the saddle at Leighford nick, his flu gone, Geoff Knight glad to be out of it. The Barlichway would take longer. The Barlichways of this world always do. But people are tough, and people are resilient. And some of them are sensible. And most of them have the capacity to love. And to care. He looked at the photograph of the auburn girl on his modelling desk, and he lapsed into his Bogart again. 'Here's looking at you, Jacquie.'

Then he opened the book at random, flicking through its many, flimsy pages and his eye fell on the strange text. It was Exodus 22:18 — 'Thou shalt not suffer a witch to live.' The lights burned blue.

THE END

THE JOFFE BOOKS STORY

We began in 2014 when Jasper agreed to publish his mum's much-rejected romance novel and it became a bestseller.

Since then we've grown into the largest independent publisher in the UK. We're extremely proud to publish some of the very best writers in the world, including Joy Ellis, Faith Martin, Caro Ramsay, Helen Forrester, Simon Brett and Robert Goddard. Everyone at Joffe Books loves reading and we never forget that it all begins with the magic of an author telling a story.

We are proud to publish talented first-time authors, as well as established writers whose books we love introducing to a new generation of readers.

We won Trade Publisher of the Year at the Independent Publishing Awards in 2023. We have been shortlisted for Independent Publisher of the Year at the British Book Awards for the last four years, and were shortlisted for the Diversity and Inclusivity Award at the 2022 Independent Publishing Awards. In 2023 we were shortlisted for Publisher of the Year at the RNA Industry Awards.

We built this company with your help, and we love to hear from you, so please email us about absolutely anything bookish at feedback@joffebooks.com

If you want to receive free books every Friday and hear about all our new releases, join our mailing list: www.joffebooks.com/contact

And when you tell your friends about us, just remember: it's pronounced Joffe as in coffee or toffee!

ALSO BY M.J. TROW

SCHOOLMASTER MYSTERIES

Book 1: MAXWELL'S HOUSE
Book 2: MAXWELL'S FLAME
Book 3: MAXWELL'S MOVIE
Book 4: MAXWELL'S WAR
Book 5: MAXWELL'S RIDE
Book 6: MAXWELL'S CURSE

Printed in Great Britain
by Amazon

47071355R00152